Remember
the House

❖

Also by Santha Rama Rau

❊

THIS   IS   INDIA

EAST   OF   HOME

HOME   TO   INDIA

Remember the House

By

SANTHA RAMA RAU

Harper & Brothers . Publishers . New York

To
Jai Peter Bowers

Remember
the House

❖

Part One

❖

THE SEASON

❖ I ❖

JAY'S PARTY WAS THE LAST OF ITS SORT THAT ANY OF US WENT to in Bombay. The momentum of postwar extravagance had carried us all up to that New Year's Eve, but after that, through the early months of 1947, people became more and more self-conscious about lavishness, they took the food rationing restrictions more seriously, for instance; gradually it became unfashionable to buy black-market gasoline for the long drives we often used to take after parties. Indian independence, only months away, was felt by most of us first as a sort of wariness about our pleasures, later as a political achievement.

Parties like Jay's already seem to me so remote in mood, almost as though they belonged to another generation or to life in a different country. But perhaps that is at least partly because my own life has altered a good deal since those days. It is quieter for one thing, and although I feel that I am very busy—there seems to be so much to occupy one in a country household—still I would find it hard to answer the question that people sometimes ask, "What do you do with yourself all day?" In fact I find that I scarcely ever make the opportunity even to visit Bombay—though, actually, it is not such a great distance from my home. It is the bridging of moods that now seems to me too much trouble.

Across the gilt-edged invitation card, over the wild boars and crossed lances of the Kalipur crest, Jay had scribbled in his semi-illiterate handwriting, "You *must* come because this is my swan song. Can you postpone your family binge? Or bring your father if he would be amused." Jay knew, of course, that my father wouldn't be amused—my father felt that the younger generation of our sort in Bombay had too much money and no sense of responsibility, and found them anything but amusing. But Jay also knew that New Year's was the only festival that my father would allow celebrated in our house, and for that reason it had become a rather important family affair. He disapproved of "religious ritual of any sort" (as he called everything from Mahashivaratri to Christmas), and said that the celebration of religious festivals "merely perpetuates prejudice and breeds an entirely unjustified sense of self-righteousness." New Year's, however, gave him nothing to complain of and ever since I could remember we had invited all my many aunts and uncles and cousins to a family dinner and to see the New Year in. It was always a placid, fairly boring occasion, with everyone eating too much and talking over old family gossip and scandals, and always ended immediately after twelve o'clock when my father would tuck away his huge gold pocket watch, hold up his half-empty glass of brandy and offer his usual toast, "May we all receive better than we deserve in this new year." I could never quite catch the gleam of malice which I was sure must glitter behind his words. But anyway, his toast always had the effect of making everyone feel rather guilty and depressed. The party invariably broke up within a few minutes.

Jay's New Year's Eve—an entirely different affair—was the first time I had ever asked to be excused from the family dinner and my father's permission had been surprisingly easy to obtain. I think this was because he was in the middle of writing what he called "a strong letter to the Law Member"—an occupation he always enjoyed. I put Jay's card down on his desk among the crystal paperweights, the letter openers, the insanely sharp pencils. "Would you like to come too? We could cancel the family quite easily."

My father read Jay's scribble carefully. "Not precisely a gracious invitation," he said, "but I have come to accept the fact that good manners are too much to expect from the younger generation. No, I think not. Thank Jay from me and tell him I cannot postpone the 'family binge.' I doubt if he would be able to understand the reason, which is that I, at least, retain some sense of family responsibility."

Feeling vaguely reproached I said, "I'm sure Shalini would love to come and hostess for you. She has always fancied herself at the head of that table." I knew that my sister-in-law's fussy ways made my father as uncomfortable as they made me, but most oppressive of all was her exaggerated deference to my father and his opinions and the flawless enactment of the Dutiful Daughter-in-Law that she always gave in our house.

He looked at me rather sharply. "I think I am still capable of entertaining in my own house without assistance." Then he stared again at Jay's card. "It's a good thing old Kalipur isn't alive to see what has become of his sons. There was a man who understood princeliness. In those days the State was decently governed."

"Decently, if autocratically," I reminded him with some sense of being loyal to my own generation, though the young Maharajah of Kalipur, Jay's elder brother, must have been nearly twenty years older than I, about forty, and was disliked by all of us for being pompous and a bore.

"Well, better our own autocracy than the British variety," my father said with finality. "In those days that was the only alternative. And old Kalipur with all his highhanded ways was concerned first of all with the welfare of his State. And one had to admire him for this, at least, that his subjects knew that any one of them had access to their monarch at any time of the day or night." He swiveled round in his chair to face me, punctuating his words with little jabs of his cigarette holder. "There were even instances when people walked into his bedroom to present some problem or demand the righting of a wrong. Once a purdah woman came to complain that her husband beat her. Old Kalipur sent her home in a carriage, escorted her himself on horseback, and from the street shouted to the husband to come out and take his punishment. He thrashed that man in the middle of the road in full view of the neighbors, and he scarcely even worked up a sweat doing it. Say what you like, men of that sort understood kingship. He had no patience with the British and their niggling rules and magistrates and tedious bureaucracy. He hated the pious way in which they tried to cover up their obvious self-interest with a show of 'good administration' and their middle-class ideas of 'stable government.' He used to say to me, 'You lawyers can only argue about regulations; it takes a prince to give the people justice.' "

My father returned suddenly from this romantic flight. "A debatable point, I admit," he said in a prosaic tone of voice. "Well, those days are gone forever." He handed the invitation card back to me. "I see that even Jay has sense enough to realize that this kind of thing is his swan song." "Enjoy yourself," he said unexpectedly as he turned back to his letter. Enjoyment was something to which he gave no thought and no importance. In the four years since I had returned from school in England and had lived continuously in Bombay, I had felt myself dominated by the atmosphere he gave to the house. I had learned to express only moderately—even furtively—my pleasure in, say, a party, a day at the beach, a new sari. We had no habit of intimacy—there had never been the opportunity for it, until it was too late to begin.

Kalipur House was built on one of the most beautiful sites of Malabar Hill. The house itself was rather ugly, combining the most meaningless decorative extravagances of Mid-Victorian taste with all sorts of haphazard additions and alterations that the changing needs or whims of successive generations had dictated. My best friend, Pria Bhutt, who had talked casually for a time of becoming a medical student, had once added that the chief advantage of Bombay was that one could learn everything one needed to know about malignant growths simply from looking at the architecture. Kalipur House would certainly have been one of her best illustrations. But that New Year's evening the curly cornices and fluted whitewashed pillars had a certain bizarre charm because Jay had arranged floodlights in the shrubbery to play on the long façade, throwing huge dramatic shadows and flattening out the worst of the details.

Pria and I arrived at the party together, escorted by her fiancé.

I hadn't yet reached the envied stage when I might go or return from a party unchaperoned. While Karan was parking the car we dawdled up the wide, shallow steps. The main door was open and flanked on each side with four of the Kalipur State retinue in their peacock-and-gold uniforms. Distantly we could hear the candied strings of a Viennese waltz.

Pria said, "Is my hair all blown about?"

"No." It was as smooth and shiny black as ever, coiled high on the back of her head and decorated with hoops of tiny jasmine, like pearls.

"That's good," she said absently. "How I hate these shy woodland creatures who peep timidly out at you from among their curls." Pria had a way of making the strongest statements in a remote, floating voice so that one never knew whether she was expressing a deep prejudice or the most transient fancy.

I'm not certain, now, why I remember with such isolated clarity that moment of standing at the top of the steps with Pria before Jay's party. It was a moment when I was curiously conscious of the almost chilly calm of our lives—not something to which I normally gave much thought. But for some reason it was also a moment of depression; I felt somehow trapped by this world, these people I knew so well, surroundings that were so familiar, the most predictable of futures. It could, of course, have been just pre-party nervousness. Pria stood half turned away from me frowning into the floodlights, her sari falling in sharply defined folds from her shoulder. She was humming the subdued waltz tune which drifted through the open house. The deep green smell of the garden was all about us. Behind me one of the uniformed men cleared his throat.

"Pria," I began without quite knowing what I was going to say, only aware that I wanted her attention or to get some kind of reassurance from her. "Scarlet is your color, all right," I said at last.

She turned to me, smiling suddenly and brilliantly. "Mm, but not an indication of my subconscious wishes, I hope. Ah, here he comes."

Karan's figure in its white achkan and narrow black trousers flickered jerkily through the pillars of light and shadow, and ran up the steps to join us. Two of the servants moved silently away from the door and led us through the house to the wide terrace at the back. There they stood still, one on each side of us, making the perfect setting for one of Pria's entrances.

Although the terrace was more softly lit than the front of the house, people still turned around as Pria walked out. In anybody else there might have been calculation in that pause in the doorway, the look of vague distress as her head turned slowly, the confident grace of the walk toward her host, the smile, the greeting first with hands folded in a namaskar and then stretched out in a less formal gesture. But Pria wasn't an affected person and was irritated by theatricality. She was simply the best-looking girl in Bombay, recently engaged at the right age and with the right amount of social publicity to one of the most eligible young men of our acquaintance.

As we trailed behind Pria in her regal progress across the terrace to Jay, I felt slightly sad for Karan and the secondary position he seemed to take. I asked, "Are these moments of being sort of an A.D.C. ever going to get on your nerves, do you think?"

Karan said, with surprise but an entire lack of interest, "What moments?"

Jay was already looking disheveled. As the evening went on he would get more and more untidy. So far he had only unbuttoned the top fastening of his achkan so that the stiff, high collar was open and one large emerald-and-diamond stud shook precariously every time he laughed. The rest of the jeweled buttons still held his coat together tightly across his short, square body. I suppose he couldn't have been more than in his early thirties then, but we all treated him as considerably older, a sort of jolly favorite uncle. And of course there were a number of stories about him—that he was fabulously generous and no one had ever asked him for money and been refused, that he couldn't resist gambling on anything whatever and was always in debt, that he married the daughter of a rich zamindar (without a title) to get back two of his favorite race horses that he had been forced to sell, that he kept a mistress in a beach house out in Juhu, that he was devotedly faithful to his wife, who was a chronic invalid, that he used to change clothes with his personal servant and go down to Kamatipura where, in some of the more exclusive brothels, he could hear the music that he loved—the classical Indian songs of devotion sung by the famous courtesans—that with the same exchange of clothes he would send his servant to replace him at tedious State functions—parades, processions and the like. . . . Actually none of us knew very much about Jay although we had been friends of his for years, and none of us had met his wife, who lived in purdah in Kalipur State.

Jay held both Pria's hands in his plump, damp grasp. "My dear," he said, "I didn't think girls knew how to look radiant these days." He turned to Karan and continued in his smoky, chuckling voice, "I haven't had a chance to congratulate you yet. I suppose you know that everyone in Bombay is wondering what you have done to deserve such good fortune." He opened his tired, innocent eyes wide. Sweat stood on his forehead. The loose flesh round his neck shook, the emerald-and-diamond button flashed, Jay laughed delightedly.

Pria's voice sounded very light and cool in comparison. "It's no use pretending it's not a great *relief*," she said. "One can stop all this talk about careers and jobs which I'm sure convinces nobody." She smiled at Karan with a great deal of affection but she sounded quite prosaic as she added, "I couldn't be more pleased."

With an abrupt movement Jay snapped his fingers at his side. At once Daulat Singh, Jay's personal servant, always brisk and angry, stepped up—he was never more than a few yards away from Jay. He carried Jay's cigar case and cutter, his handkerchief, money, swizzle stick and the large tumbler out of which Jay liked to drink champagne. Jay always insisted it should be drunk as a thirst quencher, like beer. "Champagne," he once told me in a more grandiloquent moment, "is like a footman who has suddenly been made a duke. His proper place of enjoyment is the local pub, but poor devil, he finds all his evenings taken up with formal banquets."

Daulat Singh handed him an enormous silk handkerchief, waited till Jay had mopped his face, retrieved the handkerchief, tucked it away in a pocket of the peacock uniform, gave Jay the glass of champagne, watched until he had taken a sip and then stepped back. Jay hadn't looked at him once. "Baba, my child," he said to me, "you must have a drink. No, I insist. This is an occasion—several occasions—Pria's engagement, New Year's Eve—"

"And your swan song?"

"Yes." Jay suddenly turned down the corners of his mouth, looking comical and sad, like an unconvincing clown. "After this the deluge, in the form of my brother, arrives. For the polo, you know. Next week. The Kalipur team is coming down to meet the Australians."

"Really?" Karan was interested in the conversation for the first time. "I suppose they'll be having some exhibition matches here? Will H.H. be playing?"

As the talk turned to polo, Pria muttered to me, "If there is any one thing that bores me more than chat about horses, it is chat about Kali and his horses." She steered me gradually away toward the terrace balustrade. "Poor Jay, fancy having a brother like Kali. By tomorrow I suppose the whole household will be 'in training,' keeping what ever people mean by regular hours, and the conversation will become incomprehensible—all about chukkers and withers and things. It's a form of hysteria." That was one of our phrases at the time. We used it a lot to describe a wide variety of things: an enthusiasm we didn't share, a friend's love affair, getting drunk, political arguments (as distinct from political gossip, which was a necessary part of small talk)—all were "a form of hysteria."

Pria and I took, as usual, one drink each, which we would carry with us until dinner, and joined some friends at the balustrade. From there the garden stretched in a series of terraced lawns down to the sea. Small lights had been hidden in the trees, and in the banks of pink oleanders and cannas that marked off each plane. The garden was full of diffuse light, indistinct and spreading pools of darkness, sudden sharp color in illuminated hibiscus and purple bougainvillaea falling in cascades from arbors and stone railings. In a descending scale, fountains shot upward with pastel radiance and fell glittering into lily pools.

Immediately below us, on the next wide step of the garden,

was an absurd and charming pavilion which appeared to be made entirely of roses. Jay, as he later told us—smiling happily, asking us to join his amusement at this extravagant silliness—had imported twenty thousand cut roses from Poona because, he claimed, they had a better scent than Bombay ones. He had reserved a compartment in the *Deccan Queen*—the express between the two cities—and two of the peacock-and-gold retainers were sent to pack the compartment with ice and accompany the roses on their three-hour trip. All afternoon the gardeners had been constructing a latticed cane framework through which the flowers were woven into a damp, heavy, fantastic tapestry. Now from the pavilion the orchestra played out the faded gaiety of the "Merry Widow" and "The Desert Song."

That evening, in accordance with the food-rationing rules of Bombay, there were only twenty-four for dinner. "Only Jay," as Pria said, "can say 'only twenty-four' and mean it." Still, it was a far cry from the days that even I could remember when three hundred might sit down to dinner if it were a big occasion—a family wedding, for instance—and in Kalipur House, before the war, fifty or sixty would have been the most ordinary of parties.

Because most of the guests would be coming in afterward, dinner was announced fairly early—about half past nine—and Pria and I carefully put down our drinks, still three-quarters full, and turned with the rest of the group to whom we had been talking and walked into the dining room. There, the fragrance of tuberoses was heavy as a fog on the air. At each end of the room was a bank of scarlet-and-white flowers, and down the center of the table were massed the pale early orchids from the hills. Behind each chair stood one of the Kalipur retinue gazing across the silver, the lace, the cut glass, to the terrible family portraits on the walls.

In spite of all this the atmosphere was not formal; all of us had known each other for a long time, for one thing, and anyway Jay couldn't bear to be regimented by social conventions any more than he could in a career—which was why, for instance, he had refused flatly to go into the army, which would have been the accepted thing for the younger son of a princely family to do. Jay marched in to dinner first, brandishing his tumbler and leaving be-

hind him a trail of champagne splashes, and settled himself more
or less at random somewhere halfway down the table. He beckoned to Pria. "Come and be guest of honor," he called, and seated
her next to him. Not that things would stay that way for long because Jay could never sit still through an entire meal. He would
change places several times with different people, or simply have
his chair dragged to any point at the table that interested him.
The rest of us arranged ourselves as we pleased.

Sitting opposite them I found myself between Karan and another childhood friend, Hari Joshi. An abrupt young man with
conflicting features, the full, arrogant mouth of the Mahrattas and
large, soft eyes, a manner of impatience controlled, a strong accent
when he spoke English, the troubled "r's" and sharp "t's" of
Mahratti in all his speech—an almost stagy contrast with Jay's relaxed English. He apologized for being late as if he didn't much
care. "I was driving back from Thana and got lost looking for a
short cut—"

"Lost?" Jay leaned across the table, smiling incredulously, dis-
arranging the silver. "Who with? No one gets lost alone."

"Quite alone, I assure you."

"Baba," Jay opened those childish eyes at me, "you'd better
watch your step." It was more or less assumed by most of us that
Hari and I would get married one day. We both knew it would
please our families, and I had thought from time to time—without
any great enthusiasm—that it might be a comfortable arrangement.
Actually Hari had never suggested it, and I had never indicated
that I might refuse. Curiously enough, this undefined situation
made for greater ease instead of greater constraint between us.

Easily we launched ourselves on the usual small talk of our set
in Bombay—an exchange of news about mutual friends, not biting
enough to be called gossip, a despairing irritation at the works of
the retiring British government as well as the new nationalist
government that would soon accept the complete transfer of
power, comments and condolences on how we had fared at last
Saturday's races, vague plans for a future date or excursion. Hari
often seemed not so much bored as absent from the talk. His
attitude politely showed that he could take or leave such parties,

a Bombay amusement, irrelevant more than tiresome. Silently he told you that his life sprang from his family property in Poona which he farmed with a kind of hardheaded devotion.

Food rationing limited the number of guests at a party but, in Kalipur House at least, made virtually no difference in the amount of food that was served. There was a complete Western meal first which took us, in elaborate stages of soup and lobster, wild duck and venison and various salads, through to just before the dessert. Then the Indian meal began. The china and cutlery, the wine glasses, the salt cellars and all the varied implements of Western eating were removed, and large silver thals—round shallow trays— were placed before us. Each contained a little mountain of rice surrounded by small silver bowls filled with different kinds of curries, curds, sweets and lentils. Most of us preferred Indian food to the first part of the meal, finding Western cooking, in contrast, lacking in interest and too bland. All down the table the girls pushed their bracelets up their right wrists, dipped their lacquered fingernails into the perfumed rice and began to eat as soon as they were served. The men, too, applied themselves more seriously to the Indian food; conversation was more spasmodic, servants flitted about with fresh relays of thin wheat chapatis, of sharp spiced meats or of milky sweets soaked in rose water.

We didn't rise from the table until nearly eleven.

When Pria and I came out to the terrace again we walked across to join Karan and Hari. Leaning against the balustrade a little further down were a couple of foreigners whom I had never seen before, a thin blonde girl and a tall man who had his back turned to us. They weren't talking to each other and they seemed isolated by more than being strangers at the party.

"Who do you suppose *they* are?" I asked Pria softly.

She turned, looked at them deliberately, and then said in a voice that I was terribly afraid was audible to them, "God knows. Some of Jay's Americans, I dare say. Where *does* he find them, I wonder?" She turned back with complete indifference.

"Should we talk to them, do you suppose? They look rather left out—"

Pria looked at me in amazement. "Probably they are just bored and cross. Knowing Jay, he probably didn't tell them what time to come and just said something vague like 'after dinner' or 'latish,' and I wouldn't be surprised if they've been waiting about here for the last hour for us to finish dinner—you know what lunatic hours Americans eat at. They probably had their dinner at seven o'clock." A new thought struck her. "Perhaps they're hungry, poor things."

To Karan's suggestion that they dance, she said, "Yes, love to. I've eaten my way into an absolute stupor and *must* exercise some of it off. . . ." She took his arm to walk down the steps to the lower terrace and the rose pavilion.

Hari, slender and as usual standing very straight (a trick that made him look taller than he was; actually we were the same height), still had a brandy glass in his hand and was saying something to me. I didn't listen because I was wondering how much of Pria's conversation the American girl had overheard. Certainly the girl showed no sign of having heard anything, nor did she make any attempt to talk to her companion. But it was in no sense a passive stillness. Resting against the stone, she still looked taut and ready at any moment to be active. In fact, the thing that kept my attention on her even after I had decided that she probably hadn't heard, was that air of excitement that she carried with her, as though she had just come from or was just going to the most fascinating rendezvous of her life.

"Do you," I asked Hari suddenly, "think she's pretty?"

"Who?" he asked, looking startled. "Oh, the American girl." (By then I had decided that she was beautiful.) "Well," he said disapprovingly, "she has very unusual coloring." Like most Indians Hari preferred a fair skin and this girl was deeply sunburned. Besides, he had the sneaking feeling that there was something rather disreputable about "unusual" looks. With the odd reserve he acquired in any dealings with foreigners, he said, "Would you like to meet them?"

"No," I said, embarrassed, for some reason, to admit that I would. "Let's dance before the crowd arrives."

Hari put down his glass with something like relief. The movement caught the girl's attention, and light burnished her hair as she lifted her head quickly. She looked directly at me for the first time and began a slight, secret smile but never finished it.

Under the canopy of roses, scarcely noticing the Goanese musicians with their dark, sad faces shining, with their white dinner jackets padded at the shoulder and nipped in at the waist, their air of desperate nattiness, the saris and the achkans danced. Girls hummed "Sentimental Journey" gently into their partners' ears in the scented twilight of the pavilion. The meaningless steps were all performed gravely and without abandon. Hari danced well, although I knew he didn't like it much. At some point I noticed the Americans among the dancers, taller than the rest, still silent, her temple pressed close to his mouth, not oblivious exactly, but generating their own air of privacy. Distantly, thumping away under the dance music and the shuffling sandals, one could hear the sea.

What with the dancing, the waving and smiling to new arrivals, the pauses by the whispering fountains to catch one's breath, to have a drink, to discuss people's clothes with Pria, I didn't realize it was midnight until a breathless, delighted voice somewhere near me said, "Oh, look, fireworks! Oh, how beautiful!" The bright head was tipped backward, the face of the American girl an extraordinary luminous green as she watched the stars cascading out of the night sky. She turned impatiently to her companion, grabbing his wrist. "Oh, hurry—let's go watch them fall in the sea— quickly—" a most compelling whisper. She ran past me, a flurry of silvery skirt, bare shoulders tense, down the steps to the lower terraces and the sea. Most of us standing there by the fountain turned without thinking to follow her. It seemed suddenly urgent to reach the water before the next rocket went up. We heard the mounting hiss from the bottom of the garden and without a word began to run toward it. Behind us the Goanese band was playing "Auld Lang Syne."

The falling lights flexed in the water, the broken reflections moved in on the waves to the rocky little beach. In soft explosions, rose pink, purple, an unearthly blue, the stars kept blossoming and falling in the night above the sea, the weird radiance lit the garden and the strangely still figures were caught in a magical intensity.

Unaware of any particular direction, almost mindlessly, I found myself standing behind the Americans in the darkness, and in some quick lull of sea and fireworks caught a few whispered words, ". . . loving you—"

"Oh, my darling . . ." The girl turned to look up at the man, unsmiling, like a serious child.

"A happy New Year to us," he said, as if it were a spell.

From somewhere higher up in the garden Jay's chuckling voice called, "Happy New Year everybody! You must have a drink—the first of 1947. . . ." Servants had reappeared with more champagne and people were laughing and shouting good wishes to each other. I went in search of Karan and Pria, and found them walking slowly down with Jay. "Happy, happy New Year, all of you," I said, my head still full of the bursting fireworks. "Oh Jay, what *heavenly* ideas you have!"

"It's lucky," Karan said, in his measured way, "that the blackout restrictions have been withdrawn."

But Jay was thinking of something else; he said conspiratorially, "Look, you girls have got to help me. I've invited a couple of Americans—" He looked vaguely around. His plump face shone, his eyes were nearly closed. He was, by then, quite drunk, in his interior way that didn't show in a thickening speech or an uncertain walk but in a kind of loosening of body and disintegration of feature that is hard to describe. Another couple of buttons of his achkan were undone. "They must be somewhere around. I couldn't have mislaid them—"

"We've seen them," Pria said coolly.

"Well, look. I meant to see they were looked after, but somehow— You must be nice to them because they were very nice to me. Or rather her parents were, last summer when I was in New York. They've just arrived and they don't know anyone in Bombay."

"Just as long as she doesn't want to be taken shopping," Pria said.

"And if she isn't one of the cultural ones," I added, imitating Pria's tone, "always wanting to know the date of everything. It's a form of hysteria with Americans." Privately I was rather pleased at the excuse to talk to them.

Jay giggled and said to Karan, "The ladies, God bless their feline hearts. . . . No, my dears, don't be disturbed." He waved his champagne tumbler at Pria and me. "She won't be any serious competition to you—she has a husband whom she adores, her own husband, which makes it all the more remarkable. . . . She insisted on marrying him, although he was, as they say, Nothing."

"And she was Everything, I suppose?" Pria asked.

"Well, Enough, which I'm told is as good as a feast." Jay smiled tolerantly.

Pria said, "How dreary that sounds—like rationing. A feast should be a feast with far too much of everything and people feeling sick afterward." She decided to be co-operative. "What are they doing in Bombay?" she asked.

"Oh, business. Shipping," he said in the tone of voice that relegated people "in trade" to a category something less than human. I'm sure Jay was quite unconscious of his inflection; his unalterable good manners would never have allowed him to be scornful of businessmen in front of Karan. And Karan, too, appeared not to notice because he joined in at once and said, "Oh, really? Well, I must talk to him. I expect I can introduce him to a few people."

"That would be exceedingly kind." Jay was guiding us slowly down to the sea. "He is to manage the Bombay agency for the next couple of years. . . . Her father's a director of the firm, of course—"

"Of course," Pria said softly.

"—by way of experience. He's very young still."

Down by the sea wall it was almost entirely dark. Occasional bursts of laughter, a glowing cigarette, the flare from a match, showed where groups of people still lingered after the fireworks. To the Americans, standing with, but clearly not part of, a little knot of people, Jay shouted huskily, "What? Not welcoming the New Year?" He clicked his fingers briskly for more drinks.

The girl spun round toward us, and without waiting for introductions said, in that abrupt rush of a voice I had noticed before,

"Oh, I'm so glad to meet you! I was hoping you might come and talk to us up there on the terrace earlier on—but you didn't."

Pria raised her eyebrows and turned to Jay, obviously asking first to be introduced. Jay said, "Mr. and Mrs. Nichols, Miss Bhutt—"

Pria, with far more than her usual drawl, said, "How do you do?"

"Miss Goray, Mr. Desai . . ." Jay chuckled hopefully.

Karan and I muttered something. The tall American man, smiling and hostile, returned our greeting formally, carefully repeating each name.

In the chilled silence that followed, Pria said in a very social voice, "And how are you enjoying Bombay?"

Jay retreated, still chuckling. "If any of you feel lucky later on," he called back, "come on up—there's roulette inside. . . ."

The sea breaking on the rocks below us covered over the sound of the dance music. The wind was sharper and carried a faint smell of fish. The American girl shivered and said nothing. Her husband answered gravely, "We've been here only a few days but Alix is determined to love India."

It must have been nearly three o'clock when we left the party, and we were among the first to go because Pria felt one should leave a party before it got "rowdy." Almost everyone we knew in Bombay turned up at one point or another in the course of the evening, and there were, besides, more foreigners than we were used to seeing at an Indian party and a good many of Jay's other friends—"States people," from the Indian princely states, that is, who were usually in Bombay only for a week or so on their way to Switzerland and winter sports. During the war they had been more in evidence in Bombay for the Season because European travel had been, of course, impossible. They still hadn't returned to their prewar life of millionaire nomads, but this time because their future in India was scarcely as secure as they could have wished.

Even as we were leaving, people drove up from other parties. Clearly there was an extreme of "rowdiness" ahead—the singing and laughter had begun to sound shrill. A couple of guests had decided to take showers in the fountains to sober up. Screams from the beach announced either a sprained ankle from the rock-climbing party or just hilarity. Only in the roulette room was there comparative silence. Someone had given the orchestra a lot of whisky and the music that followed us out to the driveway had lost all its early restraint.

In the car, sitting relaxed between Karan and me, Pria said, "Well, that was everything one could hope for from a swan song. What do you suppose will happen to the States? Will Congress chuck all the princes out once the British go?"

"Well, at least we won't chop their heads off or make them flee across the snow with the wolves snapping at their heels," I said, wondering why no one had ever asked Jay what he felt about it all, whether the uncertainty of the years to come troubled him as little as it appeared to.

Karan halted the car for a moment, as we always did after a party, on the crest of Malabar Hill, near the Hanging Gardens, the highest point of Bombay. From there you can look out across the whole beautiful curve of the Back Bay, and beyond to the tapering island city caught between the harbor and the open sea. Below us the crowded tangle of houses was dark; only the double line of lights that followed the bay—the Maharani's Necklace—remained sharp and brilliant as diamonds set against the nighttime city.

"I'm sure some equitable settlement will be reached," Karan said.

Quite unexpectedly I was annoyed by his complacence. "I should think the only equitable settlement would be to make them work for their living."

Karan sounded shocked. "What would they work at? Can't have our Indian princes wandering about like the Balkan royalty cadging drinks off any American on the Riviera."

I couldn't help laughing, and then I felt guilty for having attacked poor Jay when I was irritated by Karan; and after that I felt silly for snapping at Karan when it was really Pria who had made me cross—and that for her offhand rudeness to an American girl I had scarcely met.

* II *

NEW YEAR'S DAY STARTED BADLY WITH A LONG, TIRESOME
scolding from my ayah. She arrived in my room with my early-
morning tea and squatted on the floor by my bed with a look of
sulky righteousness that had exasperated me ever since I could
remember. She had rather special privileges in the house which
she was eternally trying to extend and which she used as a weapon
to bully and threaten the other servants. She slept, for instance,
on the floor of my dressing room instead of in the servants' quarters at the back of the house, although she insisted on having a
room of her own there, too, in which she could keep her two tin
trunks with their peeling paint containing all the oddments of
clothes, materials and trinkets she had accumulated from my
mother or from me over the years, as well as a loathsome collection
of photographs recording my plump and nondescript infancy, a
saccharine and curly-headed childhood and a singularly ungainly
adolescence. Whenever she especially wanted to embarrass me in
front of friends or young men that she had for some reason decided
were unsuitable as admirers, she would bring them out and display
them with a sort of half-witted devotion which I knew (and could
never convince anyone else) was completely bogus.

Once when I had tried to get her out of my dressing room and
back to her own quarters, she had produced, of all implausible excuses, her widowhood as a reason for staying on. I, of all people,
she indicated reproachfully, should help to protect her in her
widowed state when any man could take advantage of her. I gave
up the project without any further argument, without even pointing out to her that all the men servants had wives of their own far
prettier than she had ever been, or that even if they hadn't been
terrified of her she was far too old to interest them. Her tenacity,
I knew, was greater than my dislodging abilities. And she was
determined not to relinquish such a good spying post.

About the only thing that pleased me about the ayah was that she came from Jalnabad in north India and she remained my only link in Bombay with the place where I had spent most of my childhood, with the years that my brother and I had lived in my grandmother's house. To the ayah, however, it was no distinction to be associated with Jalnabad because she suffered most acutely from the occupational disease of all ayahs—extreme snobbism. Even in those days in the rare moments of privacy that the Jalnabad house afforded, when she scrubbed my head or poured warm water from the huge brass bucket over me in the bathroom, she would tell me to remember where my proper place was. "Living here is just for now. Never forget that your real home is in Bombay."

"But I hate Bombay."

"You don't even remember it. Your father's house is there—a big, broad house—that is where we will live."

"I like it here."

She sniffed. She far preferred the comfort of the empty, silent Bombay house to the noisy, shabby compound of Jalnabad with its casual living and its subtle organization. "Your father is an important man—he has a much better house. Not like this," she said, slopping water scornfully, "where all the water must be carried in from the well."

"You can go if you want. I shall stay here with Nani."

"Just wait till I tell your grandmother how defiantly you speak."

I ran out to dry my hair in the sunny courtyard behind the house. There I saw my grandmother sitting, as usual, cross-legged on a bed—a wooden frame with tape webbing across it. She was shelling peas. "Nani!" I called. "Nani, Nani!"

"What is it, child?" she looked up, entirely unfussed.

But I said, "Oh, nothing," because all at once there seemed no need to ask her for reassurance.

Somehow since those days the tradition had grown up that the ayah was allowed to lecture or reprove or correct me as if I were still a child—in fact it was due to her refusal to change her habits that everyone still called me "Baba" instead of Indira, my real name. She had been with us so long—had left Jalnabad to come to Bombay with my mother when she was a bride, had nursed my brother and then me, had returned to the north with us when my father had to travel a great deal accepting cases all over India—making his name, she used to tell me, as a political lawyer. In the end she had established herself as she had planned in our Bombay house and she didn't consider leaving even when, three years before, my mother had gone to live in the far south of India to be near her guru and the ayah might logically have left as she had come, with my mother, to be her personal servant.

That New Year's morning she made full use of her special privileges to give me a long lecture about coming home at half past three in the morning. Not, she said, that she expected me to listen to the words of a devoted old woman who had always had my best interests at heart. I was too caught up these days with all my fine friends who had learned in wicked foreign lands these habits of drinking and dancing all night. But even if I had no sense of shame left, at least I could think about my future. A Fast Girl was all very well to have a good time with at parties, but which respectable man would marry her? He would as soon marry a film star or some other riffraff. Of course it was useless to talk to me these days, I thought only of my own pleasure, but I would come to learn that there was more to life than pretty clothes and smart friends. . . .

There was clearly to be no respite for some time, so I escaped into the bathroom and turned both taps on full to eliminate the possibility of even a shout reaching me. But when I came out half an hour later the ayah was still there. She was folding clothes and tidying my room in a sulky silence, ready at any minute to start her monologue again.

The thing that saved me from that was almost as bad as the scolding itself. My sister-in-law arrived, ostensibly to wish me a happy New Year, actually to point out that she would never skip a family party in favor of gayer amusements.

"Was it as deadly as usual?" I asked. I could never resist shocking her.

"Well, perhaps I'm strange that way," she said patiently, "but I like to hear all the family news. It's only once a year that we all get a chance to be together—"

"Thank goodness."

"—and after all one wants to keep in touch with one's own flesh and blood."

From that remark it was quite obvious that I was to be given one of Shalini's impersonations. She fitted them over her character with the same conventional habit with which she chose appropriate saris for different times of the day. That morning it was the Perfect Hindu Wife (who had accepted her husband's family as her "own flesh and blood") that discussed last night's family party with me. Even her round, undistinguished features seemed to formalize themselves to fit the part. Her tika—the round red spot that most of us wore on our foreheads more for decoration than for any religious significance—was always more exaggerated than ours and made of the proper powders and spices and coloring, and now it seemed to stand out accusingly. (Pria with typical insouciance used to change the colors of hers to suit her sari, and sometimes even wore a sequin glittering between her eyebrows for a change.) Shalini never actually *said* anything to show her disapproval of Pria and me, but she made it perfectly clear by her silences and an occasional self-deprecating comment ("I know it's foolish of me to be so old-fashioned. . . .") that she found us too "Westernized."

The Perfect Hindu Wife renounces her own family and is completely absorbed into her husband's family from the day of her marriage, so Shalini recited for my benefit all sorts of tedious bits of information about "our" family. "Our second cousin is doing very well in his first year at Oxford. Poor cousin-sister is so upset because the smallest daughter has been teething, you know, and so she's running a slight temperature."

"I didn't know."

"It's hard to realize, isn't it? The child is already a year old. I'm so thankful my two are over that stage. I told her that the best thing is to make a paste of soft-cooked rice and crushed cloves and coat the baby's gums with it—"

"How revolting that sounds."

Shalini said forgivingly, "When you have children of your own you'll find out that these old remedies are often the best. Was

Hari at your party last night?"—which wasn't quite the *non sequitur* it might on the surface appear.

"Yes," I said, "and he proposed to me at last, but I turned him down."

For a second, Shalini raised her eyebrows high in unguarded excitement, and then decided I was joking. "I only asked," she said with dignity, "because Father's brother Prakash is thinking of buying property near Poona. He thought he might consult Hari."

The ayah, who had been interested in the family gossip, which she followed with fascination even though it was in English, was not going to listen to Shalini on the subject of land values and the security of property. She interrupted briskly to ask me whether I wanted to wear slacks or shorts that morning. Shalini was diverted at once, and pursed up her mouth as I said, "Oh, shorts, I think. I'm not going anywhere this morning, except possibly for a swim."

The ayah advised me, "If you are going out in the sun you'd better wear slacks; otherwise your legs are going to get burned black." Actually she disapproved of both shorts and slacks quite as much as Shalini did, but was quite determined never to side with my sister-in-law on any point—Shalini had the maddening conviction that she could "manage the lower classes," which was deeply resented by the ayah. She could be "born ten times" and never acquire an ounce of breeding, the ayah used to tell me.

Shalini said through a sweetly artificial little laugh, "I do think you're brave. I know it's *modern*, but I would never have the courage to show my legs."

"If you have thick ankles," I said nastily, "slacks are almost as comfortable."

"I'm really more comfortable in a sari than in anything else," she said, and then added, getting her own back, "For a married woman it's more dignified, I think."

The ayah understood the tone of this exchange even if she couldn't follow the exact words. In silence she handed me a pair of shorts. Shalini walked over to the long mirror and fussed with the folds of her printed silk sari. Then she smoothed back her hair, patted the fat, twisted bun on the nape of her neck and tucked the creamy frangipani flowers more securely into it. "I'll go down and pay my respects to Papa now," she said, looking demure.

"I wouldn't," I put in quickly. "He has a meeting on this morning."

"Oh, I won't disturb that," she smiled. "I'll only look in for a minute. I've brought a garland and a coconut to bring him good fortune through the New Year."

There seemed to be no way of sparing my father the irritation of Shalini's determined dutifulness, so I went downstairs with her (avoiding the ayah's eye), wished her a happy New Year and left the house to spend the rest of the morning swimming about slowly in the pool at the Country Club.

I returned home about half an hour before lunch to find a message that Pria had telephoned, and to find that my father's meeting was still going on. The door of his study was open, and as I passed it I saw his tall figure pacing impatiently about the room, as usual when he was worked up about something. He had the kind of theatrically impressive looks that had served him very well many times in the courtroom—the plume of white hair above a wide forehead, the frowning eyes, the conventionally strong modeling of jaw and chin. I think he must have been vain—it seems unlikely that he could have made such good use of his looks unintentionally. He turned when he heard me and beckoned to me to come in. Without interrupting what he was saying, he pointed to a table under the windows on which there was a large jug of buttermilk and several glasses.

I poured out the buttermilk and handed it to the three men who were sitting around my father's desk. All were dressed in the inevitable white hand-spun cotton dhotis and shirts of the Congress Party. All three had Gandhi caps which they wore indoors and out. Each smiled a brief recognition and then took no further notice of me. They looked a little sheepish, a little placating. Shalini's garland of pink roses and dahlias entwined with silver tinsel hung limply from the edge of the desk. The coconut lolled incongruously beside the inkstands and foolscap paper. I sat in a corner by the open window, half listening to the discussion in the room, half dreaming in the garden outside, in the smell of roses and the vulgar imperatives of the crows; caught occasionally by my father's authoritative gestures or the Congress Party men's fluctuating tones, occasionally thinking of Jay's party. Sometimes I listened inattentively to the political talk. Partition. The British Raj. Bapuji. Mountbatten. Jawaharlal. Attlee.

Mostly I stared at the melting ice in the bottom of my glass, still covered with a thin, milky film. Involuntarily, as it often happened, I saw myself in Jalnabad, in my grandmother's house, a small child standing in the crystal sunlight of north India. Standing in the courtyard behind the house, next to the cart of the fish vendor, holding in my hand the fragment of ice—an object of wonder—that he gave to each of the children in the house whenever he called. I would hold it on the flat extended palm of my hand and stare enraptured at the cloudy piece of ice studded with fish scales shining with the elusive colors of a sea shell, blues and greens, as I tilted my palm, a fleeting pink, almost a flame. All around me was the early-morning bustle of the courtyard, the household shaking back the night and approaching the growing day. Near by the broad figure of my grandmother would be prodding the fish suspiciously, saying in a loud, accusing voice, "Don't pretend to me that this is fresh," or "What is this—only six? Mine is a big household as you should know by now, I need more." From one corner of the courtyard came the clatter of the servants scouring pans in front of the kitchen building. Dimly, behind me, the slap of sandals as an aunt, a cousin, a remote, elderly relative crossed the courtyard from the house to the bathroom. And I would stare and stare at the fish scales in the sun, feeling a sense of loss as the ice melted in dirty trickles down my wrist, and at last only the scales remained gummed tight to the palm of my hand. I had tried saving the scales to look at later, but they lost their iridescence as soon as they dried.

Once, when the ice melted, there was a round, gray, glistening pebble left in my hand. I was turning it over with some curiosity when the cook's daughter spoke to me. She was a couple of years older than I, but since she didn't go to school she was often allowed to play with the younger children in the house. She was a malicious little girl, and I was rather afraid of her.

"Don't you know what that is?" she asked.

I shook my head, still looking at the pebble and scratching the filmy skin that enclosed it.

"It's a fish eye. If you swallow it your wish will come true."

I faced her then, to see if she was telling me the truth. But she only smiled in her sly, ingratiating way and ran off to help my oldest cousin collect her schoolbooks.

I don't know how long I gazed at the fish eye trying to make up my mind. It became grayer, more opaque, more repellent, but I knew that in my heart I believed her. In those days I believed a lot in magic. Whenever I left the house, for instance, I would stop at the gate and look carefully in each direction to be sure there was not a funeral procession coming down the road. (I had my strategy planned in case there was—I would run back home, sit down, eat some fruit, and that would dispel the bad omen.) If anyone in the house was ill I always burned a chili. If anyone admired my baby cousin—said how healthy he looked, or what a beautiful child he was—I would quickly place a black tika on his forehead to ward off the evil eye. I suppose I was never in serious doubt about swallowing the fish eye.

It must have been half an hour later that my grandmother found me near the well, outside the courtyard wall. I was doubled over, retching miserably.

"Baba!" she said in a tone somewhere between concern and irritation. "Baba, what is it? What's the matter?"

"I swallowed it. . . ." I said, sobbing and angry and dizzy. "I swallowed it and it didn't do any good because I sicked it up again."

"What *was* it? What did you swallow?" She sat on the wide stone brink of the well and pulled me into her lap.

"The fish eye." I could still taste the thin, bitter saliva at the back of my mouth. "She told me it would make my wish come true."

My grandmother stroked my forehead and said without scorn

and without indulgence, "Silly baby. What did you want enough to make you swallow a fish eye? What did you wish for?"

Her saris always smelled faintly of sandalwood. With my face pressed against the starched white cotton on her shoulder, I thought, It doesn't much matter if I tell, since in any case it won't come true now. "I wanted something exciting to happen. I wished for an adventure."

She rocked me slowly for a while in silence, and I have always carried with me the comfort of that fat, commanding body and the sane, affectionate voice. "Where do you inherit this from?" she asked. But I knew she didn't expect me to answer. It wasn't really a question.

My father's voice was saying something in a tone of exasperation. ". . . Baba! What are you dreaming about? You are wanted on the telephone."

"I'm sorry," I said, jumping up clumsily, "I was thinking."

"Thinking?" he demanded frowning. "What were you thinking about?"

"Nothing much. Jalnabad . . . Nani—"

He looked puzzled, perhaps, but turned immediately back to the Congressmen. Their talk of politics followed me out to the hall.

Pria sounded composed and cheerful on the phone. "Are you coming to the races?" she asked. "Shall we collect you on our way?"

"Oh, New Year's, yes. That should be nice." It was nearly always one of the best meetings. "What time are you going?"

"Not early. Those first two hours always make me feel hot and tatty, and anyway nobody will be there until the Governor's Cup. Karan's filly Mehri Jaan is running so we'll have to be prompt. Suppose we pick you up at half past three?"

"Yes, I'll be ready." On an impulse I said, "Pria—"

"Yes."

"Let's not go to the Club after the races. Let's go somewhere else."

"Well, where?"

"I don't know, but somewhere or something different."

"Are there any different places?" I could hear the smile in her voice.

"There must be—"

"But in any case we can't. Karan and I are meeting people at the Club for drinks."

Later I walked out to the veranda, waiting for my father's meeting to end. Outside in the garden a couple of tiny honey birds with long bills hovered near the banked jasmine. Beyond our sloping garden, across the massed confusion of city roofs, I could see the distant glitter of the sea. The gardener's children were chattering gently among themselves, sitting like a row of parakeets on the low white wall down by the servants' quarters. A woman's voice from indoors called out something indistinguishable. The children slid off the wall and scattered. In a tree in the lower garden one of the children's kites had been caught and abandoned. The translucent paper held the sunlight as a bright ruby in the branches.

Behind me I could hear the sounds of voices coming into the hall.

The Congress Party men were adjusting their caps. My father stood at the top of the steps leading down to the drive, still talking. At last they all made namaskars, and turned their separate ways looking serious and worried.

My father and I had lunch alone together in the cool dimness of the long dining room. He was still full of the morning's arguments. "I'm not a constitutional lawyer," he said, "and in any case I have no taste for Delhi and its intrigues."

"Were you thinking of going to Delhi? Is that what the meeting was about?"

"Partly. In a way, yes. This month the constituent assembly will be convened, but of course the donkey work, the *real* thing, must be done quietly by a few people behind the scenes."

"And that's what they want you for?"

"So they say—with the usual appeal to my patriotic spirit attached. But I distrust these 'advisory' jobs—too vague, too undefined. And one would have to work with such small men," he said with conscious arrogance, "each wanting to write his own private prejudices into a nation's constitution. If only," he continued, as so often, getting carried away by the grander possibilities of the situation, "if only we had men of vision—what a historic opportunity for a declaration of faith and principle that would stand for all the world as the testament of this new emerging India! But," he sounded sad, "that spirit, I'm afraid, is an outdated commodity. Nowadays, we bicker and make compromises and talk about the common man and put everything to the vote as though a showing of hands were a magical alchemy to turn caution and greed into idealism and virtue. Still," he added, "I may do it."

I was quite used to being addressed somewhat in the manner of a public meeting. But suddenly, for the first time, it occurred to me that my father was not, perhaps, the powerful, determining figure I had always accepted—the incisive intellect, the driving nationalist, admired, respected. He began to seem old-fashioned, almost pathetic. The offer of the "advisory" job sounded a little like a consolation prize, polite (after all, they had a lot to be grateful for to my father), meaningless (the fight was over now), anyway, a comedown. He should be able to withdraw with dignity, I thought. Jay, at least, was young enough to be able to make light of his swan song. My father's swan song had been on a much bigger scale. The great Belgaum Sedition Case had been a tremendous national issue five years earlier. People had talked of it and written of it in every part of the country. One newspaper had described it as the greatest single spur to India's independence movement since Gandhi's famous salt march. And when the British government banned editorials of that sort, several of the Bombay papers came out with a blank white column on their editorial page headed "Belgaum Conspiracy" with the word "Censored" printed across it, and people reading the newspapers were even more indignant than if all the anti-British arguments on the case had been openly presented.

The accused in the case had been two rather bewildered peasants from a village near Belgaum, in the south of Bombay Province. The old man (who was actually a little gaga), too old to be of any use to his family in working their land, had once heard Gandhiji speak at a public meeting on the subject of non-violence.

He had been deeply impressed by that tough, inspired realist, perhaps the only Indian of his time who could speak to all levels of his countrymen at once. Afterward he had often quoted the great man's words within his own family, at village gatherings, even in casual encounters with people traveling through his village. "We must hold to truth," he would say, interpreting satyagraha literally, "and truth cannot live in a violent heart."

Everyone in the village had been thrilled by the arrival of a detachment of troops from the Indian Army who established themselves for some sort of training course near Belgaum, within easy reach of the village. For the old man it was a special excitement because now he had a new audience.

Sometimes in the evenings the soldiers talked of fighting. The White Man's war. Indian soldiers in Burma, in Europe, in Africa. The old man would shake his head and repeat his Gandhian principles, polished and smooth from repetition. "Not by fighting. Violence will never bring good ends. We must have peace in our hearts, only then will we find the truth."

Nobody—least of all the old man—really knew how the trouble started. Possibly someone was hoping to curry favor with the British officer. Perhaps someone was genuinely alarmed by the talk among soldiers of pacifism and Gandhi. Anyway someone had reported him to the Army authorities for spreading disaffection among the ranks and undermining their morale.

I first heard of the old man when our bearer came to tell my mother—who still lived in Bombay in those days—that a couple of villagers had come to the house asking to see my father. The bearer sounded incredulous, and uncertain whether the matter should have been brought as far as my mother at all. We all went downstairs together, to the kitchen. Most of the servants had collected on the steps leading down from the kitchen door to the open courtyard in front of the servants' quarters. I remember thinking how pretty the bright solid colors of the women's saris looked gathered in a group in the sunlight—the cook's wife, particularly, standing so gracefully with a large pan of orange lentils held in the crook of her arm and balanced on her hip. It was only

a few weeks since I had come back from school in England, and
things like that still caught my eye from time to time.

The old man was sitting on the steps and talking comfortably to
the servants, telling his story, describing the journey from his
village. His nephew who had accompanied him stood aside in
silence. He seemed more ill at ease, but perhaps that was because
of his shoes, which were obviously new and constricting, certainly
the first pair he had ever owned, and had probably been bought
especially for this trip to the big city. The young man saw my
mother first and gave her a deferential greeting. His uncle smiled
but didn't get up. "May you continue to prosper, my daughter,"
he said.

Much later, for the sake of a good newspaper story, these two
were quoted as saying that they "had heard of the great lawyer
Goray, and that he undertook to defend without payment anyone
who was arrested in the cause of independence for our country."
Actually, of course, they had no idea at all who my father was,
and certainly hadn't associated themselves with the cause of
Indian independence. An alert Congress Party member in Belgaum had seen political possibilities in their case far beyond the
immediate issue. My father, too, had seen in the situation the
makings of the perfect cause célèbre.

We took the two men into my father's study. The younger one
had taken off his shoes and left them neatly on the kitchen steps;
his uncle hadn't worn shoes in the first place. My father greeted
them with great friendliness, but the establishment of equality
never came easily to him, and I can still remember the incongruity
of the picture—his tailored and somehow exact figure leaning
against his desk, gesturing occasionally with a cigarette holder, and
the two bony peasants squatting on the floor, bewildered and a
little frightened. I remember, too, a moment when my father said
heartily and sincerely, "We will do our best for you. I will fight
your case with all my strength."

And the old man shook his head, certain at least of this. "Not
by fighting," he said. "Good cannot come through violence. . . ."

Anyway, the big drama came, as we all expected, in the courtroom. The crowds, the special police to hold them back, the

banners and slogans and the shouts of "Jai Hind!" the sympathy strikes in town and later the rioting and martial law. My father was at his best in an atmosphere as charged as that, and his final peroration is quoted to this day with all its fine emotional phrases. "Who can accuse a slave of sedition? . . . Loyalty is a free man's voluntary offering to his freedom. . . . Like love, allegiance cannot be commanded. It can be earned, it can be given and it can be simply—and most humbly—accepted. . . ."

I have forgotten, if I ever knew, what became of the two villagers. They were sent to jail, of course, but I believe it was a very light sentence. Certainly the whole case was my father's most successful failure and he emerged a hero—a reputation which to a great extent he deserved. The authorities, after the Belgaum Sedition Case, were far more wary in their application of the Defense of India rules; it had been a severe example of the inflammatory temper of the country.

That New Year's Day at lunch, I think my father regretted the years of the fight when principles were clear and the leadership certain. "Still, I may do it," he said. "I don't pretend that I 'understand' or 'speak for' the people of India. No. I leave those tricks to politicians. But I still have courage—or stupidity—enough to believe that certain values are universal and good and it is from those values that a constitution for any people should spring. Even if it is a vague advisory job, perhaps I should take it."

"I wish you wouldn't," I said without quite intending to.

My father looked at me with surprise. "Really. Why do you say that?"

"Well, I don't exactly know—" I couldn't say, "Your time—the time for gestures, for crusades—is over." He and all those other brilliant agitators—the Belgaum Sedition Case had been, in a way, the swan song for all of them. Now one needed a different kind of Indian—a kind, for instance, that felt comfortable in homespun cotton and a Gandhi cap.

❋ III ❋

THE MAHALAXMI RACE COURSE HAS ALWAYS DELIGHTED ME. It is all white and green and very pretty. Clustered around the white-painted betting booths and the railings of the show ring are banks of bright flowers. Between the show ring and the open terraces and restaurants of the Willingdon and Turf clubs stretch green and smooth lawns all the way to the actual race track. From the white galleries and boxes of the spectator stands you can see across the wide sunny oval, the far ranks of stables, half hidden by trees, and beyond them the emerald sea.

Across the lawns the women stroll in their silks and chiffons, fugitive pastels or the intense colors of the south. Then there are the turbans of the men in the starched cockades of the Pathans, the careful pleats of the Sikhs, the intricate coils of Rajputana, or the sheeny brilliance of the jockeys' colors. A subdued, occasional gleam of gold—from a sari border, a sandal showing through the film of trailing georgette and a brocade jacket. Flowers in the black hair of the women; flowers flanking the paths; the trees in flower shading the lawns; garlands of flowers for the necks of the winning horses, for their owners, trainers, jockeys; great silver bowls and cups filled with flowers to be presented from a table massed with flowers.

Almost the first people I saw at the races that New Year's afternoon, standing at the railing of the show ring, were the Americans of the night before. Two tall, foreign backs in the neatly casual tailoring of obviously American clothes. Pria and Karan had gone off to talk to Mehri Jaan's trainer and jockey and to join the other owners in the center of the show ring while the horses were led round. On an impulse I walked over to the railing and stood beside the Americans but I could think of nothing but the conventional "Are you winning or losing?" remark to make.

The girl turned. "Hello," she said, rather warily I thought.

"I've only just arrived," I continued, searching for firm conversational footing, "so I haven't had a chance to lose as disastrously as I usually do."

The man suddenly decided to smile. "Do you play hunches?" he asked. "Or do you have a system—like Alix?"

She moved her brown hand, like a spider, along the railing toward her husband. "Just because it's not a very systematic system—" she said, sounding very gay now.

"Well, as long as it works—" I began.

"Oh, it works, all right. You'll see," and all at once I felt included with these two in a private ring of amusement and expectancy.

The man said, "We ought to back the Maharajkumar's horse since we are his guests."

"Whose horse?" I asked, with only tepid curiosity, and was puzzled by his quick withdrawal.

"Maybe that isn't how you address him? Maharajkumar Jaywantsinghji," he pronounced the name clumsily. "Or is he His Highness of Kalipur too?"

"No, no. You're quite right. It's just that I'm used to thinking of him as Jay," I said, trying to cover his embarrassment and realizing that I was saying the wrong thing.

"We aren't familiar with your titles—" he started formally, but his wife interrupted. "Number six," she said, "the little gray one."

In the center of the ring I could see Pria and Karan talking seriously to the trainer and I wondered if I would ever be able to explain why I didn't want to back Mehri Jaan in this race, and then assured myself that I would never have to because they would assume that of course I had. Karan walked over to where the jockey was just mounting Mehri Jaan. He patted the filly's neck and watched her stagger in a high-strung canter toward the course. I turned my back on the ring and walked with the Nichols to the betting booths to place my ten rupees on number six.

Instead of sitting in the shade of the grandstand or in Karan's box, which is what I usually did at the races, I followed the Americans across the wide stretch of grass down to the track itself and watched the horses line up in the strong sunlight. It was the moment just before the afternoon turned with a fresher breeze and a slight chill into evening. People still preferred the cooler stretches under the trees or in the club pavilions and I felt conspicuous and almost daring, standing unfamiliarly with the two sunburned foreigners as if we were on a stage, listening to their excited chatter.

"There he is, purple with gray hoops and a black cap—terrible colors."

"He looks awful small to me—"

"But he's a winner, you'll see—"

The horses fretted and jostled at the starting line. The noise of the crowd behind us and on our right in the public enclosure began to sink to that tight quiet just before a race begins. The breathy whisper, "They're off!" and then the growing shouting from all around us.

"Can you see? Can you see him?" the girl beside me said. "Look, he's pulling ahead. Oh, I can't bear to watch—" She pressed her fists into her eyes for a second.

Actually it wasn't a very exciting race because number six kept his lead right around the course and came in a couple of lengths ahead of the field, but all the same, I found myself yelling, "Six! Come on si-ix!" with my new friends, as if I had never seen a race before. Certainly I had never been as interested in a race before. At some point in those two minutes I looked to see where Mehri Jaan had placed, but she was mixed in with several other horses somewhere in the middle.

The American girl turned to me, laughing. "Now are you impressed with my system?"

"Deeply impressed. Let's go and collect our winnings."

"We're rich but will it work twice?" the man asked. "I'm reserving judgment."

We walked slowly toward the tiers of boxes. I could see Pria sitting with Karan and somebody else, resting one elbow on the edge of the box and holding in her hand Karan's racing binoculars. She looked bored, her face turned a little away from the others, staring out at the people on the lawns below. I caught her eye, and without thinking waved my winning ticket at her. She wrinkled her forehead in surprise at my companions, and then signaled toward the club pavilion to indicate that we should meet there for tea.

Jay and several other people from last night's party were already sitting on the club terrace. As usual, the number of Jay's guests had overflowed to include a couple of the neighboring tables. Pria and Karan were there sadly sipping tea and discussing Mehri Jaan's form. Hari, sitting between two very unappealing girls (whom Pria and I privately called the Weird Sisters), said desperately, "You look very cheerful. Have you been picking winners?"

"Actually, we *have*—"

Pria looked at me, astonished. "But Mehri Jaan didn't come in—didn't even place."

"I know. We have been playing Mrs. Nichols' system."

"Alix," the girl said. "Please call me Alix. I never know who people mean when they say Mrs. Nichols—"

Hari said, "I must hear more about a system that *works*," and used that as an excuse to leave the Weird Sisters and join us.

Jay called out, "Have a drink, everybody. Really, one should always have a hangover party on New Year's Day when the state of one's head is the only interesting subject of conversation." And what with one thing and another I managed to ignore Pria's cool and speculative gaze.

Jay at this hour of the day was still looking fairly spruce. Behind him, as always, Daulat Singh hovered angrily, and every now and then twirled a bottle of champagne importantly in its bucket. He leaned forward suddenly and whispered something to Jay, who immediately put down his glass, pushed himself laboriously out of his chair, straightened his wilting jacket and ran a finger painfully around his collar as if he hoped to tuck his neck more securely into it.

Standing at the head of the stairs, which led up to the terrace from the lawns below between the potted palms and boxes of bright flowers, was a tiny woman, the Maharani of Kalipur. She made a tedious point of her smallness, and had always made me feel clumsy and like the girls who were good at hockey at school. Everything about her was in miniature except her carefully shadowed eyes, rimmed and elongated with kohl, which stared out with huge and deceptive appeal. She always wore the palest of pastel chiffon saris, usually sprinkled with floating designs in silver or gold sequins. Her saris were made for her in Paris—Pria and I considered this both unpatriotic and in poor taste. We were still very careful about buying only *swadeshi* even though it was by then clear that Indian independence was only months away. Ever since Gandhi's first passive resistance movement and its accompanying "Boycott British Goods" campaigns, our families had impressed on us the importance of supporting Indian industries exclusively.

Jay walked across to where the Maharani was standing and escorted her to our table. As she arranged herself next to the Americans, a sort of fog of her perfume settled over all of us. She continued steadily on with what she had been saying, raising her voice to reach across to Jay. ". . . and His Highness and I feel that you have let us down badly—I want you to know I put five hundred on your Mira and just *look* what happened. You must change your trainer, darling, that is the only solution. . . . I am delighted to meet you Mr. Nichols. American, are you? How I would love to visit your country. His Highness has some American friends he is very fond of, Bill and Sue Parson—you *don't* know them? They live in Long Beach—"

"Oh, California. Well, I—" the American began, but the Maharani wasn't listening.

"—or perhaps I mean Long Island. They come to stay with us in Kalipur for the polo—he plays *quite* a reasonable game himself in *spite* of those hundreds of martinis morning noon and night— do you suppose he will *ever* break himself of that habit?"

"Well, I don't know—"

"No, I suppose not. But *can* you believe it, *she* has a very good seat."

"A very good—?"

"Yes, I *knew* you'd be surprised. I'm sure you always think of Sue lying about on the beach in the south of France. Well, you should see her in Kalipur—you should go on a shoot with her—" she glared accusingly at the man.

"Your Highness," I interrupted firmly, "Mr. Nichols doesn't *know* the Parsons."

"Mr. *who?*" she said in a voice of childish surprise.

"Nichols," I said, "sitting next to you."

"Then why is he asking questions about them?"

I caught his eye over the Maharani's head and found him grinning widely to me. "But I would love to see Mrs. Parson's very good seat," he said.

The Maharani looked at him thoughtfully. "You do play polo?" she asked.

"No. I don't even ride horseback."

"Don't even *ride—*" she repeated helplessly.

"Have some cake," I said quickly.

"Darling," she said reproachfully, "you know I can't. It gives me *the* most awful attack."

"Liver?" I asked, resigned to a long account of her illnesses, "or amoebic?"

"Alas, liver." She turned brightly to the American. "I am a martyr, Mr. Nicholas, to my liver. I have been to doctors *all* over Europe, and they simply don't seem able to diagnose it properly. Diets. I have tried everything. Now just the other day Her Highness Madaghar suggested the waters at Aix, but I said to her, 'Darling, *who* has the courage to go to Europe these days? Even France and England, that we always *thought* we could rely on, even *they* are Communist. Where is one safe?' Only in your country, I'm afraid, Mr. Nicholson. Anywhere else they would murder you as soon as *look* at you. But who," she looked around at all of us triumphantly, "can get the dollars to go there?"

"And who," Pria murmured, "on earth wants to?"

There was an uncomfortable silence until Karan said heartily, "Fortunately the problem doesn't concern most of us. What is Your Highness' information on this next race? I see they're lining up. Can I place bets for anyone?" He stood up and we all looked expectantly at the American girl.

"I can't tell unless I see them," she said, and pushed back her chair.

"All this activity," Jay complained. "Sit down, sit down everyone. It's too late to do anything about this race anyway."

But everyone had started to leave. The Maharani called across to Jay, "You must invite your American friends to the polo. Mr. Umm is very keen."

"No, really," the American began to explain, "I mean, we'd love to come to the polo, but I don't know anything about horses. I'm sure this must be difficult for an accomplished horsewoman like Her Highness to understand."

The Maharani turned back in surprise. "Horsewoman?" she said. "I never ride."

The Americans looked at each other in mock despair, taking for granted the laughter between them, and all of us wandered back to the show ring.

Two more things happened that afternoon. One was that Alix's system astonished all of us by proving itself again, and as we had each bet twenty rupees this time we came out at the end of the day with several hundred rupees between us. Alix said, "We must spend it all on one thing, not just fritter it away in driblets. We'll have a party, a beach party. When is a good time? Next Sunday?"

I accepted at once, caught in her pleasure and excitement. Pria shrugged and said she would have to see. Jay, of course, said, "Excellent, excellent. A beach party—we shall use my shack at Juhu—we'll spend all day—" and arrangements were taken entirely out of Alix's hands.

The other was a rather bad moment. As we were leaving the race course Alix said, "I hope we shall see you before Sunday?"

Pria said, not quite insultingly, "One can scarcely avoid people in Bombay. It's a very small town."

"With a population of two million?" Mr. Nichols asked, amused.

Pria said vaguely, "Americans are so good at figures."

Alix said with some determination, and clearly to me alone, "I was wondering whether I might ask you to go shopping with me one day. I have to do over our apartment and we don't know many Indians here who could—"

"Yes, certainly," I broke in, anxious to get away.

Pria carefully said nothing about it even in the car on the way to the Club, and only made a few little remarks like, "Why in the world does that Mukerji girl wear white face powder? It only makes her skin look quite mauve." Or, "Karan, you really must talk to your trainer, surely Mehri Jaan ought to win *something* this season. . . ."

❀ IV ❀

EVEN NOW I REMEMBER MY SHOPPING TRIP WITH ALIX WITH considerable pleasure. It seems to me that we laughed a great deal over nothing much, and somewhere in the course of the morning we became friends. All kinds of surprising things delighted her— the bright yellow hats of the policemen, a solemn child walking along the street with a single small pumpkin balanced on her head, the pale blue mosque near the Crawford market, a man with a trained canary that picked out from a bowl folded bits of paper on which your fortune was written. She insisted on having her fortune told five times—all wonderful but rather contradictory. She loved the toy shops and bought lots of foolish wooden animals painted bright colors. She wanted, she said, a really giddy bathroom because she was sick of the surgical look of American bathrooms. She was going to place the animals in rows on the glass shelves instead of the usual toothbrushes and bottles of Alka Seltzer.

At some point she told me that her husband's name was Courtney. "Which," she added, "will tell you more than I ever could about his mother." For some reason this struck me as funny though I wasn't quite sure what she meant. "Everyone," she continued, "calls him Nicky."

"Nicky Nichols," I said, "that sounds like the cry of one of those jungle birds in Kipling." And that, in turn, made her laugh. We spent quite a long time in the cloth markets, where she gasped with pleasure at the extravagant colors of the silks and insisted on taking off her shoes and sitting on the white mattress

to have a cup of sweet, tepid tea with the shopkeeper. To my
relief she didn't ask if the milk were "safe." I took her to the
thieves' market, too, where she bought several peculiar bits of
furniture. She chose a table, for instance, and when I pointed out
that the legs were broken she said, "But I don't want the legs in
any case. I'm going to make a mirror frame out of the top." Then
there was a wooden hat rack that she said she would paint white
and hang "flower pots—all different colors—filled with geraniums
or something in full bloom" from the pegs. There was one thing
at which she looked long and thoughtfully, and then remarked,
"I really think I must have that for the intellectual exercise. I
could spend hours figuring out what it can possibly be."

I wasn't yet sure how much of the time Alix was joking, and
replied seriously, "The English call it a whatnot."

"A what?"

"A whatnot."

"Not a what, a whatnot. It's mystic," she said reflectively, and
then we both started to laugh again.

She was quite useless at bargaining because she made it so clear
that she had set her heart on this or that object that there was
no point in trying to bring the price down.

After all this, of course, the furniture wouldn't fit into my
father's car, which I had taken for the occasion, and Alix suggested that we hire "one of those black horse carriages I see everywhere." In all the years I had lived in Bombay I had never ridden
in a victoria. They were cheaper than taxis but slower, and besides
we felt—I'm not sure why—that they weren't quite "nice." However, it seemed at the moment the only practical scheme, so we
sent the car home, climbed into a victoria and had the furniture
piled around us. "Twice around the park!" Alix said to the driver.
He smiled uncomprehendingly at the eccentric foreigner, and I
prosaically gave him the Nichols' address. On the way back Alix
stopped to buy some limes that charmed her by their dusty, sour
green, and they rolled about on the floor of the victoria smelling
sharp and delicious in the sunlight. For a long time after that the
smell of limes reminded me of how much I enjoyed the slow,
clattering ride through the Bombay streets with Alix.

Once, some days later, Pria said to me, "But what do you see in those Americans?" It was one of the few occasions when she sounded bewildered.

"Oh, I don't know," I replied, embarrassed, "we have fun."

" 'Have fun,' " she repeated scornfully. "You're becoming as American as your new friends."

That night at dinner I asked my father if I could redecorate my room. He seemed surprised. "What do you need? New curtains?"

"No, I mean really redecorate it. It's all so heavy and gloomy."

"As you wish," he said noncommittally, but afterward he came up to my room with me and stood in the doorway looking thoughtfully around. The room hadn't been changed for something like thirty years—since the time when my mother had first come to the house as a bride and this was her sitting room. The only things that had been added were my bed and a long mirror. The rest of the furniture was still the dark carved rosewood that had been much admired in those days, massive and uninviting and a great nuisance to the servants who had to dust and polish the elaborate wooden lace of sofa backs and table edges. There were no pictures on the walls; the curtains were an ordinary sort of brown, the old Persian rugs subdued both in color and design. The only thing really to hold your eye was a bowl of pink roses by the bed.

I tried to see the room with other eyes, to imagine it changed as Alix might change it, "do it over," I thought, in her phrase. Pale curtains blowing at the window, all the furniture low, the chairs covered in pretty but impractical materials that would show the dirt, the brooding clothes cupboard banished to another room, many mirrors, a yellow carpet, perhaps, spreading all across the floor and covering the feel of cool stone under my feet when I got out of bed in the hot early mornings that would come in another couple of months. It didn't come to life in my mind.

"Furniture was built to last in those days," my father was saying. "Probably it seems old-fashioned to you."

"No, no," I said, "it was just an idea I had."

"I have no objection," he remarked coldly.

"I know. But it would be a silly waste, really. And what would we do with all this stuff?"

"I imagine there is still a market for good furniture. It was the best that I could buy." His voice still held a note of that remote satisfaction. It had lasted thirty years, I thought.

"Yes, I dare say, but—"

"As you wish," my father said again. He sat down on one of the stiff chairs, a strangely graceful figure in contrast. "Tell me," he said in the voice of a stranger, "are things a little dull for you here? I know I am very much occupied these days—"

"Oh, no," I interrupted. "Not at all—" I had never had intimate conversations with my father. We had no language for an exchange of confidences.

"Perhaps you should have gone to college."

"I never much wanted to."

"Nevertheless, it is supposed to train your mind, give you intellectual resources to fall back on . . . books," he looked absently around the room, "things like that."

"I do some reading," I told him.

"Mm. Novels," he said with a moment's scorn, and then with a return to a more familiar tone, "However, I agree with you on the whole, particularly these days when our universities are mass-producing graduates with no thought of their own or the country's needs. No jobs for them, all the white-collar professions overcrowded. There are few things more troublesome than discontented intellectuals. Never prepared to do the hard work, always ready to disrupt a scheme or a society. It used to be different in my day. A college education meant something then, and carried a sense of responsibility besides." He continued with the theme that I had heard enlarged on many occasions, and I hardly listened, thinking more about my years of expensive schooling in England and wondering vaguely what it had left me with. Sooner or later, I thought, I must get married.

Unexpectedly my father broke into his own speech to ask, "Do you see much of Hari these days?"

"We meet at parties quite often. He was at Jay's, and then I saw him again at the races."

"A pleasant young man."

"Yes," I said rather acidly, feeling pushed. "Very responsible."
If I marry him, I thought, I shall live forever in this kind of
house.

My father looked at me sharply. "If your mother hadn't gone
away," he said on something like a sigh.

"I also met a couple of Americans at Jay's," I said, pretending
not to have heard. "I rather liked them. He is in business of some
sort and she is very nice."

" 'Nice?' " my father said as though he had never heard the
word.

"Well, I mean amusing and very excited by India. I'm going
shopping with her again tomorrow."

My father said nothing. At last he got up to go. "Enjoy yourself," he said from the door. He had said the same thing before
Jay's party but that day it had seemed to me to have a different
meaning. All of us did many things that we counted as pleasures,
but I felt then that we seldom enjoyed them, and I think it was
a kind of joy in Alix, a determination to have a good time out of
life, that made her such an exotic and such a welcome addition
to my world.

Even in the Jalnabad days there was never much consideration
of enjoyment—not that any of us were oppressed in the house; in
fact, I suppose, as children we were rather indulged. There were,
of course, the necessities of school or college that forced a pattern
on the days of our older cousins, but for the rest of the time the
crowded life of the Jalnabad house occupied us and always there
was too much activity to allow for organized pleasures. Neither
my cousin Gita (closest in age to me, and my particular playmate)
nor I yet went to school, but occasionally our days were given over
to taking care of our baby cousin if his mother was busy or ill or
went calling on friends. Besides this, there were a number of small
tasks about the compound that fell to us, never actually specified
but somehow understood, and we did them as the others did
theirs, taking them for granted as part of the organization of
Jalnabad life.

In the pale, cool, north Indian mornings we used to go out to the vegetable garden beyond the well where the blindfolded oxen were already plodding round and round turning the creaking wooden wheel which pumped up the water for the morning needs. We carried flat baskets to pick chilies for the day's cooking, and okra, pumpkins, peas, whatever vegetables were ready; we dawdled . on the way back, stopping to see if the mulberries were ripe, picking up leaves from under the eucalyptus trees that grew tall and silver gray around the outside of the courtyard, pinching the leaves under each other's nose for the first, sharp smell. Even years later, whenever I had a cold and my mother put drops of eucalyptus oil on my pillow for me to breathe in all night, I would go to sleep with the thought of Jalnabad in my head, certain that I would wake to the special brilliance of the north Indian sun and the chill of those distant mornings.

Always, by the time Gita and I got back to the courtyard, deposited our baskets on the kitchen step—no one was allowed inside with sandals on—shouted to the cook to tell him what we had brought, yelled to the ayah the reply that we *had* washed, the courtyard was already busy with people. Servants would be taking down the mosquito nets and the bamboo frames from the long row of beds where the entire family slept at night, rolling up the bedding and carrying it indoors, stacking the beds themselves on one side of the courtyard, but always leaving one for my grandmother to sit on, strategically placed so that she could watch the coming and going of all the members of the household and rule the compound almost without moving from her place. Already the long procession of tradesmen would have started—the meatman, the fishmonger, the man with the spices and condiments (the men with Benares saris, glass bangles, Kashmir shawls had sense enough to wait for a calmer moment of the day)—and meanwhile the family, in twos and threes, would be going into the long, bare dining room for breakfast. There we all sat on the floor in front of low wooden tables, all looking brisk and starched in our white cotton clothes, hair still damp from bathing, drinking milky tea out of big silver tumblers, eating bread and guava jelly and fruit, and Gita and I usually had a special saucer of cream on our little table, the cream that had been skimmed off the milk as it boiled. We covered it with sugar and ate it very slowly. My two uncles were always in a hurry, gulping their tea with great, noisy whistles, jumping up, shouting to the servants or the children to bring their shoes, where were the files they brought home last night? what was the time?

Gita and I used to run beside them to the gate making our daily requests—please bring me back a pencil box, a doll, a ball—and watched while they climbed into the bus and went bumping away along the dusty road to Jalnabad. Meanwhile, in the courtyard, my oldest cousin would be standing, dressed ready for college except for the towel across her shoulders and her hair falling loose over it. She would stand wincing while her mother rubbed oil into the hair with long, hard strokes and at last braided it too tightly. The two boys would be standing impatiently by their bicycles, saying, "Hurry up, hurry up!" They had to see her into the college bus before they were permitted to pedal off to school themselves.

My grandmother would yell commands at Gita and me: "Ask the gardener why there is so little fruit this morning. Call the sweeper—he has made his wife pregnant again, it is really very thoughtless of him." Gita and I would scurry about, always returning to the courtyard as a sort of center of gravity. At about half past nine, my grandfather would come out of the house, walking stiffly with a cane, a smiling, scholarly old man, a not-very-successful provincial lawyer with a great fondness for children and an inexhaustible stock of family stories. Gita and I always ran to him, clinging one to each arm, and he always protested, smiling and pleased. "Stories? At this hour? You children are worse than the plague!" And Gita and I would continue to laugh and beg, while my grandmother, alert as soon as she saw him, would bring out his breakfast herself, serve him and watch him, standing warily beside him while he ate and drank. "Don't pester your grandfather," she told us, occasionally, but not really meaning it. Like us, she knew he was pleased. Afterward we made our second trip to the gate to see him in to the ikka—a tiny horse-drawn carriage —his only luxury, and wish him a safe ride to his office.

At last, when only the aunts, my grandmother and the youngest children were left in the house, the day was really ours. We would finish our share of the tidying of the house as fast as possible and then rush off to the mango orchard, our favorite playground. We had to be back in the house for lunch and if we forgot, as we often did, we would hear the high, wailing voice of the ayah. "Baba! Gita! Where are you? It's past eleven thirty! Are you hiding? What have I done to deserve such disobedient charges? Gita! Baba!"

But after lunch we returned to the orchard at once, and it is really those long, long afternoons, while the grownups slept and the servants were off duty, that I remember best. My grandmother had hired a small boy, for an anna a day, to scare the monkeys away from the mango crop, but it was easy to bribe him away. We, Gita told him, would take care of any monkeys that appeared, and he could go and play with his friends. Then we would climb the most likely tree and collect enough unripe mangoes to last us the afternoon. We sat in the dusty shade of the orchard eating sour mangoes, wrinkling our faces with delight at the acid, delicious taste, clenching our teeth at the shuddering sensation it left.

Gita, a talkative, lighthearted girl, shared my interest in magic, but without the superstitious nervousness that went with it. We told each other ghost stories, cold with a pleasant kind of horror in the bright, hot afternoons. We practiced our own magic, placing small white stones in a circle and leaving them overnight to see if there were evil spirits about. We knew that a demon cannot bear a perfect circle and would feel compelled to destroy it. The next day we would run back to the orchard, bubbling with excitement to see if our circle was still there. It always was, and that, in turn, plunged us into inconclusive discussions. "Perhaps they didn't notice it," Gita once suggested.

"Oh, they'd be sure to notice it. They go everywhere."

"Well then, perhaps it isn't a perfect circle and so it didn't bother them."

"Next time let's take a plate from the kitchen and mark out a perfect circle with it."

"The cook will see us."

"Not if we do it in the afternoon."

"Well, Nani will be furious."

"She needn't know either."

"She's sure to know. She sees everything."

"Would it be too small if we used a bangle?"

Dirty and still arguing, we returned for tea when the pace of the day again picked up momentum, when the family returned from schools, colleges, offices, when there were again chatter and news and activity in the courtyard. Later the servants spread huge cotton mats on the ground and my brother and cousins sat down with their books to study. The aunts would be perched together on a bed, mending, darning, making clothes for the baby. The uncles would be engrossed in the newspapers or the files they had brought back from their offices. My grandfather sat on another bed with his hookah beside him. As it gave little bubbling gasps and sent out a fragrance of charcoal and tobacco he asked for an account of the day from each member of the family, interspersing them with comments of his own, reminiscences, analogies with previous family events. My grandmother bustled between the kitchen and the family, supervising the cooking of the evening meal, watching to see that the children were working, reminding Gita to prepare for her music lesson, seeing that my grandfather was comfortable. It was a lovely time of day, and I would lie on the bed behind my grandfather listening to the whispering hookah and to the chatter and stories and dreaming deep into the sky as it darkened and the evening drifted over the courtyard wall. Sometimes if dinner was late, or if we pleaded, or if my grandmother found her work done and her hands idle, she would fetch her huge tattered copy of the Ramayana from the house, and as she crossed the courtyard would call out, "Fetch the children! I will read this evening."

The boys were allowed to stop their homework, the servants' children crouched around her bed, and all of us listened to the great legends of Rama and Sita and Ravana, of gods and heroes and demons and monkeys, of loyalty and treachery and evil and justice. She scarcely needed to look at the pages, she knew the stories so well, but as it grew darker one of the servants would place a lantern at her elbow, the listening figures would become shadowy and featureless, the night noises from the garden would gradually begin, and at last she would close the book with a snap and shout to the cook in a loud, sensible voice to ask if dinner was ready.

While we ate, the great, filmy cubes of mosquito nets would again appear in the courtyard enclosing the rows of beds. One lantern would be left on all night—no reading in bed; we weren't encouraged to waste kerosene. In the half hour before bedtime Gita and I often climbed the courtyard wall and sat on top of it trying not to remember the ghost stories we had told each other earlier in the day, sitting close together in the dark. Sometimes we saw the moon rise beyond the orchard, whitening the tops of the mango trees. Sometimes we just stared out at the far lights of Jalnabad trembling in the dust haze. It seemed a long way away though actually it was no more than, perhaps, a mile and a half, but ours was a tight protected world, circumscribed by the high walls around the garden, the orchards, and more closely by the courtyard and the house. If I longed for adventure, it was only against the background of this sure protection. If I wanted exciting things to happen, it was probably because I felt I could afford it—the Jalnabad house was so safe.

Until I went to school my life seldom took me outside the compound. About the only expeditions we made were to the temple, which I found quite exhilarating, and to call on friends, which I hated because it was accompanied by such an inordinate amount of hair brushing and face washing and instructions from the ayah about behaving well and eating enough to compliment the hostess but not so much that she might think we weren't well fed at home. On those occasions we all wore our "good" clothes: silk saris for the women, for the boys and the uncles tight pajamas wrinkled into neat folds at the ankles and achkans buttoned to the neck instead of their usual loose pajamas and flapping shirts. For Gita and me, still too young to wear saris, there were full silk trousers caught in a tight band at the ankle, and over them flowered silk tunics, and a gauzy scarf thrown over the shoulders. The baby was the most uncomfortable of all in his little velvet jacket trimmed with tinsel; he could hardly help being overheated and cranky.

Occasionally the world, in a sense, came to us—a second cousin who would come for a visit lasting several months, full of horrifying stories about her mother-in-law's cruelty and demented perfectionism ("She makes me grind all the spices myself," "I can never speak to my husband in her presence," "She makes me massage her feet at night."). A widowed great-aunt, who, of course, had a right to expect protection from any member of her husband's family, sometimes came for a month in the summer, unobtrusive and busily useful knitting blankets and shawls that the family would need for the cold north Indian winter. From time to time the family itself would bring the world back with it in the evening. Once, for instance, my oldest cousin came back from college with her sari wildly stained with red ink. Laughing and confused, she explained to us, "I was waiting for the college bus—I don't know what got into them, the men students, I mean—they were standing on the corner with a bicycle pump full of this red—" she gestured at her sari. "I don't know what got into them, they squirted it at me—I was so embarrassed—"

My grandmother wasn't smiling. "Why should they do such a thing?"

We all realized she was angry. "I have no idea," my cousin said. "Preparing for Holi, probably." That great, abandoned springtime festival that brings all of north India onto the streets in celebration, allows the boys their practical jokes, permits all the young people to throw colored water at each other, was only a few days away.

My grandmother said, "But why should they choose you?"

"Nani, I don't *know*. I was just the first one they saw, I expect."

"Nonsense. You must have looked at them."

We all knew exactly what my grandmother meant. "I *didn't* look at them," my cousin replied indignantly, blushing and angry.

"Why else should they choose you?—a girl from a decent family. They wouldn't dare."

"I *didn't*—I can't help it—I *didn't*—" she ran weeping into the house. I realized for the first time that evening that my cousin was remarkably pretty. After that Gita and I often discussed the various young men she might marry.

There was a time, too, I noticed, when the boys came back from school with a different kind of joke; Gita and I didn't really understand it, for they still teased us in their usual rowdy way, still scuffled among themselves, but now their laughter had a private sound and their conversation was full of hidden meanings and they stopped talking when the grownups were near. Gradually, I suppose, the relentless evolution of the family was bringing us to a knowledge of the world. Surrounded by the different generations in the house we slowly became aware of our own stages, a little at a time saw the possibilities, the promises and the threats of our own lives, but always wrapped around by the family, enclosed by the compound walls, measured by the secure progression of the Jalnabad years.

It was scarcely surprising that when, at last, I came to live in Bombay our house there should have seemed lonely and forbidding, and the life of the city should have seemed empty of the excitement I had once wished for or the warmth that the house in Jalnabad generated.

❖ V ❖

IN THE DAYS THAT FOLLOWED OUR FIRST SHOPPING TRIP I SAW Alix often, her husband less often. Alix and I went out a number of times to buy the many things she needed or fancied for her apartment. Sometimes we lunched downtown at the Taj Mahal Hotel, where we enjoyed ourselves enormously making small bets on whether the orchestra would play the "Warsaw Concerto" or not, steadily raising the odds and finally giving up the game because whoever said it would, always won. We giggled over the senseless skill that went into the elaborate ice sculptures in the middle of the cold-buffet table. And always Alix would want me to point out all the various people I knew and tell her what they did and what they were like—she was endlessly inquisitive. She loved the clothes, deplored the Western-style food and always ordered from the Indian menu, was enthralled by fragments of other people's conversation.

The scrap she cherished most, even after I had explained it, was the chance overheard remark, "But you can take our mystery for the evening," made by a very solid-looking woman with no touch of fantasy about her. Alix repeated it to me, adding with incredulous delight, "What can she possibly *mean*? Isn't it *heaven*? Imagine getting a mystery on loan."

Half convulsed with laughter myself, I said, "Not mystery, Alix, 'mistri'—she must have said 'mistri'—"

"Oh, *don't* tell me! If it's something ordinary, I mean, I'd much—"

"But it *is*. Very ordinary—only a cook—" But we went on laughing anyway.

She never liked to sit (as Pria and I did) at one of the tables by the big windows looking out across the harbor and the dark green islands to the far hills of the mainland. She wanted to be in the middle of everything.

Afterward, in those January afternoons, Alix and I went back to her home or mine and either flopped on the hard wicker chairs of my veranda or sank into her deep cushions, heads tipped back, legs stretched out, feet on the coffee table, and talked and talked.

The most surprising thing to me about Alix—shocking, in a way, but very attractive, too—was her frankness about herself, the openness of her demands. It was all part of that special excitement that she carried with her as a birthright. "India is just my meat," she told me once—I can't remember now in what context—but I was struck at the time by the appropriateness of the phrase. It was an appetite, this grasping for experience, this immediacy, this involvement with life. A big, healthy appetite, I thought. It was only much later that it seemed like greed.

"I suppose," Alix was saying, "the main thing in our lives—well, Nicky's anyway—is ambition. And don't ask ambition for what because it doesn't matter. Anything will do, or best of all, everything—money, work, people, social standing, even love—you know, to be better than good at everything and to be envied."

"It doesn't sound very restful."

"No. Well, we don't think too much of rest. Think of all that time to think."

"I do believe that's an epigram," I said, at a loss.

"And that's going to be the most difficult thing for Nicky about India."

"I don't see why he can't be ambitious here as well as anywhere else."

"Don't you? Well, look—you can only know that you are successful if you can measure it against other people. And in India you would never know."

"But you know Indians," I argued, rather puzzled but interested.

"I know you."

"And Pria and Karan and Hari, Jay, all the rest you've met in Bombay—"

"If you don't see *that* difference you don't see what I mean at all."

Actually I did see a little of what she meant—it was what had made me cross with Pria at Jay's party. "Anyway, there's a big foreign community here," I said.

Alix sat up suddenly. "But that's exactly what I don't want! Nicky wants me to join all these paralyzing clubs and go to bridge parties with the ladies and I keep telling him that it's silly to come all the way to India if you aren't *in* India. I can join clubs in Westchester."

"And you? What are you ambitious about?" I asked, expecting to learn something.

"I'm ambitious to be the kind of woman I'm ambitious to be."

"Oh, *now* I see," I said, laughing.

"I'd like to always be able to do the things I want to do, to have a good marriage, to travel, to have wonderful clothes and a special way with decorating rooms. I'd like to always be good company and always enjoy things and have people wonder who I am when I come into a room—" she broke off giggling at herself, and added in a tone of parody, "I don't ask for much—" But still, she smiled at me from her big silk sofa, asking me to reassure her on these silly points. And I smiled back, thinking of the holiday my family and I had once spent in Kashmir. I had stayed in bed much of the time with some complicated kind of flu, and when, at last, I was allowed to get up it was only for half an hour, to sit on the hotel balcony, heavily wrapped in blankets in the mountain sun. I heard my mother, calm and anxious, turning the pages of a book beside me. But I didn't read, just sat there extraordinarily pleased, warmed by another warmth, coming slowly back to life with a different vitality. There were echoes of all that in the afternoons I spent with Alix.

Her drawing room suited her much in the way her clothes did —everything chosen with an unsentimental eye to the woman who would be wearing it. There were no greens or blues because she said they made her look like an oyster. There were no ceiling lights as we had in our house, only table lamps, cushions the colors of nasturtiums, the gramophone playing very softly, almost inaudibly, the tunes that she used to hum or dance to in college, and massive low chairs in which Alix looked extremely slender and rather pathetic. I think it was, besides, what Alix thought a house in the tropics should be. Certainly it looked cool (though in point of fact it wasn't; or wouldn't be in a few months—too much silk, too much and too deep carpeting, nothing to keep out the glare from the sea), and was, I imagine, very far in feeling from the house in which Alix grew up. The house in Connecticut which her mother had furnished with American antiques (I remember thinking that I must tell Pria that phrase, 'American antiques'—it would make her laugh) at a time when they weren't particularly fashionable. "Now, of course," Alix told me, "they are and every morning when Mother gets up she looks around the house and is pleased all over again at her good judgment. She says that those months—years, really—when they were buying the stuff for the house were the happiest in her life. Week ends she and Dad used to go to country auctions and bid very cautiously for things and cart them home and spend days scraping them and waxing them. Dad used to laugh at her and say, 'Well, if it makes you happy to live in a junk shop. . . .' but she didn't mind and would ask his advice a million times about where this table or that cobbler's bench should be placed. She still does that, but it doesn't matter what you say because she's still going to move it a million times until it looks right to her." It all concerned a jolly sentimentality I had never known.

Alix often talked about how much in love her parents still were, and I don't think she ever noticed that the information embarrassed me or that the whole idea of one's parents being in love seemed to me even more inexplicably foreign than her descriptions of the Connecticut countryside or college week ends. "Childhood sweethearts, the boy next door, a small town only fifty miles from where they still live, Sunday dinners with the family, and they still adore each other, a typical American story. . . ." So far away, so unfamiliar.

But if Alix was able to talk so easily and so intimately about herself, she expected a comparable frankness from me. Her questions, which seemed to me at first alarmingly straightforward, were, I later realized, only what most people asked inside their heads in any case. "Are you rich?" "Your father is supposed to be famous, isn't he?" "Are you in love with anyone?" I tried to answer them honestly—"Not really, by Bombay standards. Compared to my grandmother's kind of life, yes." "Well, he used to be at the height of the nationalist movement. Not so much now." "No. No, I'm not in love—never have been."

"Oh, how sad for you!" Alix said with extravagant concern. "I can hardly remember a time when I wasn't in love—with a boy at dancing school who hated to dance, with Cary Grant and then Van Johnson, with a Princeton boy and a boy I knew summers at the beach (those were sort of the same time) and a Harvard graduate student and finally Nicky. Well, with Nicky it was rather different and I knew that as soon as I saw him. Parties were different during the war anyway. But we agreed at once on certain things—how to live and making a particular kind of impression—although we had different reasons. He was in uniform at the time; you can imagine, he looked very handsome. I let him kiss me the first night we met."

I could imagine very easily, and with rather romantic coloring could see them dancing, anonymously, in the kind of night clubs I had seen in the movies, or holding hands at a dimly lit table somewhere, driving out late at night to the Connecticut house, leaning back in the front seat of the car (I hardly ever sat in the front seat of our car, next to the chauffeur), kissing, saying, "To-morrow we will do this," or "Let's do that." I thought of Karan and Pria—I even thought fleetingly, and with a sense of inadequacy, of Hari.

In a rather flat tone of voice I said, "Well, I do expect to get married sometime."

"That's not the same thing."

"I know."

"Who will you marry?"

"Hari, I suppose. My family consider him very suitable." Hari, I thought. No surprise there. No sudden recognition at a party. No moment of dawning romance. A good marriage, though; I should consider myself fortunate.

Alix said, "But my God, if you aren't in *love*—"

"It's not thought to be necessary if the match is suitable."

"Well, my family thought Nicky highly unsuitable—" She got up to stand looking out of her big windows to the sea. "At low tide you can smell the seaweed quite strongly," she said.

I thought, anyone in Bombay could have told her that, an apartment like this on top of the rocks. What about the monsoon? The road outside will be flooded and the water will get into the engine of the car in the garage.

"Perhaps it will happen to you," Alix said, turning to me and smiling from some exclusive world. "Perhaps you'll fall in love some day."

Sometimes, talking of love, Alix would spring up from her chair saying, "I must call Nicky—it makes him furious!" and run to the telephone to dial his office number. I used to listen to her end of the conversation, feeling fidgety and neglected. The slightly gasping voice, the soft laughter, "Mr. Nichols please . . . his wife. Hello, sweetheart, are you busy? . . . Well, you'd say that even if you weren't. . . . Nothing really, just— Oh, I know, I know.

. . . Incorrigible is the word you're looking for. . . . Nicky, listen, one last thing—who do you love? . . ." Examining minutely
the fabric of the chair cover, I would think, How long can it take
him to say, "You, of course you." Alix's audible smile in her words,
"Just checking . . ." and she would come back smiling. "He gets
so embarrassed. Can't you imagine him sitting at his desk, looking
stern and efficient, trying to pretend it's a business call?"

"Does Nicky like India?"

"You don't *like* India, you get bewitched by it. He'll be fine as
soon as he feels more at home."

"Which would seem to miss the point of being in India."

"Well, you know what I mean—as soon as he makes friends,
then."

To myself I wondered whom he would make friends with.
Karan? Hari? Jay, in a mutual-obligation way? But I said no more
about it to Alix.

Eventually, on those afternoons, Nicky would come back from
his office, slam the door, shout to Alix. She would run to meet
him in the hall and I would stand up and stare uneasily out of the
big windows over the sea, listening to the deep personal silence
behind me, stronger than the faint music from the gramophone,
imagining the long embrace.

They would enter the room together and Nicky would throw
his jacket on a chair, say, "What a day!" or "Anything new?" turn
up the gramophone, mix drinks. And each time I would see him
a little differently, knowing Alix a little better, watching an expression I could interpret, a significant mannerism, a turn of phrase I
would understand, studying him as one would an adversary, someone to be dealt with. It was a curious, rather spooky feeling,
getting to know a man through his wife, hardly ever seeing him,
or not for long—strangers virtually, but intimate.

❋ VI ❋

T HERE HAD BEEN A FRIGHTFUL MUDDLE ABOUT ALIX'S BEACH
party. On the Saturday before it was supposed to happen, or
rather when the Nichols thought it was going to happen, Alix
telephoned Jay to ask what they should bring—who would provide
the food, the liquor, the cars? Jay, in his foggy early-morning
voice, had been polite but puzzled. "Beach party?" he said.
"Which beach party do you mean?"

"Well," Alix had said in some confusion, "we talked about it
at the races on New Year's Day—"

"What a nice idea." Jay had sounded most cordial. "I wish I
could come—"

"But don't you remember? We were going to spend all the
money we won off my system, all on one party."

"Excellent, excellent," he had chuckled in his jolly way. "I
meant to ask you about that system. It must be most ingenious to
be so successful—"

"But you won't, I mean you don't think you can do it?"

"Unfortunately. The first polo is on Sunday. H.H. is playing,
and of course I must be there."

Alix had been silent, not knowing quite what to say next. Jay
continued cheerfully, "I know what. Why don't you and your
husband come to the polo—he's a great enthusiast, I understand.
And then—yes, this will be much better—then we can have the
beach party at my shack the next Sunday. You've never been to
Juhu? Then I insist that you allow me to introduce you to it.
We'll go out in the morning—we'll spend all day—excellent,
excellent—"

When Alix reported this conversation to me later in the morning she added glumly, "As for polo, neither of us has even seen
a polo match." We were sitting in the deep veranda of our house,
from which wide steps led down, between boxes of tuberoses, to
the garden. Alix, in the painted wooden swing that my mother

had brought from north India when she was a bride, was holding herself steady with one foot on the floor. We never used the swing any more, but never thought of taking it down. Frowning and unsure whether to be cross or not, she jabbed forward with her toes. Slowly she swung away from me and back again. "What do you suppose happened? Did he just forget?"

"I don't know." In any case Jay was certain to seem to her either thoughtless or inexplicably rude.

"But you had expected to come, hadn't you? It was a definite date?"

"Oh yes," I said, lying. Like Jay I had known about the polo but had been so taken by her delight and high spirits in winning at the races that I, too, had wanted nothing to damp her at that moment. And Jay, particularly, was incapable of discourtesy, always fostered pleasure in another person.

"Well, I'm lost," she said, swinging away.

In an attempt to change the subject I said, "I'm sure you'll enjoy the polo."

"I don't know that Nicky will want to go."

"Do talk to him. I think he'll like it. The Kalipurs always have lots of foreigners—I mean . . ." I didn't know how to salvage that remark.

Alix considered her hand on the painted bar of the swing for a moment. "I'll tell him," she said.

With an effort I said, "I'm afraid I was rude."

"Nicky is very sensitive, you know. He needs a lot of reassurance."

"Was the beach party so important to him, then?" I felt that Alix was making a lot of drama out of an insignificant incident.

"Oh well, you know how it is," she said vaguely, catching the tone of my voice. "You hadn't really planned on it any more than Jay, had you?"

"I suppose not. Though I would have come."

"Mm. Whom did you have a date to go to the polo with?"

"Nobody. Since it's daytime I can go by myself."

"Daytime?" Alix said, sounding more friendly. "What does that have to do with it? Do your parents object to your going out alone at night?"

"Well, I'm not supposed to, though I don't think my father would really notice if I did."

"And your mother?"

"She doesn't live in Bombay."

"Imagine!" Alix stopped swinging and stared at me, immediately interested. "Are they divorced?"

"Goodness no!" I said, horrified.

"Or separated? Or what?"

"No, no! Well, yes—in a way—" I looked out to the garden in embarrassment, not knowing how to put a situation so long accepted.

Alix quickly covered her mouth with her hand in the gesture of a small girl. "Shouldn't I have said that? Oh Lord— Is it a secret?"

There was no space for secrets in the Jalnabad house, or for private scenes. We all knew what was going on behind the slammed doors of the indoor living room which we used only in winter. And where could my mother hide her swollen eyes and her despairing expression? To Gita and me, squatting in the passage outside, her words were clearly audible. "But what am I to do when there is no room in his life for me? Politics—endlessly politics and conferences. If I could even comfort him that would be something."

And my grandmother's cold reply, "There is always a place for a wife. It is by her husband."

"No!" my mother said violently. "It can make no difference whether or not I am with him. Am I to have nothing? Not my children, friends—even a home?"

"You have a home with him."

"A meeting here, a case there—traveling about—"

My grandmother said, as if it were of no importance, "In any event you cannot return to live in this house. The children are another matter. I, of course, would prefer them to stay, but if he insists on this scheme, his wishes must be respected."

"It won't do—it won't *do*—" Outside the door Gita and I could hear the helpless weeping.

"He has said that he wishes you to return to him, and there's an end to the business. Naturally you will go."

Gita and I walked quietly away from the door, and when we reached the courtyard, still without a word, both ran to the orchard although we were schoolgirls now and had far less time or interest for our old games and imaginings. Usually we looked forward to my mother's visits to Jalnabad because she arrived, twice or three times a year, with great baskets of presents for all the family, new clothes for the children and stories or descriptions of distant cities. This time we avoided her as much as possible, and in fact it was my grandmother who, some days later, called my brother and me into the house to tell us something. She spoke with the complete formality she adopted for Important Moments in the family.

"As you know, your mother will be leaving us again soon to join your father. Now that you are both old enough to take care of yourselves, they feel that you should go away to school."

"Away?" I asked, not yet apprehensive.

"To England. An English school can offer you more advantages than we can provide here in Jalnabad."

"*Mother* wants us to go?" I said disbelievingly.

"Your father wishes to give you the best education that he can afford. She, of course, agrees with him. So you see, Baba," she said smiling at me to forestall any protest, "you are to have your adventure after all."

To Alix I said, "It's not a secret. It's just hard to explain. I think she had wanted to leave for a long time, but she actually went away only three years ago. To set her life in order, she told us at the time. Now she lives in a small town in the south to be near her guru—her teacher, that is—"

"Her *teacher!*" Alix said, almost laughing.

"She goes to him every day to learn and to listen. And then, she spends a lot of her time in meditation."

"Well, if that isn't the most *peculiar*—" Alix suddenly checked herself, feeling I might be offended. "I'm sorry, it's only that I never heard of such a reason for leaving your family."

"It's not thought particularly odd here. Almost anyone comes to a moment in their life when they feel that the part that belongs to other people is finished and they must discover the rest."

Alix shook her head. "I still don't get it. Didn't you *mind?* Didn't your father try to persuade her?"

"How can you persuade about something like that? You don't know what the other compulsions are, and if you do perhaps you'd know better than to try to persuade. I was nearly eighteen, old enough to keep house for my father. I'd been back from England for over a year. I couldn't talk to her about 'rights.' "

I suppose I sounded severe because Alix, suddenly apologetic, said, "Pay no attention to me—I talk too much—but I wondered, of course—" As though she were offering me a tangible recompense she added, "I tell you what. I really will talk Nicky into coming to the polo. I'll tell him I want to—I'll ask him to do it for me—which is mean, but effective."

As it turned out, the polo afternoon, to begin with, anyway, was quite a success, even though the Maharani of Kalipur didn't recognize the Nichols and said to me in a penetrating whisper, "*Who* are your friends? Oh, *Americans.* What an extraordinary color she dyes her hair."

"I don't think it's dyed," I muttered.

"What? Oh it *must* be, darling, and such a bad job. All streaky."

I hoped, without conviction, that they hadn't recognized her because she was practically obliterated by enormous sunglasses and a pink silk sunshade which gave a feverish color to her skin and greatly inconvenienced the people behind her. Jay was talking earnestly to one of the Kalipur people, but waved and called out to us, "Meeting afterward at the Club for a drink. . . . must come . . ." We walked further down the stand and sat next to Karan and Hari—Pria never came to the polo because it didn't interest her.

Karan enjoyed himself explaining the game to Alix, pointing out to her the strengths and weaknesses of the players, and the Nichols sat in the sunlight watching the horses canter and turn, listening to the sharp wooden reports from the polo sticks and pleased, I think, by the novelty of the occasion, the unfamiliar flamboyance of the peacock-and-gold uniforms, the amusing incongruity of the Kalipur military band in the state colors but wearing white spats and huge turbans as they marched in formation during the interval or played, solemnly and neatly, a Sousa march or "Rule Britannia."

Alix immediately took sides and yelled for the Kalipur team, her voice ringing out clearly above the subdued comments of "Good shot!" or "Nicely!" from the rest of the spectators. Karan was a little embarrassed and made a point of applauding the Australians whenever he could. Nicky listened to Karan intently and asked a lot of questions about the training of polo ponies and how to tell a good player.

Hari, sitting next to me, had been mostly courteous but quiet. In the second half, when it became clear that the Kalipur team was going to win easily, he turned to me with his usual noncommittal inquiries about my family. What news from my mother? How were my brother and sister-in-law? He meant to call on them soon, before he left Bombay to return to his Poona land. And my father?

"I hate to see him disappointed," I told Hari, hoping, I dare say, for some reassurance from him. "I feel he is trying to hold on to something that he has already lost. Sometimes he seems to me so old-fashioned—that is only to be expected, I know—but it is more than the ditch between generations. His India is gone, and suddenly, suddenly he is in a strange land, dispossessed."

Hari never offered me sympathy. "As you say, only to be expected."

"But he has worked so hard!"

"Oh yes. And fought so effectively. But that alters nothing. It was always for an idea, you see, never, really, for people."

"You talk with such authority," I said, chilled by his callousness.

"Of course," he said with his implacable Mahratta confidence. "I am a farmer—landowner, if you prefer—and my people have always been. Our tragedies are matters like famine and too little water."

A thin burst of applause announced the end of the game. The

band played. The players, swinging their sticks, moist and smiling, their caps pushed back, cantered off the field.

"What are you doing this evening?" I asked Hari on an impulse. "Come and have dinner with us—just family, nothing special."

"Thank you very much," he said in a casual voice.

At the Club the Kalipur party, scattered among a number of tables, took up most of the terrace and spilled over onto the lawn. I found myself separated from the Nichols, and finally caught sight of them sitting some distance away, among some Kalipur State people, Alix looking oddly defenseless and Nicky ready to be pleasant but not quite sure whom to be pleasant to. Then someone asked me some routine question about the races or Bombay gossip, and I turned back to the people at my table.

The waiters in their long white coats and broad green sashes scurried about with chit books, drinks, bowls of nuts and savories. Music from an inside room reached us unobtrusively, and through the tall glass doors of the card room we could see the dedicated faces of the bridge and poker players. The polo teams arrived late with shiny clean faces and wet hair still holding the stiff furrows of a comb. Pria arrived later still, in the palest of yellow saris with red roses in her hair.

Apart from Kali's massive unconvincing gallantries to the various girls ("Ha ha, must make new ground rules—none of the beautiful Bombay ladies allowed on the polo ground. Too distracting. Can't keep your mind on the game. Ha ha."), and the Maharani's monologue about the state of her health and the state of the world, most of the conversation was about polo and horses and more horses and polo. Jay was always withdrawn and rather quiet in front of his brother, and only smiled and nodded when Kali called across the tables to him remarks like, "Shockingly out of condition, what? Never make a player out of you, Jay," and laughed loudly.

Pria said, "How long can we possibly stand this?"

"Another ten minutes, not a second longer," I said. "I must get back in any case; Hari is dining with us."

Pria looked at me and didn't quite smile. "We'll probably stay

on a bit longer. Karan seems to be enjoying himself, so I might as
well get used to it."

The Nichols were sitting together being offered drinks and food
but not being talked to. Even Alix seemed a bit uncomfortable.
When I went over to them to say good-by, I noticed that they
were holding hands under the table, but there was an antagonism
behind Nicky's voice, and in Alix's bright stare a kind of hurt.

"If you are as bored with this party as I am," I whispered,
"come with us. I'll drop you home."

"We won't trouble you—" Nicky said.

"Oh darling, let's not—" Alix began, her hand on Nicky's arm,
an appeal of some sort in her voice.

He interrupted, "We don't want to impose on anyone. We can
get a taxi here, can't we?"

"Oh yes," Hari said helpfully, "just tell the clerk at the desk.
He'll telephone one for you."

"Fine. Well, we'll do that."

Alix looked at me imploringly, I thought; Nicky with a mysti-
fied hostility. "Let's lunch tomorrow," I said to Alix, and when
she nodded Nicky turned to her with a gesture of such exasperation that I was glad I couldn't hear his comment.

As we were leaving I asked Hari if he thought the Nichols were
annoyed.

"Why should they be annoyed?"

"Perhaps they expected me to take them home."

"What outlandish things you worry about. He said he would
rather get a taxi."

"Nobody was talking to them. Perhaps that's why"—which, I
could see, appeared as no particular disaster to Hari. "I think he
thinks that Alix is too much with Indians. Too much with me,
that is."

"Oh really?" Hari said blankly; then probably thinking he ought
to say something, he said, "They don't seem to mind going to
Jay's parties."

"Well, princes are different."

Hari nodded at the accepted fact. We had already talked too
much about the Americans.

We decided, as we often did, to drive by Chowpatty, that short stretch of beach between Malabar Hill and the long crescent of the Back Bay, to buy some bhael-puri, a hot, sour-sweet mixture of various cereals and chutneys and pickles. Out on the beach at this time of evening the stalls of the vendors had been set up, each lighted by a glary kerosene lantern. Crowds of people were walking along the beach or gathered around the stalls; there was a man with two trained monkeys doing tricks, and the excited laughter of children. The lights that formed the Maharani's Necklace were just going on, the black promontory of Malabar Hill was pinned here and there with lighted windows, the headlights of cars sweeping down the drive illuminated for an unreal second the massed trees and then fled on up the hill. Hari and I plodded back through the sand, each holding a newspaper cone full of bhael-puri, remarking as usual that we would never be able to eat any dinner after this, commenting as we always did on the mystery of the mixture, how the vendors throwing the ingredients together in the most casual way, mashing it all together with their fingers, should be able to produce every time this delicious mess. You can never do it properly at home.

Shalini was waiting for us when we got back to our house. She was sitting on the veranda lecturing the bearer about putting too much sugar in her lime juice and water. She scarcely greeted me as I joined her. "Don't your servants know that there is rationing?" she demanded. "The waste that goes on in this house!" The bearer retreated thankfully now that I had arrived to listen to Shalini's scolding. "I know you have your own way of doing things, and I don't want to be interfering, but I do think you should keep the stores locked up. It's a constant temptation to the servants, and it's really no kindness to them—"

"It's not supposed to be. It's just more convenient for me and less trouble."

"Goodness, what do you do all day that you can't take a little trouble over the running of this house?" There was no answer to that, and Shalini continued her complaint. ". . . spoiling the servants . . . the least you owe to Papa . . . can't blame them when they are practically asked to steal. . . ."

Hari, who had gone into the study to see my father, now came out with both my father and brother. Three disconcertingly different men. Hari, not tall, but straight and moving easily, a serious, irregular face with its full, curling mouth and striking eyes, heavily lashed and deep. My father, tall, precise, handsome, gesturing characteristically with his cigarette holder, and my brother, who had not inherited my father's good looks, short and round, like a bun with alert black eyes and a drooping, childish mouth.

As soon as Shalini saw Hari she became coy and knowing. "What a stranger you have become! We never see you. But I dare say you have better things to do with your time than see dull old married people like us."

During dinner she was even worse and said things like, "Baba moons around the house all day; I wonder whom she is dreaming of?"—with a sly smile at Hari.

"Oh Shalini, do shut up," I said, not really caring.

"But only before dinner," she said in her most injured voice, "you were telling me that it was too much trouble to run this house. Then what is it that occupies all your thoughts?"

Well, anyway, not Hari, I thought. There had, however, been a time when I had developed a mild hero worship for Hari. During my second year at the English school, my brother and I had returned to Bombay as usual for the summer holidays. That year my mother had taken both of us up to Poona to escape the worst of the hot weather in Bombay. Since she, with the standards of her childhood, considered it bad form to stay in a hotel if you have relatives or good friends in the district, we all stayed with Hari's family on their Poona land.

It was an eventful summer for me. For one thing, Hari taught me to ride, and for another, he told me one of the secrets of the self-possession he had displayed even as an adolescent. "Whenever I am scolded I pretend to be Shivaji"—he was, of course, Hari's hero. "Then I can say to any grownup (not out loud, naturally), 'You can't punish me. I will ride away across my land and hide in the mountain fastnesses.' " Even at the time it seemed to me a splendid chapter of history, and I listened entranced to

Hari's stories and references from the turbulent past of the Mahrattas.

I could imagine, as he described it, that strange, poor, tough army of Shivaji successfully holding back the Moghuls, defeating the Muslim armies—the kind of glorious triumph of wits and morale over superior force that, at school, was connected only with the British against the Spanish Armada. To his soldiers in the seventeenth century Shivaji had offered practically nothing except pride and glory. Each man was issued a horse and a sack of grain and after that he was expected to fend for himself, to eat off the countryside, to use his ingenuity to find himself quarters for sleeping or living, to take care of his own wounds, to manage somehow. A tough, realistic army raised from a poor part of India and paying off in success through its mobility, its guerrilla tactics, its very poverty. An army that could be assembled overnight, that could, when necessary, simply melt into the land, into the lives of farmers, peasants, mountain herdsmen. It all came to life as Hari talked in the old days. Shivaji the bearded hero, the flashy military genius, the arrogant Mahratta, the unconquered Indian—one never heard about him in school in England and I was proud to be allowed to be one of his horsemen—even a minor one—in the wild games that Hari and my brother played that summer. When we rode in the Poona hills, I used to imagine I was with Shivaji waiting in ambush beside the great trade roads of the Moghuls with the guerrillas in hiding all around. When the great, ponderous caravans of the Moghul came down the road, magnificent with elephants, loaded carts, sacks of gold, companies of heavily equipped horsemen, enormous stocks of food and rare foreign delicacies for the palaces in Agra, tents and paraphernalia for their huge, luxurious camps, Shivaji and his men would sweep down from the hills, fight, loot, never take prisoners—only horses—and vanish again into their dry, scrubby land. With Hari, I was caught in admiration of that great, burning, unsentimental patriotism of the Mahrattas that made them—even now—call their province simply Desh, which means Land, as if there were no other land, as if that stretch of hills and plains and insufficient rivers needed only the word earth—so grand and so ordinary—to identify it forever as a special place, the only land worth considering.

There was a legend, Hari used to tell me, that Shivaji had a secret overland route between Bombay and Poona, so that he didn't have to go the long way round the Trombay inlet, and he could ride in an hour from the sea to the hills. It has never been discovered since, and I used to dream of discovering it again after all those years.

On occasion, Hari and my brother and I used to act out even the one time when Shivaji was captured—but only because it ended so well. He escaped from the impregnable prison of Agra in a basket of sweetmeats. I always felt it served them right—those luxury-loving Moghul emperors who would be fools enough to allow sweets into a prison as a matter of courtesy. And afterward all they could say to themselves was, "Witchcraft! Witchcraft!" and call Shivaji the Mountain Rat to shrink his stature in their own minds and save their self-esteem. Afterward we would canter about the Poona land yelling like maniacs, "Hurr! Hurr! Mahadev!"—Shivaji's battle cry that had at one time been the most frightening words in half of India. My grandmother would have thought the whole thing most unseemly, but she never heard much about that summer because that was the year my grandfather died, and her mind and time were fully occupied settling the property and coping with the dispersal of the family in Jalnabad.

I decided to tease Shalini—the impulse was always too much for me—and said to her, "I'll tell you who occupies my thoughts," and when she looked up in her sharp, inquisitive way, added, "I dream of Shivaji the unconquerable."

Shalini frowned and said in exasperation, "Really, Baba!"

Hari, who had a way of handling knives and forks inexpertly, as though they were clumsy instruments ill-suited to the business of eating, pushed them away with some relief and smiled at me affectionately across the table. "Will you never grow up?" he asked.

My brother was munching his way steadily through dinner and my father was silent and rather sad, thinking, perhaps, that he had

done as well as he could by his children, that there is no knowing
how things will turn out. Shalini, I'm sure, was thinking, She'll
never get him this way, missing a perfectly good opportunity to
blush and look down, or to smile at him meltingly. No, no. Sweet-
ness, a certain womanly gentleness, an appreciation of his wishes,
a helplessness combined with domestic competence—that was the
way to catch a husband. Those, for instance, were the qualities
she had displayed to my brother before their marriage. And once
she had him in the mood to marry her, she had shown extraordinary grit and determination in having the matter settled at
once. He had met her after his first year at Oxford, when he was
back in Bombay for his "long vac.," as he called it. I, too, was in
India for the holidays before my last year at school, and we had all
gone to the wedding of a distant relative of ours.

Just what happened between the time when he met Shalini as a
wedding guest that day and the time a couple of months later
when there were long conferences in my father's study and sulks
and defiance from my brother at home, I never discovered. Possibly, less at ease in Oxford than he had been at school, watching
his friends going out with girls, finding the center of life shifting
from studies and sports to social or emotional things, uncomfortable and frightened with English girls, he, too, had felt the need,
if not for marriage, at least for an excuse.

Anyway, he had made an issue of it—strongly supported by
Shalini and her family, who were pleased to have her settled so
well with so little trouble. My father couldn't even persuade him
to wait until he graduated, and finally consented to the marriage,
although I think his real grief was not Shalini's entrance into the
family but my brother's refusal to become a lawyer. Shalini
wouldn't leave India, and my brother, therefore, could not consider the long years of study, of being called to the bar, of training,
away from his wife, in London. He returned a couple of years
later to enter, with my father's influence and pressure, a respectable banking job with "a future." He seemed to be content with
his life, but I had no real way of telling. We hadn't grown any
closer through the years since his marriage, and the rides and
games and shouts of that Poona summer seemed to be no part of

the solid, quiet man at dinner in Bombay. As for Hari, I felt
pretty sure that there was no longer any room for romance in the
commonsensical devotion he now gave to the Poona land, and
even in the old days the dreams of Shivaji had been, in a way,
only an insulation against the rest of the world.

❋ VII ❋

Banganga, on the shore of malabar hill, a sort of
village within the city but no part of the city's life, is the oldest
remaining part of Bombay.

Fishermen live there mostly, and a few dhobies and their families. It has its own tiny bazaar, and the ubiquitous paan and biri
stalls. Its crumbling temple still shows every sign of active life
and worship; the images are regularly smeared with kum-kum,
offerings are placed before the shrine, children run madly about
kicking aside the withering flowers of past devotions. In front of
it, occupying more room than anything else in the village, is the
huge, ancient bathing tank with its tiered, uneven steps, its glassy
expanse of fresh water, and beyond that, half obscured by dusty
trees, the huddled huts and houses of the people. It was from this
fishing village that the city grew. But you can't drive there because
the only road connecting it with the rest of Bombay cuts sharply
up the hill in a series of shallow steps, and if you walk up them
you emerge bewildered at the busy corner and tangle of traffic at
Teenbuthi. Impossible to believe that only a couple of minutes
separate the turbulent anonymity of the city from the intensely
personal life of the village.

The other approach to the village, the one that Alix and Pria
and I took one night, is a narrow foot path along the rocky shore
that brings you up from the sea into a short alley and then to the
edge of the sudden dark and sobering oblong of the temple tank.
Nicky had gone out alone to a stag dinner and Alix had telephoned me while Pria and I were sipping our after-dinner coffee
on my veranda.

"I was planning to eat a sandwich and a glass of milk, and give myself a manicure, and write a letter home, and get to bed early and things like that but I don't feel the least bit like doing that. Why don't you come over and have coffee here?"

I was still amused at Alix's American way of framing requests. "Do you want to turn the light off?" when she meant "Will you please turn the light off?" or "Why don't you come over?" instead of "Please come over." It lent a foreign color to even her most ordinary conversations.

"Pria's here," I said.

A pause. "Would she care to come too?"

"Better still, let's all go for a drive."

Pria raised her eyebrows but made no objection, and after we had picked Alix up, I suggested that we watch the moonrise from the village, knowing by then something of Alix's tastes, the disproportionate pleasure that the most ordinary Bombay sights gave her—the driveway of somebody's house decorated with lights and paper flowers for a wedding or a prayer meeting, the Mahratta women in the burning colors of their cotton saris, with their big nose rings, toe rings, anklets, usually employed where some city construction was going on, walking erect to balance the shallow trays of stones on their heads.

The moon was already up when we got there. My father's chauffeur waited in the parked car while we walked the short distance to Banganga.

"Oh, what nights you have in India," Alix said. She stared at the pale slice of moon and the dusting of stars, and stumbled on the stony path.

"They get better in the hot weather," Pria remarked. The sky comes down closer then, and the stars grow with meaning.

We walked round the tank to the little temple. All about us was the spiced and smoky smell that no Indian ever forgets, the breath of the country inextricably a part of cities and villages or any place where Indians live. A small pot of live charcoal glowed in the temple. On a bench an indeterminate shrouded figure was asleep, its head covered. When Alix lit a match, a full-breasted stone woman danced out of a wall and retreated immediately, impossibly slender of waist, shadowed, jeweled, her face worn to nothing but a faint, knowing smile.

Across the tank was an angry little kerosene light from a paan stall; a few indistinct figures stood around it. Over the water an occasional spurt of laughter reached us, a word or two from some-one leaving, saying, "It's late, let's go." We sat on the parapet around the tank, turned sideways to the great dark hollow, watching the moon tremble on the water.

"Before I came," Alix said, "I thought all of India would be like this—sort of mysterious, and making you feel very small."

"The darkness is an advantage," Pria said. "It looks better when you can't see the dirt."

Alix continued in a wondering voice, "I had such a clear picture of India knowing nothing about it, just bits of this and that picked up from all over, movies, a book or two, and, I don't know, just hearsay I guess. There was to be dirt and diamonds and nothing in between, elephants in procession, women in purdah and Untouchables. People bathing in the Ganges in incredible squalor, a very romantic Kashmir (lakes and lotuses) and, of course, any number of mystics." She laughed softly. "And here I am in India and my pictures were all wrong. I haven't seen any of those things, or anything like them. It's all so wonderfully un-expected—"

Pria interrupted in her dry, cool voice, "But it's all here, in India, I mean. All those things and everything else as well, just about."

"Even the mystics?" Alix asked, making her own comment on Bombay society. I thought, Pria shouldn't treat her like a fool.

"Oh yes," Pria said vaguely, "but mysticism is apt to show up in rather unpalatable forms. It makes it difficult to accept."

"You find it so?" Alix pursued.

"Oh no, we don't."

"I see," Alix said in irritation. "You know something? When I was—" I felt her sudden recoil against me, and heard her sharp intake of breath. From somewhere close by, unseen in the shelter of the parapet, a figure emerged, trailing a dirty white cloth. It crouched sleepily at our feet, and seeing Alix's long legs stretched down the wall, it touched her feet and her ankles, and began the familiar, sexless beggar's whine about no money and no food and being hungry. . . . I felt Alix tremble against me. "—get him away—"

"It's nothing," I said.

Her voice was on the edge of control. "What does he want—get him away—"

"Hush," I said again. "It's nothing. A beggar."

A couple of coins clinked in Pria's hand. "Here," she said, "clear off. Buy yourself a biri." The figure tottered away into the far shadows. I could still feel the electric tremor of Alix's shoulder against mine. "He touched me," she whispered.

"It's a terrible racket, this begging," Pria said absently.

After a silence Alix said in an ordinary voice, but unable to help herself, "Was he—do you think he was a *leper?*"

"Oh no," I said.

Pria said, "In any case, it's not nearly so contagious as everyone thinks."

In the moonlight Alix's face looked pale, her hair ashen. She seemed to be in need of protection, and I thought, Nicky can't protect her here, only in his own world.

On our way back in the car we left Pria at her house first, and when we reached the Nichols' apartment, Alix said, "Come on up and have a drink. I don't want to sit around alone waiting for Nicky."

But upstairs Nicky had already returned from his party. He was standing at the liquor cabinet, glass in hand, looking abstracted. He had taken his tie and jacket off. He was rocking gently back on his heels, at loose ends. I wondered if he had had too much to drink. He put his glass down when we came in and turned alertly.

"Where were you? I was worried." He nodded briefly at me, not really conscious of my presence, and looked back to Alix.

"Fix me a drink." Alix sounded exhausted. "What about you, Baba? Just water? I don't know how you do it. . . ." She kicked off her shoes and crouched in one of the massive chairs. "There are moments of the day—between half past six and seven is the worst—when you must have a drink to tide you over, it's such a difficult stretch. . . . Do sit down, everyone."

I smiled at Alix and sat opposite her. Nicky came over with her drink and stood there looking down at her. "I thought you were going to stay in. I thought you were going to get an early night."

"I was." She made a slight gesture of raising her glass to me and sipped her drink. "We went out instead."

"Out? Where did you go out?" Nicky sounded inexplicably stern.

"Where was it, Baba?" she asked languidly.

"Banganga," I said, pleased that the name meant nothing to Nicky.

"Where? Where did you go?" He looked badgered.

Alix complained, "I was lonely. I can't stand to be lonely."

Nicky muttered, "Oh God," and turned away restlessly, back to the liquor cabinet for more ice, as if he were unwillingly entangled in some petulant, insignificant women's dispute. "All right, all right," he said, "I only—"

Alix sat up and said sharply, "Does it matter where we went? We went for a drive."

"I only wanted—"

"I acted sort of silly and I don't want to think about it."

"Look, I only wondered why you were making such a mystery of it."

"It's no mystery."

"If you want a mystery," I said suddenly, "I'll lend you mine for the night."

Alix looked straight at me and her face began to crinkle and then we were both laughing uncontrollably, bent double in our chairs, laughing and laughing. "What? What?" Nicky said, look- ing expectantly from one to the other, waiting for a signal to laugh with us. I could almost have felt sorry for him except that I was laughing too hard. "Nothing," I said between helpless gasps. "Just . . . a foolish . . . joke."

Alix sat up wiping her eyes. "Lord, Lord. I have a cramp."

Nicky smiled stiffly at us. "I get it. A private joke."

"They're no good if you explain them."

"Well. I think, if you'll excuse me, I'll get some sleep." He was very angry. He strode loudly from the room, leaving his half-finished drink on the table. Silence settled slowly over the room with Nicky gone. Alix and I avoided each other's eyes. A minute or two, not more. I could imagine Nicky unheard, banging furiously about the bedroom. Undressing with large gestures, feeling left out.

Alix jumped up suddenly. "Oh, why do I have to be so mean and irritable? I can't bear it when Nicky and I quarrel."

I, too, got up. "Was that a quarrel?"

"Lord, yes. Couldn't you tell? I must go and make it all right with him." As I turned to leave she caught my arm. "I'd hate it, you see, if he *didn't* worry about me." She smiled. "We have lovely reconciliations. He's really very sweet."

"I'm sure he is."

"Lunch tomorrow?" Alix asked, as an apology.

* VIII *

THE NEXT DAY, WHEN ALIX AND I WERE LUNCHING AT THE Taj, we saw Pria and Karan at a window table. Usually Pria would have dragged Karan over and joined our table, but that day, smiling and remote, looking very beautiful in her precise way, she scarcely nodded, and when we looked around again both of them had left.

Pria phoned me that evening and asked me to come and look at her trousseau saris, which was her way of assuring me that we were friends. Actually, she hadn't even brought the boxes out of her dressing room because Pria had her own kind of directness. We sat on her bed, drinking lime juice and water, and we talked about the Americans. Pria never used the hypocritical prefaces of "It's none of my business but—" or "I may be wrong but—" She said, "I think you're being a terrible fool."

"Seeing the Nichols?"

"Well, seeing so much of them. One expects to meet Americans at parties occasionally, not our parties of course. But every day, and so conspicuously—giggling in public, riding about in victorias. It must be a kind of hysteria."

Irritated and somehow guilty, I said, "But Pria, I like them."

"I dare say. You 'have fun.' But you know how these things end."

"What things? Friendships?"

"Oh, friendship," Pria said in exasperation. "Do be sensible. As if one can be friends with them. I mean how people like the Nichols end in India." She added more kindly, "You know it as well as I do."

"They aren't anti-Indian," I said, answering Pria's real comment.

"Of course not. I didn't say that they were stupid. Nobody is anti-Indian these days. It isn't chic. Only Cheltenham colonels and Anglo-Indians and red-faced clubmen and people like that are anti-Indian in the old-fashioned sense—and they are as much a joke to the foreigners as they are to us."

"Then," I said obstinately, "I don't know what you're talking about."

"Yes, you do. You just won't admit it."

I got up and wandered about the room, touching the chiffon sari that Pria would wear that evening where it lay over the back of a chair, staring at the neat pile of laundry that had just come back from the dhobi, picking up the family photographs in silver frames. "How can foreigners ever be friends with us if we don't let them be friends?"

"I can't say that's any ambition of mine," Pria replied.

"I dare say. But you can see, can't you? that this thing that they have—whatever it is—this vitality, this joy or discovery in life, you can see that I find it attractive. They suggest—or rather Alix suggests—something lacking in my own life—"

"Well, that can hardly be surprising since it is a different life."

"Then, let us just say that I find them stimulating, though that is only half the truth."

"And the other half, I suppose you think, is that she will give you a key to something or other. But you know perfectly well that it is without significance in your life."

"If I knew what was significant—"

"You do, really. Your whole childhood must have taught you that."

"Family. Responsibilities. Duties—"

"You deliberately make it sound dull."

If only Pria liked Alix, I wished. Rather slyly I thought, Perhaps she will respond to a predicament, see Alix as making a brave try, admirable at least, if pathetic. "Listen," I began, "they've come to India—"

"That's what they never realize," Pria said, refusing to be wheedled into sympathy. "They've come to *India*. Think of that silly fuss she made in Banganga—a beggar, after all, is nothing to get excited about. One needs a good amount of realism to live here I suppose."

"Even the mystics?" I asked, quoting Alix.

"Well, they are probably the ultimate in realists."

I said nothing, and after a second or two Pria added more gently, "At least let these Americans of yours get used to us. Why should all the effort be yours?"

"When do we ever give them a chance?"

"You can't give people chances; they make them. Baba," she said in a suddenly affectionate voice, "don't you understand what I'm saying?"

"Yes," I said, knowing that she was afraid I would be hurt.

"It always starts in such tiny ways. The food upsets them, or they get bad tempered in the heat, or an Indian is late for an appointment—"

"And then, all at once—"

"Not all at once. But at some point it seems that it's more than they bargained for. Then they get homesick, and they seek out their own kind. It's a sort of retreat—"

I knew what Pria meant; that retreat occasioned by fear, perhaps, or bafflement, or the pressure of the others who were retreating.

"—and we see them less and less," Pria was saying, "they go to a different kind of party, more drunken—"

"Jay's party was pretty drunken."

"Yes, but that's different." And arbitrary as that sounded, Pria was right, it was different (because "States people" were different, empty-headed, many of them, but not in retreat in the same way. And besides Jay was deeply rooted in India, in the life and the legend and the welfare of Kalipur. It was, most fundamentally, his source, a spring to which he returned for several months out of every year when we didn't see him, but knew that the important part of his life was there).

"And in the end," Pria said with a curious authority, "unless they have extraordinary courage they are defeated."

"Or entirely unaffected," I supplied.

"Well, that kind doesn't matter."

"But, Pria," I protested, for the last time, despairingly, "so much of it is our fault."

"Oh nonsense," she said briskly, "we are Indians, *they* are the foreigners."

❖ IX ❖

I SUPPOSE IT WAS THAT CONVERSATION WITH PRIA THAT MADE me notice particularly the small happenings that I came to think of as "the Nichols episodes"—none of them was decisive, but cumulatively they had unshakable authority. One morning I had stopped at Alix's apartment to ask her if she would like to go into town with me and do errands, quite amusing ones, an earring to be mended (which meant an excuse to yearn over the huge, inexplicable pieces of old-fashioned jewelry in the shop), a few moments' pause at an antique shop to see if the dealer had come down on his price for a bronze Parvati that I liked—that kind of thing.

Alix was in her bedroom, a room that always made me uncomfortable for some reason. The walls were the color of cocoa and everything else was very white. On one side there was an enormous mirror with harsh lights on each side of it. "You have to be ruthless with a dressing table," she told me once. "You can't allow yourself to be flattered by your own mirror. Then afterward you can be quite secure because other people will see you by table lamps and candlelight."

She was standing in the middle of the room staring at something when I came in. She didn't even smile at me but said at once, "Look at that."

A gray taffeta dress that had apparently just come back from the cleaner's was hanging up on the cupboard door. "It's very pretty," I said, disconcerted by her tone.

"It's ruined. I don't think they even cleaned it. Probably washed it or something."

"It *looks* very nice," I said, conciliating. "Has it shrunk? Have you tried it on?"

"It's hopeless. I told them, I explained very carefully that these are unpressed pleats—though any fool could have seen they were." She sounded disproportionately upset.

"Perhaps they could be ironed out?"

"Of course they couldn't. The lines would be there forever. Oh *Goddamn* them! It's simply ruined!" There were tears in her voice. "Damn them! Damn them! Surely the idiots can grasp something as simple as cleaning a dress. Why are things like this always happening here?"

I said nothing while Alix angrily lit a cigarette, but I wished I hadn't come. Eventually I said, "Perhaps it will look all right when you put it on. Perhaps you'll be able to wear it anyway."

She said, "Would you like some coffee? It's probably stone cold by now." I trailed along behind her as she walked out to the drawing room. "I must phone Nicky," she said. "He's the only one that can cheer me up."

I sat, as usual, in a big chair, looking out to the sea, and listened to her voice becoming slowly warmer and more relaxed. "Nicky? . . . Oh darling, tell me something nice. . . . Well, I love you too, but that's not what I meant. . . . Just anything to make me feel better. . . . Yes, my good taffeta—your favorite—the cleaners

ruined it. . . . I know I should expect it but. . . . Oh sweetheart . . . Well, I remember too. It was fun, wasn't it? . . ."
Then laughing, "Nicky, what an idiot you are! . . . Wouldn't it
be wonderful? . . . Of course I will. . . . Yes, some day. . . .
Me too. . . . Come home early, darling, will you? . . ."

She came back from the telephone smiling. "Well!" she said.
"Shall we have some coffee?"

"What did he say?" I couldn't help asking.

"Oh nothing. 'What's a dress?' and 'One day I'll buy you Paris
originals and you can throw them away after you've worn them
once,' and 'Remember the times we . . .' Well, really nothing
much." She was still smiling.

In a way it was the ruined gray taffeta dress that gave Alix the
idea, though she had often asked me how one put on a sari. She
telephoned me, full of excitement, to tell me that she had decided
to wear a sari to the big dance the American Women's Club was
having—an annual affair in aid of Indian charities—could she bor-
row one of mine and would I help her dress? With some mis-
givings I said I would, not wanting to seem either ungenerous or
dampening.

She chose a brilliant parrot-green sari of thin Kashmir silk
mottled all over with tiny gold stars to wear over a plain gold
choli. She made me promise not to tell Nicky; it was to be a surprise. We dressed her in great secrecy, buttoned her into a long
white evening coat of her own, and I saw them off to the Taj
Mahal Hotel and then went home—I hadn't been invited to the
dance as I was not among those few Indians who "went around
with Americans," as we used to say.

The next day, though, I heard about the evening from Alix.
Nicky had been rather pleased with Alix, unfamiliar and exhilarated in her sari, until he had heard the comments of the other
foreigners. Then he had been very angry with her. Why did she
always do such crazy things? Why did she always have to be
different and make an exhibition of herself? He was trying to
make a position for himself here and it was her job to get along
with the other wives, couldn't she see that? Couldn't she see that

as strangers they had to be specially careful? After all it was only
sensible to watch the people who had lived in India for years and
take the advice of people who knew the country far better than
they, the Nichols, did.

"I told him," Alix said, still angry from the scene of the night
before, "that I would never *think* of asking anyone's advice on
what I should wear to a party. And he kept talking about 'going
native' and always wanting to be the center of attention. The
thing that happened was that old Manning, who was pretty high,
anyway, took Nicky aside and told him that *his* wife thought I
shouldn't wear a sari—she knew, she said, that I didn't realize because we're so new here, but if I would listen to a word of advice
from an old India hand, the Indians didn't understand this kind
of thing. 'It makes them,' old Manning said, 'think less of
Americans.' " Since Manning was the acknowledged head of the
American business community in Bombay, his wife's word carried
weight. "The old battle-ax," Alix said. "If she'd said it to me I'd
have spat in her eye."

I didn't know the Mannings, but I had seen them and had
heard of them, and the picture of Alix spitting in her eye pleased
me.

"It's nothing to laugh about," Alix said. "You've no idea what
a fight Nicky and I had. Things like that matter a lot to him. If
you knew his mother you'd know why. She's always acted terribly
poor but proud. They hadn't much money and that makes all
kinds of crazy things important. It's supposed not to matter but
it does make you worry." Alix, pulling crossly at her cigarette,
added, "I wish you'd been there. You could have told them that
you helped me dress in a sari, that you *like* Americans to wear
saris, couldn't you?"

"Well, ah, yes," I said, not quite quickly enough.

"Well, don't you?" Alix asked slowly.

"I don't think that Indians think any less of Americans that
wear saris." I couldn't very well say that Indians are apt to find it
a little ridiculous, and to think of the American figure as rather
ungainly in a sari, or even in some cases to resent it as a form of
condescension.

Alix looked at me rather shrewdly. "That's not quite what I meant. Do you *mind* when I wear a sari? Do you dislike it?"

"Oh, not you—" I said, feeling tangled.

"Well, an American, then?"—not accepting the compliment.

I decided to be at least partly honest. "The thing is that there's a kind of foreigner that gets smitten with India—sort of like being stage-struck—and usually, in the past, they've been the ones that wear saris, and they're sometimes rather figures of fun—"

Rigid, Alix said, "Figures of *fun?*"

"Oh, Alix, not *you!*"

"Mm. Maybe."

"And there's another kind that think they'll get *in* with 'the natives' by doing it, sort of getting down to *our* terms, being— you know—democratic." I knew I had said too much.

"I see. I guess the old battle-ax does make sense after all."

"But, Alix, her reasons are all wrong—"

"I'm not so sure." She stared at herself in the mirror over her dressing table. "On a blonde a sari probably does look pretty peculiar."

Somehow things were going astray, and sitting on Alix's bed watching her, striped with sunlight from the venetian blind, pushing her hair back behind her ears, I couldn't think of where to begin putting it right. I was sorry—but helpless—predicting to myself the consequent stages. Pria seemed after all to have been right. First, probably, it would be only a regret at having been angry with Nicky the night before, a wish to restore his evening's worth of lost prestige. And from there the rest would follow, a wariness, never again that easy trust, a pulling back into a surer life. After all, it would only be a short time in India.

It was on one of the mornings soon after that Hari telephoned me. "What are you up to these days?" he asked, which meant he was about to invite me to something.

"Nothing very much. The usual things."

"You've been seeing a lot of these Americans?" Hari remarked, somewhere between a comment and a question.

"How things get about in Bombay," I replied sourly, sensing or perhaps imagining a criticism. "I suppose you disapprove?"

"Why should you suppose that?" In Hari's undaunted view one always appeared unnecessarily complicated, fussed by trifles.

"You should say something like, 'Of course they're not my cup of tea. . . .' even if you can't bring yourself to say, 'I can't think what you see in them. . . .' I mean since it must be a puzzle to you. We have no foreign friends."

"Surely not because of disapproval?"

"Well, because of something. Perhaps we are afraid of them."

"Are they a threat?"

"Aren't they? To our way of life?"

Hari's heavy-grained voice sounded like a judgment. "I don't think so, since they have no place in what you call 'our way of life.' "

"You sound just like Pria."

"What I don't understand," he said reasonably, "is why you should make a situation of it. After all, you went to England when you were relatively young and I expect that is why you find things in common with foreigners."

"I can't think why you say 'after all' in that tone of voice. We are talking—aren't we?—of qualities in people. Nationality, where you (or they) are born, has nothing to do with it." I knew I sounded carping.

"I expect it has. Nationality and all the bigger things that go with it. Or smaller things. It depends on how you look at it. Anyway they are a part of you, learned before you know you're learning."

"How complacent you are!" I said, upset by his calm voice and thinking, How could one love Hari? and rather surprised to find myself thinking so openly about love. "Europe, I know, was no contagion to you—"

"I was much older," he interrupted matter-of-factly, "and then, it was only two years."

I could imagine those two utilitarian years in a Welsh agricultural college with Hari working hard and after classes dutifully drinking beer in pubs with his fellow students, even, perhaps, taking a walking tour in the damp mauve hills on a long week end, considered by everybody a nice chap—quiet, you know, but no side to him. He, himself, had too little self-pity in his system to see it as an exile. Was he ever homesick for his Poona land? I wondered. If he were he probably would have considered it an irrelevance, something to be ignored until the immediate jobs of learning and acquiring were complete. I said, rather loftily, "I couldn't expect you to understand."

"Are you quarreling with me, Baba?"

"Well, trying to. One can't quarrel with you very satisfactorily. I suppose that's a sign of some sort."

Hari laughed. "A good one I should say. Now perhaps you'll let me tell you that I'm going up to Poona next week end. Pria and Karan are coming, and my mother will be there" (letting me know that we would be properly chaperoned—as if I could ever suspect Hari of an impropriety). "Would you like to join us? It's the first sugar pressing of the year, and that usually means something of a party."

"I'd like to very much. May I invite the Nichols? I think Alix would love the Poona place."

A pause. "If you wish."

"Yes, please."

"Very well. I suppose we can all drive up together."

✳ X ✳

IT WAS ONE OF THOSE MORNINGS, TOO, THAT MY AYAH CAME to me looking especially pious and asked whether she and a few of the other servants could take the following afternoon off because there was a very famous yogi who was coming to the Mahalaxmi temple, a few hundred yards down the hill from our house. He would recite and give darshan—blessings—meditate and, as a final act of discipline and austerity, would allow himself to be buried that evening. He would continue in his state of controlled and suspended life for three weeks, and at the end of that time he would be taken out of the grave, still alive. They wanted to see the interring, and, if possible, receive darshan from him.

While she was talking to me, Alix telephoned and I mentioned the matter to her because I thought she would be interested.

"But that's absolutely fascinating," she said, very excited. "Can we go too? Do let's."

"All right," I said, "if you don't mind hundreds of people." And late the next afternoon we pushed our way through that strangely casual, strangely exhilarating thing, an Indian crowd. They made way for the foreigner, smiling or staring inquisitively at her clothes and her fair hair. One woman, carrying a sleeping baby balanced easily on her hip, said to me as we passed, "Is she old?"

"Not very. About the same as you."

"Her hair," the woman pursued, "has been like that since always?"

"Yes, yes. She comes from America."

"How many children?" the woman asked, and when I told her, "None," she clicked her tongue pityingly.

We moved slowly on past the big stone tank where the men in loincloths, their hair knotted on top of their heads, crouched on the steps leading down to the water. Beyond them we could see the tall stone gates of the side entrance to the temple, elaborately carved with figures of gods and scenes from the epics. They had been whitewashed many times, and as the paint peeled off in long curls you could see the darker streaks of previous layers, and occasionally the stone itself. Massed all around the tank and spreading to the gates and the outer walls the crowd stood, the dark, moving heads, the white clothes, broken here and there by groups of Mahratta women in the strong colors and cotton saris of Bombay Province. On the far side of the tank the yogi sat cross-legged on a white sheet spread on the ground, a slender, erect figure with open eyes and no expression, in a white muslin loincloth and a thin black string slung over one shoulder and across his chest. Around the edges of the sheet were piles of flowers, coconuts, rice, and beyond them sat groups of priests and disciples chanting and rocking gently back and forth.

Before that intense, oblivious group a deep hole had been dug. When we came closer we could see that the dark earthen walls of the pit had, near the bottom, been braced with wooden planks and the floor, too, was covered with wood. It seemed like a long time but I suppose that it was really only half an hour that we stood shifting and murmuring with the crowd. There was no particular moment when the chanting seemed to reach a conclusion, but as if they had a prearranged signal, the men around the yogi stood up. At some point, I noticed then, he had closed his eyes and they remained closed. They lifted him as he sat, rigid but seemingly without strain, and to a sort of whispering sigh from the crowd, long drawn out, almost of pain, they lowered him into the pit. They returned to their places and picked up raggedly, unconcernedly, their chanting.

"What are they saying? Tell me what they're saying," Alix whispered to me urgently.

"I don't know," I said, not wanting to talk. "The Vedas, probably, I don't know Sanskrit. . . ."

Alix stirred uneasily beside me. "Now what? Are they going to fill in the hole?"

"Ssh," I said. "I don't know. Probably."

First, wooden planks forming a low ceiling were placed deep in the hole over the man's head. Onto that a couple of men who looked like laborers, sweating with the exertion, began to shovel earth into the pit from the high pile beside it. The crowd pressed closer around us. Some of the people picked up handfuls of earth and threw them in. Slowly the hole was filled and the men prosaically stamped it firmly down. On top of it all a huge flat stone was placed. The tomb was sealed. The men wiped their foreheads with their arms, one blew his nose with his fingers, and turned away without emotion.

Now the crowd broke forward to touch the stone, to scatter flowers on it or the red powder we call kum-kum. Movement boiled around us. Only the chanting continued unbroken and the disciples in their watching rows remained unmoving.

"Are they going to leave him like that?" Alix asked, trying to stand still against the crowd.

"I suppose so. I don't think anything much more will happen. Would you like to stay and see?"

"No. Let's go."

I wondered if perhaps Alix was disappointed and so I suggested that she might like to see the sculpture in the other courtyard. It is older and rather beautiful with its voluptuous figures standing out warmly from the nearly obliterated details. But Alix said, "No, no, let's get out of here."

We walked slowly back to the main gate, and for once Alix paid no attention to the beggars, the sick, the lame, the lepers, that clustered along the way, or the demented old man with his rags and his happiness that called to us, "*Hari-bol! Hari-bol!*" as we went by. She edged ahead of me, thin and straight but far less pliant in her walk than an Indian, the heels of her sandals sinking into the dust, her tangerine dress clinging in darker patches to her back and waist. A child ran laughing in front of her, shouting over his shoulder something to a companion in the crowd. She stopped abruptly as though this were an extraordinary sight. Somebody offered me garlands of marigolds and roses to buy. A general relaxation had entered the crowd; people were talking in louder tones, gossiping, exchanging news.

At last we reached the gate where my father's chauffeur had been waiting for us. He signaled to me and ran across the road into a side street to bring the car to us. Evening had arrived suddenly, as it does in Bombay. Far overhead the sky was deepening, the hawks circled and dipped for the last time, there was the first fragrance of wood fires being lighted for the evening meal, of something being fried with spices. People were dawdling home from work, golden light slanted between the trees onto walls and houses, the different life of the evening had begun.

Alix seemed unaccountably upset by the whole thing. "Come on home with me," she said, as if she didn't care whether I did or not. "I need a drink." In the car she stared out of the window at the twilit city, at the plaster extravagances and surprising balconies of the houses on Malabar Hill, at the figures in their white cotton clothes sitting on the sea wall, silent and at ease, or the bright saris blowing, or the activity and laughter around the stall of a street vendor. She looked very American huddled in the corner of the car, thin and tense and far away. "Do you," she asked suddenly, "believe in all that?"

"In yoga, do you mean? Mysticism?"

"I don't know what you call it," she said impatiently. "I mean do you believe in that man?"

"Well, I'm not a follower of his," I said, conscious that she was asking something different.

"But he must be a phony of some kind. There has to be a trick to it."

"Oh, no," I said quickly, a little shocked, "I don't think there is any trick. I'm sure he is sincere—"

"Oh, sincere," she said helplessly. "I don't understand—"

"He's a famous man," I insisted, not wanting to sound a fool but feeling, rather unreasonably, slightly insulted for my country. "He has thousands of disciples, a great reputation—"

Alix turned frowning to look at me. "At night," she said, "they'll open that thing up—his friends, accomplices—disciples, whatever you want to call them—"

"Of course not. How could they? I mean, there'll be priests and people sitting on top of it all the time, in relays, singing and praying and reciting—"

"Baba," she said anxious and angry, "do you *believe* that? Nobody can live without food or water or air for three weeks. It doesn't make sense."

"Well, it happens. Stranger things than that happen."

"What things?"

"Oh, Alix," I said, "I can't explain it. I know it seems peculiar, but there are other laws besides the everyday ones."

"Besides everything that we know from life and science?"

"But we don't *know*," I said, thinking of my mother and wondering how she would answer. "Who *knows* about life?" I asked, feeling silly and pompous.

Alix smiled. "All right. We'll see. It's only three weeks."

"When he comes out alive after that," I said, "how will you know that there wasn't, after all, some trickery?"

She sighed deeply. "Mm. I certainly do need a drink," she said again.

In her apartment we sat in front of the big windows looking out across the darkening sea to the last green fans in the sky where the sun had set. Distantly from some temple we heard the dissonant clatter of bells. The room held its own twilight, darker and more foreign than the land and sea outside. In stiff folds on each side of the window the fantasy of taffeta curtains reached the floor. Even before the monsoon came the salt air of Bombay would eat into the material; in a year they would hang in ghostly and extravagant shreds from the rod, the down cushions would smell from the rains, the white leather top of the table would fester grayly with mildew.

Alix was saying, "Are you sure you won't let me put a little slug of something in your drink? We drink too much, I guess," she added.

"Americans do seem to drink a lot."

"It's an occupational disease—like success. When I was a child," Alix said dreamily, "my father used to tell me that success didn't matter, that nothing mattered except that I should be happy. But by the time I grew up I knew it wasn't true, and I knew that he didn't think that it was. But by then *that* didn't matter because I'd had a happy childhood and that stays with you."

"How do you mean 'happy'?"

"Well," Alix said smiling, "successful. My mother worried about my clothes and hair and teeth and whether I went out with the right boys. My father acted amused about everything, and would come up with special surprises for birthdays or Christmas. I think he worried sometimes that I might turn out to have an intellect, but I didn't. I never worried about anything except who would take me to the Yale-Harvard game. By then, you see, I knew it *was* important to be successful, that my father couldn't have given my mother and me all the things he did if he hadn't been, and that I couldn't be happy unless I was."

"I see," I said, suddenly aware of how different her intonation was from mine.

"And now I know," she continued, almost as if I weren't in the room, "that Nicky and I can't be happy unless *he* is successful.

I love him, you see. My father understood that and that's why he took Nicky into the firm."

She held up her glass. "To happiness," she said, laughing.

I sipped my lemonade and laughed with her. In Jalnabad, I thought, no one made much of a point about happiness. We were given, and we accepted, almost without thinking, certain precepts. The importance of the family—the one we were born to or the one we married into. Our place in a certain structure, a pattern of life, of birth, marriage, children, peace and death. Our debt to a world could be defined, but the promises were all unstated. Within our framework we would make our own happiness. It was never suggested that we pursue happiness. We were not encouraged to waste our time.

Just before my mother left Bombay to go to the south, I had asked her, "But why are you doing this?"

And she had replied, "I cannot explain the rewards except to those who already know what the rewards are. You see—I am already talking in false terms, for the rewards are not the point."

"Are you unhappy with us? Is that why?"

"The only unhappiness is inside myself. I must do what I can."

When Nicky came into the drawing room he had already changed for dinner. He walked across the room to shake hands with me and to kiss Alix. "I didn't know you were back," he said.

"Had you forgotten? We have this consular party tonight."

"Oh God," Alix said.

"You'd better hurry and get dressed," Nicky said rather sharply. "We don't want to be late."

As I got up to leave Nicky said to me in almost a conciliating voice, "Sure you won't have another drink?"

"No thank you." I stood uneasily by the window. "I must really be going home."

Suddenly and charmingly, Nicky smiled. He put a hand on my arm. "Don't go. Stay and talk to me while Alix gets dressed." He walked across to the cabinet with its many bottles and many-sized glasses, stopping along the way to turn on the gramophone. Gradually the whine of a sad American song that I didn't know came into focus. "The old tunes are still the best," Nicky said with his back to me. He returned to sit in my chair while I still stood awkwardly looking into the drifts of shadow in the far corners of the room. "They are really very lovely," Nicky said looking up at me, "these gowns—these saris that all you Indian girls wear."

I glanced down, surprised, at the crumpled gray chiffon. "Thank you," I said as Alix would have—there seems to be no way of acknowledging a compliment gracefully in English. "They're really very practical."

Nicky laughed. "Thank the Lord they don't look it."

"I mean, you can wear them forever and they fit anybody—"

"No styles? Don't the fashions change?"

"Not really, you just keep collecting. I'm still wearing my grandmother's saris."

"Now I know why I envy Indian men," he remarked jovially, and I searched for a way to change the conversation because I knew he was making an effort to be nice to me only because he was irritated with Alix. I thought he felt me a bad influence.

"Alix and I," I said abruptly, "have been at the Mahalaxmi temple to see a yogi being buried." It sounded very odd as I said it but Nicky didn't smile.

"That's very interesting," he said. "We haven't many opportunities to enter Hindu temples."

"Anyone can go in, you know, except into the innermost shrines."

"I always thought," Nicky said politely, "that you Hindus cremated your dead."

"Yes, we do."

"Only the holy men are buried?"

In the deepening evening I could see Nicky's face indistinctly. He looked bored but his voice remained pleasant. I said, "This swami was alive."

There was a pause, and then Nicky said laughing, "Next you can tell me about the rope trick—"

"No really, ask Alix—"

Quickly he said, "I know amazing things can be done with mass hypnosis. I was reading an article in, let me see, one of the magazines, I think it was—"

"Americans read an awful lot of magazines, don't they?" I felt like Pria.

"Well, we like to keep up with world events."

"I dare say that keeps you very busy."

Nicky said carefully, "Of course we don't know nearly as much as we should about India. It's a very complex country."

"Yes. Neither do we." I looked out at the shifting white line where the surf broke on the rocks. The sea was already black. We could hear the gasping of the tide pulling between the rocks, and inside, the room was full of soft foreign music.

Alix said from the door, "What are you two doing sitting here in the dark?" She switched on the light. Guilty as lovers, Nicky sprang up and I moved away from his chair. "Waiting for you to get through beautifying," Nicky said just as I said, "I was about to go home."

❖ XI ❖

THE POONA ROAD MEETS THE WESTERN GHATS WITH A SENSE of impact. Suddenly before you are the flat-topped hills, a jungled wall and, on each side of the road, the level caramel-colored fields of the littoral. We all felt a slight rise in spirits as the car turned onto the first of the sharp bends that would take us in giddy stages up the Ghats to the small hill towns and eventually to the Poona plateau. Jammed into one car (after a careful pooling of gasoline coupons), all six of us had until that moment held a conventional early-morning silence, Pria and Alix staring out of the back windows of the car at the dull landscape of first tenements and factories, then the short respite of the Thana creek, lost again in the scrubby countryside and haphazard villages. Sunk down between them I gazed at the backs of the heads of the three men in the front seat and watched the whitening sky freckled occasionally by a flight of paddy birds. We had started early to avoid the mid-day glare. Hari, driving without strain, one elbow under the rolled-up white shirt sleeve propped on the window edge, left hand spread easily on the wheel, had made good time, and we felt the chill air of the Ghats before we had entirely lost the freshness of early Bombay mornings.

"The only bore about this drive is that one gets hungry at such exotic hours." Pria frowned at her wrist watch. "Here it's only eight and I'm ready for lunch."

Hari said, "We'll stop at Khandala for coffee, if you like."

So far I had been in a dream, half left behind in the sleeping Bombay house. There was always something portentous about a departure before my father was awake; the servants still in their quarters, the night watchman not yet released from duty and the only activity from the sweeper grimly washing the veranda floor. Now, at the idea of coffee, I entered the day and waited impatiently for the swinging road to bring us to the top of the Ghats. From each turn one looked out at the plain below, hazy and seeming, through the netting of bamboos and leaves on the roadside, impossibly barren, burned, a hostile, unyielding land cut by the black line of road.

The coffee shop where we stopped was an undistinguished affair of wooden trestles set out on the street in front of the dark shed where the proprietor crouched over a charcoal stove. We climbed out of the car, smiling at each other with the creaky look of people who have just woken up. Alix held her arms tight across her chest and hunched her shoulders. "You can feel the difference in the air," she said, "or is it just that the smell of coffee always makes you feel alert? You know something? It's ridiculous, but I still can't get used to *every* day being sunny. I wake up any morning and think, 'Ah good—it's a lovely day,' before I remember that of course it's a lovely day. It would mean that something cosmic had gone wrong if it weren't."

Pria laughed and said, "That's a philosophy, not a comment on the climate."

"But just think—you could plan a picnic or a trip like this or a day at the beach six months in advance and *know* it would be fine! Or a garden wedding—think of the mental anguish an outdoor wedding causes back home. What if it rains? The marquisette dresses ruined and the bridesmaids resentful and the bride's hair stringy and everyone in the wrong mood. Oh no, we can never be serene while we have to take such enormous chances—"

"Wait till the monsoon," Karan said. "That will make up for all these months."

Alix shook her head vigorously. "I shall enjoy the monsoon, I know I will. I have it all planned. I'll sit inside my house and drink gin in a disillusioned way, and watch the rain come bucketing down beyond the windows, and tap cigaretts on my thumbnail and feel like a real Somerset Maugham character—"

"Can I have my coffee black?" Nicky asked.

Alix looked at him quickly with a slight frown, and Hari said, "I'm afraid they make it with the milk already in."

Nicky caught Alix's eye and mumbled, "Doesn't matter," but he pushed the cup away, and we all knew that it was because he was afraid the milk wasn't safe. The rest of us drank the hot, sweet coffee from the thick cups, and feeling as though the weekend had, at last, really begun, we started again on the road to Hari's farm. If he had been unenthusiastic but accommodating when I had asked if I might bring the Nichols with us to the farm, now as we came closer to Poona he was more warmly welcoming to us all from his own private anticipation.

On the left, some way outside Khandala, was a wooden sign that said TO THE CAVES, pointing crookedly to a dusty cart track and beyond to an eroded mound of land. "What's that? Oh, what was that?" Alix asked, twisting round to look back at the sign.

"Karla," I told her.

"But caves? What kind of caves?"

"Buddhist, mostly. Very beautiful." Karla was one of my favorite places, darkly lovely, set obscurely in its crumbling hills.

"Oh, I wish we'd stopped!" Alix said.

"It's a wickedly long climb," Pria said, feeling, like me, suddenly and uncertainly protective of the caves.

"And actually, at the top," I added, "there isn't much beyond the central cave and the pillar. Even then, it's not to everyone's taste."

"On our way back, perhaps, if we have time," Karan said, and we were both grateful to him.

At last we turned off the road onto an unpaved track which we followed for a couple of miles, passed quickly through a small village, rounded the great, useless, ruined walls of a Portuguese fort and stopped at last by a long white house backed by acacia trees.

Hari's house pretended to nothing. Its only charm, uncalculated if not an accident, was the great falls of purple bougainvillaea that hid the pillars of the veranda, made a bower of the doorway and covered the uncompromising lines of the roof. The veranda and the front rooms were filled perpetually with an after-sunset light, incongruously romantic, a light for lovers. Otherwise the house looked as though no woman had ever set foot in it, though this, of course, was untrue. Hari's mother had lived there for all the years of her marriage and, even now that she was widowed and the house was Hari's, it was still her home because her other children were all daughters and she did not consider it proper to impose on sons-in-law. She visited her daughters only when they were pregnant, and if they could not, for whatever reason, return to bear their children in Poona. She liked to be on hand for confinements, and felt it her duty to help in the house after the birth. Recently she had taken to making journeys to visit her own relatives—sisters and brothers—and what started out as a short stay melted, apparently without her realizing it, into months. She was daunted, perhaps, by the masculine atmosphere of the house and the kind—but surely impatient?—manner of her son. We scarcely saw her all weekend.

The rooms were square, the windows gave only light but no view. The walls, painted an unthinking yellowish cream, were bare except for calendars of the sort that are annually distributed by cotton mills, or airlines. Gray cotton mats covered the stone floors of some of the rooms, and on them the massive furniture of wood and cane was settled with a terrible air of permanence. Like everything else it was built to live a long and useful life, was indestructible, virtually.

Hari, in his Poona mood, yelled through the house for the servants, coffee, lime juice, were the rooms ready? were the evening preparations made? Just a moment, he had to go and talk to one of the tenant farmers, please make ourselves at home, ask the servants for anything we need, anybody like a glass of beer? shandy? Have both and then decide. He left us sitting on hard chairs ranged along the living-room walls, staring at each other across the gray matting, across the high round table in the middle of the room, staring like enemies in the purplish light.

A servant came in with an array of drinks on a tray, another followed with coffee for Pria and me. Here, on the farm, they did not wear uniforms but loose white cotton trousers and shirts hanging out.

Pria said, "In a little while we'll get used to ourselves," and gradually the bracing common sense of the farm and the life there told on us. When Hari returned, Nicky asked him many questions about the new sugar mill, learning, in his conscientious way, the facts about the country, setting his narrow, good-looking face in lines of intelligent interest. Karan, listening carefully, at last seemed to feel some affinity with the American. I imagined him thinking, "You see? get them onto a good practical subject, deal with them on neutral ground, and they're just like you or me." Nicky perhaps was deciding, "Well, finally an Indian I can cope with, finally a man that makes sense, is getting something done. He knows his country cold, too." Alix was liking everything much better because Nicky was interested. She crossed the room to sit next to him and slid her hand into his.

Pria smiled at me from time to time, and after a while said, "I'm sorry to be insistent, but let's have an early lunch. It ought to be teatime and yet there is still the whole afternoon. . . ."

We ate simple Mahratta food and after lunch we rested, Pria and I together in one room which had, in the usual Indian way, the beds pulled into the middle of the room and reed blinds drawn across the windows against the afternoon glare.

"For some reason this house reminds me of Jalnabad," I told her. "It doesn't look at all like it, but it has the same atmosphere of ordered living of a casual sort."

"Mm," Pria said lazily from the other bed. "It's a good house for a large family. If you marry Hari you must have lots of children."

"Goodness," I said startled, "I can't really see myself as the head of a family."

"I expect you will, one day."

"Possibly," I said, knowing I wouldn't.

That evening there were great festivities. Under the big colored canopy outside the sugar factory, a Brahmin priest sang prayers and offered prasad—blessed food—to all of us. A professional singer, very popular at the moment in Poona, had come out to entertain the crowd, and her voice blared out over a loud-speaker. Colored lights were looped about, throwing a dim radiance on the factory front. The workmen and their wives crouched about talking, children scurried among the groups clutching sticks of sugar cane. Soon the charcoal fires were lit to roast the millet that we all ate along with the big discs of unleavened bread with chutney.

Hari, with his Poona confidence and a pleased expression, sat on the ground and watched it all, as solidly appropriate to this place as the acacia trees or the sugar crop. The factory staff had thoughtfully provided two straight chairs from the office for the foreigners, but Alix insisted on sitting on the ground with the rest of us and pulled Nicky down beside her, and the chairs were left, back to back on the grass, looking silly and abandoned. It was only for a short time, though, because Nicky's knees got stiff and he moved onto the chair after all. Alix, meanwhile, was enchanted by the party and full of her questions and comments. "What does it mean when they wear gold rings in their nose?" "They're better looking than Bombay people." "Do they let the children stay up as late as they like?" At one moment, immediately in front of us, there was a quick exchange of words between one of the women and a man, in a hurry, not looking where he was going, who bumped into her. She answered his remark with a high, witty insolence and all the people around burst out laughing. "What did she say?" Alix wanted to know. "How different they are! Not a bit retiring in the way you sort of expect Indian women to be, are they?" She wanted to know the words of the songs, and how the food was cooked and whether women worked in the factory. It was quite some time before we discovered that Nicky, sitting slackly in his chair, had fallen asleep.

Alix looked from Nicky back to us, at something of a loss, not sure, apparently, whether to be embarrassed for her husband.

Karan said, "Sensible chap. I think I'll go along to the house."

Pria smiled at Alix. "A little folksiness goes a long way, I have to admit."

Hari nodded to them absently as they strolled away toward the house. "Good night, good night," they called above the music.

Alix jumped up to stand behind Nicky's chair, leaning on his shoulder. "My poor angel! I'm so dreadful, I can't see how you stand me!"

"What?" Nicky said, and then waking up a bit more, "Alix?"

"You work so hard, and I never think about how tired you get. Poor darling!"

"Must be the altitude," Nicky said, smiling sleepily at the three of us but particularly at Alix I suppose, because he was pleased with her excuse. And I thought, Alix will always apologize for the wrong things in India.

Hari shouted, "Sleep well, ask for whatever you want," to their retreating backs as an afterthought. To me he said, "What about you, Baba? Tired?"

"I think I'll stay on for a while."

He nodded again, and we settled back, hardly talking, to watch the festivities rise with laughter and jokes and noise, and then, perhaps an hour later, gently flicker out. Children were flopped, asleep, on the mats all around us. Just within the shelter of the canopy a group of men were gambling and would probably continue late into the night. Women gathered in tight, crouching clusters around the low embers of the fires. The trilling voice of the singer had stopped, and someone was disconnecting the microphone. The colored lights bobbed about in the chill wind that had started.

"Come along," Hari said, "we'd better be going in."

"A much better party than the kind we go to in Bombay."

1st august
pressing of you.

Hari said complacently, "Well, it's a real celebration, not just a party."

"I dare say that's the difference." We walked quickly back through the cold darkness to the house.

* XII *

THE FOLLOWING WEEK I DIDN'T SEE SO MUCH OF ALIX because I was helping Pria with a number of tedious jobs for her wedding—sending out invitations, being sure that proper presents had been bought for appropriate relatives, writing thank-you notes for presents that had already arrived. But that Sunday late in February we were all to spend the day in Juhu.

The beach-party muddle had never been sorted out properly. The Sunday after the polo, the American Consul and his wife had asked the Nichols to go with them to Elephanta, an island in the Bombay harbor, to see the caves there and the magnificent carvings in them. The Nichols, apparently thinking that Jay's suggestion of changing the beach party to that Sunday had been only tentative, had accepted the Consul's conflicting invitation. When Alix telephoned first Jay and then me "to be absolutely sure," as she said, "that no one was going to get stood up," we were all, naturally, quite astonished. As Pria said, "After all, they were the ones who made such a fuss about the beach party. You'd think they might be polite enough to go now that Jay has taken so much trouble to arrange it."

"Perhaps," I suggested without conviction, "they can't refuse a consular invitation."

"Ridiculous," Pria said. "They're business people. They aren't compelled to lick the consular boots. It's a kind of hysteria, this mad enthusiasm about something one minute and complete indifference the next."

Jay, when he came over to have a drink with us one evening, only suggested that perhaps they were offended about something.

"What could they be offended about?" Pria asked belligerently.

"Not that I'm in a position to know. Baba, of course, sees her practically every day. Have you said something, Baba, to annoy them?"

"I don't think so. But even if I had, why should they be rude to poor Jay?"

Pria said, "Well, you can never tell with Americans. . . ."

And Jay said, "In any case it doesn't matter." So the beach party was canceled again, but the disturbing idea that the Nichols might have found some impoliteness in the manners of one of us apparently stayed in Jay's mind because he arranged the beach party again several Sundays later and the Nichols accepted it with pleasure. This time it seemed very strange to us that the Nichols took the whole thing with so much equanimity, and didn't insist (after all that Jay had done) that it be their party.

We all drove out to Juhu that Sunday, in several cars, arriving at various times in the late morning. Jay's servants had been there since early morning preparing elaborate meals for the day, massing flowers in the rooms of the small house, lowering the reed mats along the edge of the veranda against the early sun and glare.

Compared with the marble palaces and the huge, ugly concrete houses of Juhu, Jay's "shack" was modest but far more charming. You drove along the sandy road that runs parallel to the incredible sweep of sand and sea that makes up Juhu beach. At the very far end, where the beach houses are set farther apart from each other, you turned off the road into a coconut grove. There was no formal driveway, and your car would go bumping and stalling between the palms until you came suddenly to the little house set right on the sand. Jay used to say that if you were going to have a house on a beach it had to be right on the beach; if you were going to have a road in between or even a garden you might just as well live in Khar (a rather dreary suburb).

When you entered the house you walked directly into the dining room, which he hardly ever used. Although meals were set out on the table there, we usually piled food on our plates and took them back to the living room, where we sat, looking out at the beach, to eat. The living room was really only a deep veranda which ran all across the front of the house, open on three sides and separated from the dining room by two coconut palms which grew through the stone floor, making gray, irregular pillars, and on through the coconut-leaf thatched roof. Two bedrooms opened off the dining room, one on each side, and those were seldom used for anything except a place to sleep off a particularly heavy lunch or to change in after a swim.

We didn't often see Jay in the mornings and he seemed that day to be rather quiet, rather tired but still spruce in his short white achkan. Daulat Singh was chivvying the other servants around in the background, and soon they set out an imposing array of bottles and glasses on he veranda. Suddenly Daulat Singh rushed out of the house down to the beach to stop a man who was walking along selling young coconuts. They argued angrily for a few moments. The man turned to leave, and then came back. Daulat Singh said something contemptuous and began to walk toward the house and then returned. Eventually he bought half a dozen of the coconuts. The vendor sat down and with his sharp, curved knife sliced away the outer husks, neatly scooped off the top, loosened the soft, creamy meat around the edges of the shell and then waited as Daulat Singh carefully carried them up to us, two at a time.

We were still sitting on the veranda, sipping the sweet milk from the young coconuts, not talking much, in that kind of entrancement that falls over people at a beach, when the Americans arrived a little after noon.

Nicky said anxiously, "Are we late? I'm very sorry."

Jay raised his eyebrows, "Late for what?"

"I mean, I wasn't sure what time you said."

"I don't think I said a time." It was clear from his tone that he couldn't understand why it mattered.

Alix said gaily, "Oh, heavens, I never know. We're always too early or too late or *something* in India." She smiled happily around at us all. "We brought you some champagne, *and* a bucket of ice to keep it cool in, *and* some very cheap glasses that we can smash against the wall afterward. I've always wanted to, and this seemed like a good moment."

Again I was caught in her high spirits and said, laughing, "Oh, so have I!" The atmosphere in the little house had changed entirely.

Pria said, "That is most kind of you," taking the gesture as some kind of apology, and was much nicer to them all day than she usually was. Actually I think the Nichols had brought the champagne simply as a spur-of-the-moment good idea without any thought of making amends—if they were aware of amends to be made at all. Daulat Singh was the only one who was rather put out, and with an expression something between resignation and a pout changed the glasses on the table, set out the buckets of ice, chilled the wine and generally flapped napkins about.

Alix, still exhilarated, was leaning against the veranda railing. "My God! Why did nobody tell me? What a beach!" She spun around to say to us, "Are you all just going to sit around here in the shade?" She held out her hand to Nicky. "Come on—we have to get out there. Did you know it would be like this?"

Karan in his sober way said, "You must be careful. This is a very hot sun."

"That's for me," Alix said, not really listening. She had turned back to the beach.

"But it is treacherous. You'd better wear a hat."

"And ruin my tan? Most of my life seems to be taken up with getting an absolutely smooth tan with no stripes, no patches, no shadows—"

Karan shook his head doubtfully. "At least sunglasses—"

"I had so hoped," Alix continued, "that India would be like this. Lots of sun, but a tanable sun—and now the beach. But people here," she said on a question, "don't seem to get out in the sun much? Imagine—in *February!*"

In the end, she and Nicky went off to change and Karan and Hari, rather reluctantly, out of politeness, joined them. Pria and Jay and I stayed on the veranda, Pria because nothing would persuade her to get her skin darker in the sun, Jay because he never swam and I because (although I wanted to be with the Nichols, laughing and making silly jokes in the waves) a vague sense of allegiance to Pria kept me in my chair still holding the rough tan shell of the coconut, a small courtesy to Jay.

We watched the four of them run down the sand toward the water, the two tall, skinny Americans, an odd orange patina on their skins from the Bombay sun, the two Indians, murkier of color, more compact and graceful of build. For a few seconds, through the light wind and the sound of the surf, I could hear Alix's high, excited voice, and then only Jay's chuckle beside me, "Such energy! Ah youth . . ." and the four little figures were puppets moving jerkily and pointlessly at the water's edge.

Altogether it was a peculiar day. I discovered a number of new things about people I had known for years, and found myself in some—for me—very odd experiences. I got drunk, for instance, for the first time in my life, and for the first time I was kissed.

Fortunately everyone was accustomed to very flexible hours for meals for it was late when the swimmers came back to the shack —though actually I don't remember eating lunch at all that day. Wet and laughing, they shook themselves like puppies on the steps of the veranda and we called out to them questions like, "Was the water cold?"

"No, no. Perfect. You should have come."

Or, "Any undertow?"

"Not yet" (this from Karan), "it won't be dangerous until just before the monsoon."

"Jellyfish?" Pria asked with a shudder.

"No jellyfish," and then Karan gave us a short lecture on the habits and movements of Portuguese men-of-war.

Already the water was drying on their shoulders and leaving little scabs of salt. Alix, perched on the veranda railing, was swinging one foot with its incongruous scarlet toenails, smiling and bemused; Nicky, standing next to her, was staring with longing back at the sea, pointing far away to where the sun made flat gray shadows of islands and distant beaches. "What's out there? Is that still Juhu?"

"Madh Island," Hari said. His family owned some property there. "Even better sands than Juhu."

"Oh," Alix said, alive again, "let's go there one day, let's do."

"It's rather a long drive with gasoline rationing—"

"We can manage it somehow—do let's."

Out of a reserve that all of us—Indians—shared, Karan said, "Silver Sands is closer and almost as nice."

"I want the best," Alix said without noticing. "I want an island and no houses and miles of beach and—"

Jay with his half-audible chuckle said, "What about opening the champagne?"

Daulat Singh, waiting for his signal, immediately began to twirl bottles, whisk his napkin, walk sedately to the end of the veranda, and with a sense of showmanship gave us a longish pause before the satisfactory explosion of the cork. Normally I didn't drink champagne, but watching Alix hold up her glass and say, "This is the color hair I'd like to have. To us. To India," I sipped from my glass too, first wincing at the brisk taste and then with a feeling of being dashing and pleased. "This is much nicer than I expected," I said, and was pleasantly surprised when everyone laughed.

The real trouble was, I suppose, that I had several glasses of champagne too quickly. I remember at one moment saying very earnestly to Alix, "I do so admire you and Nicky. You enjoy your life and each other so much. It's a special quality." I noticed with a certain interest that everyone was listening to me. I noticed, too, that Pria was looking at her champagne glass, untouched beside her, which she had taken to be gracious, with her thoughts apparently on something quite different. I wondered if my voice was louder than I thought.

"I don't think Nicky and I are anything special," Alix said lightly. "Life is supposed to be fun."

"Ours isn't."

"What would you prefer?" Hari asked suddenly.

"Oh, I don't know," I said with the heady feeling that I was being very lucid. "Anything as long as it is so different or so exciting that I can't think about anything else."

"Good God, Baba," Jay said affectionately, "I had no idea that you had such a sense of adventure."

"I haven't really, I suppose. I just wish I had. If I *did* have, I expect exciting things would happen to me, and they don't. But

I have such a panicky feeling of the years slipping by and nothing to show—"

"Oh, you'll settle down one of these days," Pria remarked.

"No, no!" I said rather desperately. "That's just what I don't want. I want things to change and—"

"*Things?*" Pria said in a sharp voice. "You can't change things enough to make much difference. You can only change yourself—what else have you to work with? You live as you must with society and people, but you make what you can of yourself."

From Alix I got immediate support. "But I agree with Baba. That's why I can't abide the foreign community here—they're so *settled*, so stuffy. Indians are much more exciting!"

I looked around at Pria, Karan, Hari, Jay, and couldn't help laughing.

Pria said, "I suppose the other person's world always seems so."

Nicky could control his irritation with Alix no longer. "Alix, for Christ sake don't *talk* like that. Things like that always get repeated and it does us no good with—"

"But I don't care!" Alix cried.

"Well, I do. You might, for once, consider my wishes."

Pria said, "It's one thing to be thought amusing, and quite another to be an eccentric. One must come to terms with one's world."

Nicky looked at Pria gratefully and was about to say something else, but before it could become a quarrel Jay interrupted. "Let's have some more champagne."

All the colors seemed to be heightened, the dark yellow of Alix's bathing suit, golden across her breasts where the material was drying, the flashing peacock of Daulat Singh's uniform as he moved about filling glasses, a slow red across Nicky's shoulders where the new sunburn had begun to show, even the white of Pria's slacks or Jay's suit acquired a new intensity. Like figures in a stylized dance they moved with a special assurance, with great distinctness of gesture. Behind them the brilliant sea of early afternoon glittered and tumbled distractingly.

"I'm going in again," Nicky said, and I could tell he was still angry with Alix. "Who's coming with me?"

"I am," I said, and got up, impelled much more by a tremendous restlessness and energy than by a wish to swim. "I feel wonderful." I laughed as though I had said something witty. As I changed in the cool twilight of a bedroom, amusement rose like bubbles in me, and then I left the house by the bedroom door, pleased to be alone, and ran giddy and delighted down the sands toward the water. I swam out beyond the surf, considering most clearly the difference of temperature between the tepid surface of the water and the cool depths that I kicked up. Turning lazily over I lay with my eyes closed against the sun, rocking gently in the swell.

Nicky's voice beside me said, "Are you asleep?"

"Of course not," I said, amused by this fantasy. "It would be lovely, though, to sleep in the sea."

"Awful cold at night."

"Not in Juhu."

"We must try it some time," he said casually.

The sun was exploding in bright green stars behind my eyelids. After a moment Nicky asked, "Are you going to float about here forever?"

"Yes, I think so. Like seaweed," I said rather dizzily.

I heard him laugh and then say, "You seem so different."

"It's the champagne."

"It suits you." He bubbled and splashed beside me, and I suppose swam away. Eventually I swam back and plodded heavily out of the waves. Halfway up the beach Nicky joined me, our squat shadows sliding over the sand ahead of us.

"Don't you feel wonderful?" he kept asking. "Isn't the water terrific? Aren't you glad you came?"

"Yes," I said, "Yes, very." The combination of the strong sun and the wine was making me feel stupid.

"We must do this often," he said, and, with a certain tension in his voice, "Come with me while I get some cigarettes out of the car."

It occurred to me in a hazy way that Jay always had plenty of cigarettes, but together Nicky and I walked around the side of the house to where the cars were parked in the coconut grove. I remember the sharp, criss-crossing patterns of the shadows of the palm leaves on the sand, and the feel of the hot metal of the car through my bathing suit as I leaned against it. I remember Nicky's hand resting uncertainly on the door handle, the questioning look on his face and the sudden grip of his other hand on my shoulder. But the feeling of his kiss I hardly remember at all, except that it was salty and rather shocking. I was conscious of the sweetish, slightly sickening smell of foreign sweat, and then I ducked under his arm and went into the house.

The bedroom was blindingly dark after the sun outside. I sat on one of the beds and stared at my feet becoming slowly visible as the gloom lightened, shaken by unfamiliar excitements and a hard sort of wariness. From the door to the dining room Pria's voice said, "You were gone such a long time. Don't you want any lunch? We've all—" and then, with a note of concern, "Are you all right? You're cold."

The skin of my arms and legs was rough with goose flesh. Pria fetched a towel from the bathroom and started to rub my arms and shoulders briskly. "The wine," she said. "You shouldn't have drunk so much."

"I'm quite all right. Really. It's so dark in here."

"Would you like some coffee?"

I couldn't help laughing. "No, I'd hate some coffee. I'm perfectly all right. What I would really like is another glass of champagne."

Pria said in a cold voice, "I don't think you'd better."

"Perhaps not, but that's what I'd *like*." I got up to look for another towel to dry my hair. In the bathroom there were only face towels, so I opened the chest of drawers thinking vaguely that there might be some there, half watching Pria in front of the mirror tidying her hair. In the drawer there was a pile of folded saris, some underwear and an open cigarette box full of hairpins. I called Pria over to look. I asked, "Do you think it's true? Does he really keep a mistress here after all?"

"Couldn't be the servants'," Pria said. The saris were simple cottons but obviously expensive, decorated with the fine white embroidery of Lucknow—almost a tracery—on the white muslin.

"What secret lives people lead," I said.

"But where could she be?" Pria asked. "Does he send her away when he has a party here?" She closed the drawer with a bang. "There is probably some very dull and respectable explanation."

"Yes," I said, not convinced. "I wonder what his wife's like."

"In purdah," Pria said, "probably pretty, all wrapped up in the children, thinks Bombay is a *fast* town—"

"Do you suppose he loves her?"

"His wife?" Pria asked, surprised.

"No, this other woman."

Uncomfortably Pria said, "There probably isn't any other woman."

"One knows so little about people. You and Karan, for instance, are you happy? I never asked you."

"Of course I'm happy." Pria turned away quickly. "This is what I've always wanted—"

"Karan?"

"What extraordinary questions you ask."

"A good husband," I chanted, feeling that somewhere Pria could tell me the truth, "a marriage, children."

"Impossible, isn't it?" Pria said lightly. "That's our life—"

"And you love each other," I insisted.

Impatiently Pria said, "Good heavens, Baba, what a child you are. Yes, of course."

"Well," I said, at a loss, "and Jay loves *his* wife, and—"

"Who loves whose wife?" Alix asked as she came in.

With a furtive feeling of superiority I muttered something like, "Just gossiping . . ." and closed the bathroom door behind me.

All that day I carried around a certain atmosphere with me, hard to describe but quickly communicated to people I was with. Even Hari, who had known me for years, who probably had even thought about marrying me, looked at me with a kind of discovery and for the first time with genuine attraction. Pria and Alix, too, watched me, puzzled, wary, vaguely respectful. All this, I thought, from a kiss, the power that one has or can generate. What could have been going on in Nicky's mind I had, at the time, no idea.

Whenever I caught his eye he smiled cozily at me and seemed entirely at ease; more so, in fact, than ever before.

At teatime the Maharani of Kalipur arrived, this time in mauve chiffon and high-heeled gold sandals like claws. The sea air was filled with her perfume and with her came the incessant stream of trivial talk that accompanied her like the humming of a motor on a long drive wherever she went. ". . . quite impossible dust so I had to pull my sari across my face all the way. If I breathe it in, my dear," she patted her chest delicately, "I suffer for days. Really, I can't think what you people see in a beach. Now in a place like Cannes or Nice where no one is expected actually to go on the beach . . ."

Jay, who had, in any case, been quiet most of the day, became even more remote and excessively polite, offering her champagne or tea, deprecating with a gesture the shack that we all liked so much, listening attentively to her complaints. Daulat Singh arranged a little table by her, piling on it sandwiches, cakes, sweets— all of which she left untouched—filling her teacup, at intervals, picking up her napkin. ". . . so sorry that H.H. couldn't come though he was longing to have news from umm," she indicated vaguely the Americans, "about our mutual friends the Parsons. . . . so much to attend to . . . leaving so soon . . ."

"Are you going to Europe?" I asked.

She looked at me with wide, reproachful eyes, "*Darling*, not this year—how can we? All these dreadful little political types are going to be deciding our fate and we must wait and see what happens. H.H. may have to make a special journey back to Kalipur soon to see how things are going there—"

"Are you going to spend the hot weather in *Kalipur?*" I asked, astonished.

"Certainly not. You don't *know* what the heat in Kalipur is like—my health would never stand it. No. We shall go to a hill station—Kashmir perhaps—it will be uncomfortable and dull—" she shrugged her shoulders in resignation.

"What is going to happen to the States? Do you worry?" I put the question more to Jay than to her, but she answered anyway.

"They would never let us leave—" with indignation.

"Who? Congress?"

"No. The people—our States people. They love us and they owe
so much to us. Darling, when you *think* what we do. The Divali
celebrations alone cost the palace two lakhs. The lights, the
decorations, the sweets that are handed out to the poor people—
every year I tell H.H. that we must think of some means to
economize. Would the new government do all that for the people?
Certainly not. You'll see that there will be a very strong protest
from the people if the new government tries to break up the
States—we will voice the protest for them—"

I tried not to smile as she continued with rising irritation
"—after all, we do everything else for them. We will tell these
Congress-wallahs, these *dhoti*-wallahs what our people think. They
trust us. They would want us to—"

"What do you think? Jay, what do you suppose will happen?"

Quietly he said, "I hope they will allow us to live there." He
corrected himself. "I mean, I hope they will allow me to live
there."

The Maharani gasped. "*Allow?* Who will allow?"

Jay waved his hand, brushing his remark away. "Well, whoever
it is—"

"But we allow. We are the rulers." Confused by Jay's remark,
she suddenly told the truth, "If we weren't rulers, why in the
world would we want to live in Kalipur?" In agitation she drank
her tea. "Ridiculous attitudes," she was saying, "spineless behavior . . ." when more guests arrived.

And then the evening had come and the change of pace that
the day takes. We stood or sat about on the veranda drinking
and talking. Once when I found myself next to Nicky he touched
my elbow lightly and then his fingers moved down to the bangles
on my wrist—bangles that I had worn for years, always wore, given
me when I was a child by my mother. "Pretty," he said, before
we were caught in another conversation.

Pria, Karan, Hari and I all drove home together that night,
Hari and I in the back of the car and Karan driving. The arrangement made it impossible for any of us to talk or behave as we
wanted to. By then I was feeling sober and depressed and rather

guilty. I wanted to ask Pria if I had behaved badly, made a fool of myself, but, of course, couldn't in front of the men. Hari, I knew, wanted to talk to me alone, more intimately in the light of his disturbing discovery of me. Every time Pria and Karan talked to each other in the front seat, he would turn to me and begin a separate conversation—nothing special, just to be talking just to me and having my full attention. Perversely, I would bring the others into it with remarks like, "Did you hear, Pria? The Weird Sisters are going up to Mahableshwar in April to see if they can find husbands there."

"Hill stations are notoriously happy hunting grounds," Pria would say lazily.

I suppose she and Karan, too, wanted to be alone and talk only to each other, though I never could imagine it with Karan. In any case we all, between long silences, made comments about the party and the people in a half-annoyed, friendly way. Pria even admitted, "Those Americans really aren't too bad once they stop being nervous."

Beyond the car windows the featureless, shabby suburbs of the city moved darkly behind us, a big mosque, the causeway onto Bombay Island, the riding lights of the fishing boats moored in Mahim bay rocked against the night, the bright busy bazaars, the blue curve of Worli, and in a few minutes after that I was home. As I got out of the car, thanking people generally and saying good night, Hari caught my hand. "I'll phone you," he said as if his words had some special significance, "tomorrow."

In my room, before I went to sleep, I stared at myself in the mirror for a long time, feeling that it was a dramatic moment, but could see no change.

❧ XIII ❧

REALLY, WHAT I WANTED TO SAY, INAPPROPRIATELY STAND-
ing in that crowded room from which all familiarity had gone to
make space for the cocktail party, was, "But you're supposed to
be in love with Alix. What does it mean?" But of course it was
impossible to ask Nicky such straightforward questions because
during the winter that I knew him I never understood the mysterious games of which his life was composed. In any case his eye
kept wandering to his other guests to be sure that everyone had a
drink, that Alix wasn't allowing people to "get stuck," as she said
—the certain sign, apparently, of a bad cocktail party. So, standing
by the gramophone, helping him choose a new set of records, I
said, "Nicky, that day at the beach—"

He looked at me for a second, smiling. "It was fun, wasn't it?
We must go to Juhu again soon."

"But why? I mean, I don't understand—"

"Something bothering you? What's the problem?" It was a very
indulgent voice and should have been answered with something
small and feminine like, "Does this shade of lipstick look awful in
the sunlight?" or "Am I too fat to wear a Lastex bathing suit?"

"Why did you kiss me?" I said by mistake.

Nicky, furtive and sobered, looked quickly around to see if anyone could have heard. "Just a second, I've got to go and say hello
to those people."

"Nicky, I must talk to you."

"Back in a flash," he said, and I stood and listened, for the first
time, to the words of one of those songs that the Nichols were
always playing, a list of things that someone had enjoyed with
someone—sunlight on the shore, castles on the Rhine, that sort
of thing—while Nicky went across the room to greet an American
vice-consul. On his way back he said to me, "Come into the
dining room and help me fix a couple of drinks," and standing

there by the long white table he said, "I didn't mean anything. I'm sorry if I annoyed you."

"I wasn't annoyed."

He immediately looked cheerful. "I guess we were both a little drunk."

"I know *I* was, I didn't think you were." I hadn't meant it to come out sounding reproachful.

Nicky fidgeted. "Oh, women always say that to excuse the things they do."

"I'm not 'women.'"

"No woman thinks she is."

"Well . . ." I said. I didn't know how to go on with this conversation. I should never have started it.

"Look," Nicky said urgently and rapidly. He put a hand on my arm and quickly withdrew it when my bangles clinked together. I felt certain he was inventing a lie. "That day—the beach, the beach I suppose is what did it, it reminded me a lot of a place we used to go summers at home—that day I felt very far away from America and sort of lonesome." He didn't say, "surrounded by Indians with whom I have no contact." He didn't say, "Somehow I had to get back at Alix." He picked up two drinks from the table. "Did you tell Alix?" he asked casually.

"No. Of course not."

"Good girl. Shall we go back and join the party?"

And there it ended, with nothing properly explained, although the repercussions were felt in both our lives, the beginning of the last of the "Nichols episodes" and Hari's new awareness of me—urgent to him, obviously, not entirely pleasing to me.

There were a lot of Americans at the party and some Britishers. Alix, better dressed than any of her guests, came bustling by, holding two empty glasses. "How do you think it's going?"

"Very well. Everyone seems to be talking like mad."

"They always *talk*. But are they enjoying themselves?"

From their smiling faces, from their hands restless with cigarettes and drinks, it was hard to tell. "They're drinking a lot if that's anything to go by."

"It's a good sign. Oh, how I *love* the middle of a party!"

I laughed, from habit, with Alix, and a few minutes later left without saying good-by to either of the Nichols.

The next day I felt guilty about this and afraid that I had been rude. I telephoned Alix to apologize and make some excuse about having had to get back for dinner. She, apparently, hadn't noticed and only said, "God, I feel terrible. They're playing the 'Anvil Chorus' inside my head."

"Are you ill?"

"No, only a hangover. I don't know why I say 'only'; at the moment I would prefer double pneumonia. Come over and cheer me up, but remember to whisper."

When I got there Alix was still in her dressing gown sitting dejectedly on the edge of the bed, surrounded by rumpled sheets. The curtains were still drawn across the windows and on the table by the bed there was a full cup of coffee.

"Come in," she said, "and tell me that the party was a success— not that I care. It went on till all hours. Nicky got quite drunk and gave a very funny imitation of a Marwari businessman coping with an American client." She smiled reminiscently. "You know, waggling his head and saying, 'I'm telling you sir . . .' in that crazy accent."

"That must have been after I left," I said, feeling obscurely hurt. We made fun of Marwari businessmen among ourselves, but that was altogether a different thing.

Alix caught the inflection and looked up quickly. With a sigh she said, "Indians are so touchy."

"Don't generalize about us, Alix, for heaven's sake. It's such a depressing pastime."

"I expect we seem rude," she said thoughtfully, "but, you know, Indians can be so cold, so absolutely self-contained—"

"But we're the most emotional people in the world!" I said, surprised.

"There you go, generalizing about Indians," Alix remarked, and we both laughed rather formally. "Let's talk about the party," she continued in a different tone. "Did you have a good time? You left early. Who did you talk to?"

"To Nicky mostly."

"Yes, I noticed that. He should have made you circulate. Were you bored?"

"Not terribly," I said, feeling vindictive.

Alix stared at me. Slowly, with a question in her voice, she said, "He can be fun when he puts his mind to it. Probably he's scared of you."

"Oh, I wouldn't say that." In a shameful way I was enjoying my superiority and thinking of the Juhu beach party as though it had happened a long time ago.

Apologetically she said, "You see India is the first time he hasn't been quite sure of me and I can't play all those tricks that are supposed to keep a husband comfortable. You can understand —can't you?—how that might upset him."

"He doesn't seem so. Rather confident of himself, if anything." Already I was beginning to feel guilty for my unkindness.

"I can't help it if you don't like him," she said absently. "I did hope you'd see that he's honest."

"I see that he's very much in love with you."

Alix said suddenly and very sharply, "What *is* this? Has Nicky been making passes at you?"

I had never heard the phrase before, but, of course, I knew immediately what it meant. "What do you mean?" I asked.

"You know—kissing you, holding hands in dark corners, necking on someone's terrace, secret lunch dates at small restaurants—"

"Oh, *no*—" I said, horrified.

"Well?"

"There isn't that kind of restaurant in Bombay."

"You should know."

"Alix, *please*—" I said, and stupidly, in a panic, added, "It was nothing."

"So there *was* something."

"I was rather drunk. He only kissed me because of you. He was angry with you and he had to do something."

"How corny. An American classic, really—kissing your wife's best friend. It should have been done getting the ice cubes. That's the conventional way."

"It meant nothing. We were both drunk." I slipped easily into Nicky's excuse.

"Of course it means nothing," Alix said angrily.

Neither of us looked at the other. Alix lay back on the bed and gazed at the ceiling. There wasn't even the movement of a fan to catch her eye; the bedroom was air conditioned. "It's India, you see. It betrays you," she said. She couldn't have found a better way of wounding me. "Poor Nicky. When I stop being mad at him I shall be sorry for him. He's out of his depth. So am I. But it's my fault. I started this and I think that I wish I hadn't—I *think*—because how will it end?"

"And me?" I asked, hoping for some kind of pardon.

"You? But you're Indian," Alix said without emotion.

She walked with me to the door. As we went through the living room she paused a moment to look around. "I'm beginning to dislike this room," she said peevishly. "I think I did it all wrong."

"I think it's very nice."

"I'd do it differently, if I had it to do over again. . . ." Her voice trailed off.

* XIV *

As IT HAPPENED HARI DIDN'T PROPOSE TO ME FORMALLY UNTIL some time after the beach party. We saw each other often, as we always had, but now these were made occasions, charged with some intensity. That March we went to a good many parties together, met, as usual, at the races, went for drives or sailing with Karan and Pria, watching Bombay recede, across the harbor, into an irregular line of spires and domes. Hari, though, with his big, absent eyes, was seeing all this differently. Now, ever since the beach party and my new authority, I was in his consciousness with a new compulsion.

One evening, after we had been to the movies—a big Technicolor nonsense with Esther Williams—Hari dropped off the others before he took me home. I suppose he must have planned this, but not with a sense of romance—the late, quiet night and the sleeping house. Our night watchman was asleep on the front steps, wrapped in a brown blanket as if he had a fever. At the sound of the car he jumped up, still more asleep than awake, and jangled keys with stiff, incompetent fingers.

"Are you tired?" Hari asked me. "May I come in for a drink?" We often stopped at somebody's house for a drink after the movies but Hari had never before asked to come in unless there were other people there.

I was still feeling rather petulant about the bad film and as I led the way through the waiting house, through the dark dining room, switching on a light here and there, to the kitchen, I kept complaining in a tepid way. "Why in the world do people go to a dreary film like that? It was packed, did you see? I suppose it's all those legs and half-naked girls, though you'd think they could do better simply by spending the day at Juhu. . . . Do you want a real drink or just soda?"

With our glasses of soda we went to sit on the veranda, where for the first time the unconventionality of the moment embarrassed me and I couldn't stop chattering on about the film, plans for the hot weather—any silly thing that came into my head. With a sort of desperate impatience Hari at last interrupted me. "Baba, listen. I came in this evening to ask you something." He stopped suddenly as though he had bitten his tongue.

"Yes," I said, knowing what was coming and thinking about Hari's family. His mother seemed to me very old, living like a ghostly nomad, always gentle and self-effacing, entirely uncritical of Hari, her only son, the youngest of five children. All his sisters were married and all except one had moved out of Bombay. Even the one that remained was almost a stranger to me. She had married a government servant, a conscientious official in the Housing Department, and her life with its social work and civil service friends hardly overlapped ours at all. She, I imagine, thought us giddy, and we thought her dull. Hari as a child. I remembered him, surrounded by all those women, not spoiled, exactly, but adored and cherished, escaping into a world of fighters, horsemen, people of the land. In that dense, feminine atmosphere he grew up tough but self-contained, anesthetized in a way against emotion and against loving. But people said of him—had always said of him—What a good son, or What a devoted brother. So he was. His duties and responsibilities were most meticulously fulfilled, there had never been a time of rebellion in him, but where in all that neutral excellence was his heart? It all made our moment on the veranda oddly without communication.

"Are you listening?" he asked. "What are you thinking about?"

"About your family. I don't know them very well."

Hari sounded relieved. "If we get married you will soon learn to know them. My mother, I can assure you, will make a very unexacting mother-in-law."

"I dare say. But what would our life be?" I wanted to get up and walk about but I was afraid that would seem impolite.

Hari laughed reassuringly. "I wouldn't take you away from the life you know. Don't worry. We will divide our time between Poona and Bombay—unless you liked it up there—"

"Oh, I'm not worried about that—"

"I, of course, much prefer it—"

"But Hari. Oh heavens. What I really mean is, why should we get married?"

"One has to get married."

"Has to?" I said in annoyance. "Surely there should be something else?"

"Don't worry," he said again, very gently this time. "That part will all be all right."

"This is ridiculous," I said, and could almost see Hari recoil. "I don't understand you at all. I suppose you have things or people or something that you feel about—"

"Of course."

"But I don't know them or know what they are. I don't really know you. I don't," I ended despairing, "know what you want."

"Damn it," Hari was angry for the first time that I could remember. "I want to marry you."

"So you said."

"Is that so complicated? We've known each other for years—you know everything about me, my family—"

"Your finances, your work, your friends," I finished rudely. "Yes, it had occurred to me occasionally that you might one day make up your mind to propose to me."

With a return to his usual tone, he said, "Baba, my dear. I think it would be a successful marriage."

"I dare say." I wanted very much to laugh. "And think how pleased everyone would be. My father wouldn't have to ask me if I am bored or lonely and your family would be so pleased to have you settled with such a respectable girl and Pria and I could go shopping and talk about having babies and I would remember to lock the storeroom so that it wouldn't be a temptation to the servants and of course—"

Hari smiled and got up a little hesitantly. He came and sat on the arm of my chair. "I take it, then," he said, "that the answer is 'yes'?"

"No, no," I said, jumping up and almost knocking poor Hari over. "No, the answer isn't yes—couldn't possibly be. I still think there should be more to life than just settling down." Hari stood facing me for a second and I wondered if he was going to kiss me, but he turned away. "I'm so sorry," I said. "I mean if I gave you the wrong impression. I wish I knew how to explain it."

"Not at all," he said politely. "I'm sorry too."

"Hari, listen—" but he had turned away murmuring that it was late and he really must be going.

"We shall be meeting," I said.

"Oh yes. In any case, I'm going up to Poona soon." He walked easily away down the veranda and I waited, listening to his footsteps on the stone floors until I heard the mumbling of the night watchman and the closing of the front door.

✤ X V ✤

NEAR THE END OF MARCH THE HOT WEATHER ARRIVED VERY
suddenly. In our garden and along many of the roads on Malabar
Hill the flaming blossoms of the golmohur trees were out. From
the hill behind our house you could hear the chilling shriek of
the peacocks. In the evenings all along the sea front and on the
walls above the harbor thousands of people sat to catch the breeze
that blew up at sunset. The pace of the city became slower, the
parties fewer. Most of us got up earlier in the morning to make
the most of the cool hours, rested in the afternoons and dined late
in the evening. People began to talk of going away to the hills
until after the monsoon broke. Outside my window the big
jacaranda tree flowered and, in the mornings when the sun came
from that side, filled the room with a bluish light like snow. All
over the house the wide blades of the ceiling fans whispered, and
under them Pria and I sat for hours practically every day drinking
lime juice and water and discussing the details of her wedding.

The propitious day had been chosen—the tenth of April—by the
family Brahmin (though as Pria said, "He's so saturated with
bhang that I don't see how he can read the calendar, let alone our
horoscopes"), his price had been fixed (eighteen yards of cotton,
ten of silk, a sack of rice and twenty rupees) and the invitations,
properly engraved in silver on a white card, had been sent out. The
presents from Karan's family had arrived and Pria had described
them as "very decent, I must say." There was a long string of very
beautiful family pearls, "which, after a reasonable interval, I shall
have shortened and made into a two-string choker so that they can
be seen." There were the conventional gold bangles (new) and two
magnificent bracelets (old) which were made about a century ago
in Jaipur with flat, rough-cut diamonds set in gold, and enameled
on the back with a charming design of parrots and flowers. There
was a hideous ruby pendant ("I bet she just threw this in to get
rid of it." "Can't you have it melted down?" "That would cost

more than the nasty thing is worth."), and three sets of very useful earrings, one diamond, one emerald, one rubies and pearls, and
the usual plain gold chain.

Pria's future mother-in-law had also sent her six Benares saris
so heavy with gold embroidery that Pria said she couldn't possibly
wear them; it would be like living in the Mint. The traditional
crimson wedding sari wouldn't arrive until the day before the
marriage, and Pria wouldn't see it until she was ready to be
dressed in it. Then the silver presents had been arriving from
various members of Karan's family, a quantity of rose bowls,
glasses, trays, boxes, sweet dishes, and an enormous silver tea
service in which the teapot was shaped like an elephant. The
spout was the elephant's upraised trunk, the handle was the
elephant's looped tail, and the whole thing stood on four squat
legs; the sugar bowl was a crouching elephant and the milk jug
was a standing one, with his trunk pulled in between his front
legs, his tail as a handle, and a groove in the top of his head to
pour from.

As for the presents from her own family and from her friends in
Bombay, those were mostly in the form of checks. Her father had
given her 5,001 rupees (the extra 1 rupee because it is bad luck
to give a round number without giving the money something to
grow on), a complete set of diamonds, necklace, earrings and
bracelets, a complete set of rubies, her mother's big, round diamond to be reset in platinum as a ring, an emerald ring and an
emerald-and-diamond bracelet, a thick, old-fashioned gold choker,
no sapphires because Pria was superstitious about them, but
various other pieces from her mother's jewelry that she had always
admired—an enameled pendant, long, dangling earrings set with
nine different stones, the nauratan that is supposed to bring good
fortune, opals, a pearl pin in a wide lacy design. Her family supplied as well, of course, her household silver both for Indian
meals and Western meals, her linen and the saris for her trousseau.

But there were still any number of things to do and talk about
in those early days of the heat. Pria hadn't, for instance, decided
where they would go for their wedding trip, Kashmir or Ceylon.

"The trouble with Kashmir is that we'll know everybody, and

we won't even be able to go for a walk in Srinagar without meeting people and they'll try to be tactful with the 'young honeymooners' and that will be a very great bore."

"You could go trekking in the mountains. It's very beautiful."

"I dare say, but I think it's a great mistake to start out married life in a tent. There'll be quite enough embarrassments as it is."

"Are you embarrassed with Karan?" I asked, unable to imagine Pria without her composure.

"Oh, not really," she said vaguely, and I thought she wasn't going to say any more. "But one leads a very separate life. Thank goodness," she added.

"I rather wish one didn't—"

"Oh, well, you, so intense, always wanting things to happen, reading novels—" a mixture of scorn and affection. "One day you'll want to be peaceful."

"After the movies the other night Hari asked me to marry him." I saw the smile begin on Pria's face and quickly said, "I said no."

Pria only said, "Poor old Hari," but I could tell she was angry and I launched into elaborate and rather confused explanations. "That night just before Jay's New Year's party I had a moment when everything seemed so ordered to me. We would never change, I thought. I looked at the next twenty years as though I had already lived them. But now it seems to me that other things are possible, and—I don't know—"

Then Pria broke in, very cold and hostile. "I do. Hari doesn't fit the part of the perfect romantic lover. What a fool you are, Baba! Obviously you've been infected by these American friends of yours. You've even begun to think like a Westerner, and you've lost the chance of the best marriage you could have."

"It's no use scolding me."

"I suppose not. Though I must say one would think that the most unobservant person would be bound to see that the Nichols, like us, can only function within their own limits. Ours are different, though no less satisfactory. I expect you'll find that out for yourself eventually."

Pria had a way of closing a subject very firmly, so when she said, "Perhaps Ceylon would be better after all," I knew that we wouldn't ever discuss Hari again unless I forced her into it. Besides that, she was careful and considerate about never pairing me off with Hari at movies or parties or going home in cars, as most of our friends had more or less fallen into the habit of doing, as if we automatically belonged and wanted to be together. That night, for instance—or one of those nights—when we went to dinner with the Kalipurs, she took Hari off to sit with her and I found myself at the other end of the table, next to Kali himself, depressingly enough, but at least without the necessity of chattering through Hari's rather tense courtesy.

I asked Kali—because I was chronically short of conversation with him—whether he had enjoyed his trip back to Kalipur, expecting the usual banalities about horses or a local polo match ("Jolly good show our people put up") or, at best, "You ladies don't realize how lucky you are. No work, families to keep you in comfort, ha ha. While we men, lots of things to attend to, don't you know. Files, conferences with the ministers, tours. Burdened with responsibilities, what? Can't spend all day in bed or five hours making ourselves pretty for a party, ha ha."

But for once Kali seemed to have lost his leaden jocularity. "Troubled times," he said seriously, "troubled times."

"Politics?" I asked, half expecting him to say, "Racing going to pot. Trainers are all a lot of crooks."

"Yes, politics. These Congress types have sent a pack of agitators up to Kalipur. The fellows are making a lot of trouble. Constitutions, voting, rot like that. What do they know about it? Go around the countryside telling people a lot of lies, promising them anything. Of course our chaps believe it all."

"Of course," I said, but I was glad that Kali didn't catch the sarcasm. I wondered while he was talking whether one really could blame him for his obtuseness. His education had been designed to turn him into a fake Englishman, a good athlete, a stupid, well-meaning man. Under the old system he had managed to get along beautifully—no conflicts with the British government, no trouble in Kalipur, advised by a good Prime Minister, willing to back reforms in the state—schools, hospitals, that sort of thing—possibly only because it seemed to be the thing to do, but certainly he was not oppressive like some of his colleagues. And now, a bewildered, disturbed man. A cricketer suddenly finding himself playing chess.

If it had been Jay, if he had been the elder son, how much more he would have understood. But then, he only understood as much as he did because he hadn't been trained as an elder son, had, in fact, rebelled against the whole thing in a way—loved it, loved Kalipur and its life, but, in his own terms and context, an eccentric—and what would he have done in all the years up to now? Would he have been a Splendid Chap to the British? Probably he would have been more like his father, less dramatic, but disliked and uneasily respected by the foreigners, entirely comfortable and sure in Kalipur.

". . . of course I'm not gravely worried about the loyalty of our chaps," Kali was saying. "When it comes to the test they'll stick up for us, but meanwhile it's damned unsettling. Poor show altogether."

"How do you mean stick up for you?" I asked. "Fight?"

Kali looked flustered. "It'll never come to that," he said, moving his big shoulders inside his British Guards' uniform as though he wanted to scratch his back. "The constitutional assembly will settle all that. The States will be independent, of course. We expect to have loose ties with the central government, naturally. After all, the administrative problem—communications and so forth—would be too complicated otherwise, but the States will have to be independent. They can't depose us—more than six hundred princes, after all." He sounded as if he would have liked to add, "It wouldn't be sporting."

Most of the people at the table were listening, and the Maharani at the far end was flushed with indignation. "It's scandalous," she burst out, "putting all these ideas into people's heads! After all we've done for them—"

(Very softly beside me Jay muttered, "And after all they've done for us.")

"You have no idea how ungrateful people can be! H.H. simply wore himself out touring the state and making speeches—"

"I'm not very good on my feet," Kali said. "No gift of gab."

"—and telling people not to worry, that we would look after

them as we always had. Tell them," she commanded, "tell them
what happened at that big meeting. I was never so disgusted in
my life as when I heard about it! Go on, tell them!"

Kali said, "No, no, really," and "Politics don't make good
dinner-table conversation," and "We won't bore the ladies with
all this heavy talk," but eventually we did hear the story. Kali's
advisors had told him that it would be a good thing for morale
purposes and for a general calming effect if he toured his state
and made a series of speeches to his people. It might even, they
told him, help to quiet some of the agitation and perhaps the
old, traditional loyalties—taken for granted over so many years
—could be given a new strength and impetus. After all, a Maharaja
still had status among his people; attitudes established over cen-
turies are not changed overnight, as the political parvenus would
soon see. Kali had never done much of this sort of thing, and except for state occasions or ceremonies at which he had to appear—
state marriages, certain festivals, a durbar—left most of it to his
ministers. He was uncomfortable in his formal Indian clothes
(which of course he had to wear at those times—"I feel like such
an ass"—) and he was a man without a gift for pleasing the public
or a feeling for the magic of crowds.

However, on this last tour, he had been persuaded of the necessity of doing all this, and, I suppose, must somewhere in his heart
have been confident of the emotional power of his rank. He had
made some speeches with moderate success, had dutifully in-
spected a troop of Boy Scouts, of school children, had traveled to
a couple of villages and encouraged farmers, had visited a couple
of factories and encouraged mill workers. His biggest speech was
to be held in Kalipur itself. It was open to the public, attended
by crowds of people, some who wanted to see the Maharaja, some
who were pleased by the excitement of any unusual occasion,
people with nothing to do of an evening, with their wives, children, people on an outing. And of course a number of college
students and, presumably, the Congress "agitators."

They had all assembled in the Kalipur Central Park and
Botanical Gardens to watch the royal procession arrive. They
watched Kali and his retinue climb onto the wooden platform,

which had been erected in the Park and which was covered with carpets and draped with the Kalipur colors. They listened while the Kalipur State Band played, and they listened while the Prime Minister said a few respectful words.

But when Kali got up to speak he managed to say no more than, "My people—" A tremendous commotion broke out in the back of the audience. Obviously it had been planned, because almost simultaneously groups of students and Congress sympathizers placed strategically in every part of the audience began yelling him down. "Mahatma Gandhi *ki jai!* Jawaharlal Nehru *ki jai!*"

Afterward some of the palace retinue told him that they had even heard—and this, incredibly enough, from Kalipur people, not the outside students or agitators— "*Inqilab zindabad! Inqilab zindabad!*" A Congress government, after all, was one thing, but revolution was a horse of quite another color.

When the uproar became so great that there was danger of a real riot—and there was clearly no way of resuming the speeches and ceremonies—the palace party and Kali had retired with as much dignity as they could manage. The police had, of course, tried to reach the troublemakers and had taken some of them into custody. ("They will be dealt with properly," the Maharani said with restraint.) Most of them had simply melted into the crowd. But there had been a further sign of planning. While the meeting in the park had been going on, people had painted up slogans on walls and houses on the royal route back to the palace—they hadn't been there on the outward trip. Pro-Congress slogans, of course, and sometimes just a huge, crude drawing of a spinning wheel. It was all very embarrassing for Kali. His account of it, without any of the color or details that all of us could fill in from imagination, was short, dry and curiously pathetic.

For the rest of the evening all of us talked strenuously about other, brighter things and only the Maharani kept up a steady, outraged complaint to whoever would listen to her. But there was a note of warning in all our hearts. Maharajas were the obvious, the immediate effigies, but were any of the rest of us secure in our justifications? It was only a matter of degree. Possibly that difference would be sufficient to allow us to decline unnoticeably rather than to plunge with drama.

Later in the evening at some point I asked Jay if he were worried by Kali's experiences, and he shrugged in his smiling offhand way and said that if he wanted to put his mind to worrying it would be about the Prohibition laws they kept threatening us with, not the future of Kali or of Kalipur.

"Oh, do be serious, Jay."

"I was never more serious. I'm going up to Kalipur next week."

"To see what you can do about the agitation? To make speeches?"

Jay laughed, and made his plump clown's face. "God, no."

"Then why?"

"Because I like it there."

After the party, driving home as usual with Karan and Pria, when we stopped by the Hanging Gardens to look out at the lights of the city and the Back Bay, I told them that Jay was going back to Kalipur and that H.H. and the Maharani were spending the summer in Kashmir.

"That settles it," Pria said. "We go to Ceylon."

"I'll get the tickets tomorrow," Karan said, "just to be sure you don't change your mind again."

"And Hari leaves for Poona soon, and I am going south," I continued, "and next Saturday is the last race meeting. The season really does seem to be over." Karan started the car again. "Will Bombay ever be the same again?" I asked.

"I don't see why not," Karan replied.

Pria touched my hand in the darkness. "We'll all be back in the cold weather."

It must have been about a week before Pria's wedding that we met Alix in town. Pria and I had been to the shoemaker's to order her gold wedding sandals which had somehow been forgotten in all the preparations, and had decided to lunch at the Taj Mahal Hotel. We sat at our usual table by the window and saw, across the room, Alix lunching with another woman whom we guessed from her clothes to be American. ("Standard Oil, Mrs. Number Two, I think," Pria said.)

Alix waved and, when they were leaving, stopped at our table. "Haven't seen you for ages." She sounded distracted.

"Not for ages."

"Do call me. We'll have lunch or something. Will you do that?" Before I could answer she went on, "I lunch here practically every day because of the air conditioning. It's gotten frightfully hot, hasn't it?"

"Simply grilling," Pria drawled in an exaggerated English-public-school accent.

Alix's friend stood uncomfortably a little behind Alix, present, but pretending not to be, and looked everywhere about the room except at us.

"As a matter of fact," Alix said, "I haven't been very well. Nothing serious—you know, just Bombay tummy or whatever they call it—but it makes you feel awfully unenergetic. I guess I haven't been too careful about drinking boiled water and things like that. Still—" she seemed to forget what she was going to say. "Well, I'm going up to Kashmir next week. It should be lovely, I think. It sounds so romantic—Shalimar, and, well I've always wanted to. So do call me before then. You will do that, won't you?"

"Yes, of course," I said and we both knew I wouldn't.

"And we'll have lunch or something."

Pria's only comment after they left was, "She really is very pretty."

* XVI *

THE DAY BEFORE PRIA'S WEDDING I WAS IN MY ROOM PACKING for my annual visit to my mother in south India. Usually I left at the beginning of April and stayed with her until after the rains had broken in Bombay—they broke in the south a week or ten days before the monsoon winds reached Bombay—but this year I had stayed on in Bombay for Pria's wedding and would not be leaving until the day after. There were a couple of suitcases open on the bed, and my ayah was helping me sort out the clothes I should need in the south. Between rude comments about the dhobi who had pulled buttons off my clothes (just to make extra work for a poor old woman whose eyes were failing), and had torn a petticoat and folded it so that the tear wouldn't show, she put in her familiar pleas to be taken south with me. What would she do in Bombay alone? Yes, yes, Baba always said there was a house full of servants, but Baba of all people should know how cruelly she was mistreated by them, how they resented her and were jealous of her and only waited until Baba left to make life a misery. How many years had it been since she had seen Baba's dear, saintly mother? Surely more than three? Even now she wept.

"You should have gone south with her, then."

Ah, perhaps, but she wasn't one to think only of her own wishes. Who would have looked after Baba? Who would have waited up for her at night and mended her clothes? . . .

"Listen," I said. "Why did my mother go away?"

The ayah looked cross at being interrupted. She told me, without much interest, that the time had come for my mother to think of herself. After so many years of taking care of me and my father and all our little concerns. (Like my mother, she had the trick of dismissing politics—my father's work—as irrelevant to the business of living.) "She had to follow the more important path."

Pria came in, said, "Complaining again?" briskly, gave the ayah ten rupees to spend on sweets to celebrate Pria's wedding, and told her to go away and meditate on her good fortune and her easy job. Full of smiles and blessings, the ayah touched Pria's feet and disappeared to gloat in the servants' quarters.

"I've escaped," Pria said, fidgeting around the room with most uncharacteristic nervousness. "The house is full of relatives talking family scandal in every room, on all the verandas, even in the kitchen messing around with special this and we must have that —not a moment's privacy, I'm going mad." She riffled through the folded saris on the bed. "Do you always wear cottons in the south?"

"Mostly. It's very hot down there."

"How horrid."

"How torrid." Pria smiled gratefully. "Actually," I continued, just to be saying something because she seemed so ill at ease, "I don't mind it at all. The heat's much more bearable in the country than in Bombay. Besides, you don't try to do anything, and that keeps you cool."

"I suppose so. I bet Ceylon will be boiling hot, too, even Kandy. Oh God I wish it were all over."

"Don't fret—"

"A bride," Pria said with rather careful control, "is allowed to fret as much as she wants on the day before her wedding, and should be indulged." Suddenly she asked, "Do you know what that bitch has done? She's gone and sent me an absolutely impossible sari. I cannot, cannot wear it."

"The wedding sari? Have you looked at it?"

"Of course." Pria closed a suitcase impatiently. "Nobody really expects you not to. It's made of that bloody awful stiff gauze. I'll look like a balloon. I'm not going to wear it, that's all."

"Can't you get it softened?"

"Oh, use your head. How could I possibly get it softened? There isn't any time."

"If you pay them extra—"

"No, I'm going to wear something else. I don't care."

"But Pria, you'll have to—"

"Don't tell me I have to," Pria shouted. "I don't have to. I don't have to do anything. I don't even have to marry Karan."

"Pria, Pria," I said helplessly.

She sat down in a chair and started to cry, not at all prettily. In a hoarse, jerking voice, with tears streaming down her face, she said, "I can't see how I'll stand it. So pompous. And he enjoys all that polo talk, I mean really enjoys it. And businessmen to dinner, and that—that woman for a mother-in-law."

"Pria, it'll be all right. You'll see. This is just nerves."

"Oh, I know, I know. It's entirely conventional, and next week I'll be embarrassed about it, and for a few months I'll be ashamed whenever I think about it, and in a couple of years I'll have forgotten about it altogether. Don't ever remind me."

"I won't."

"But just now," she said, hiccuping, "I'd give anything to be fifty years old."

The next day, however, when I went to Pria's house in the morning, she was standing in the middle of her room being dressed by her own young sister and Karan's two sisters, in the stiff, gold-embroidered gauze that she hated, and in which she looked extremely beautiful. Apart from a certain irritability about details she showed no signs of nerves. On the chairs, the bed, and on the floor twenty female relatives sat about, and Karan's mother, with the position of honor, was directing the dressing of the bride. Pria was allowed to do nothing herself and I could guess how uncomfortable she must be feeling—nobody but you yourself can drape a sari properly on you so that it falls right and you are happy in it. I guessed that probably later on Pria would excuse herself to go into the bathroom and redo the whole thing to her satisfaction.

Meanwhile, with admirable patience, she stood while her sister and tomorrow's sisters-in-law tied her petticoat, fastened her choli and wound the six yards of crimson and gold around her. The soles of her feet, the palms of her hands and her fingernails had been stained a dull reddish-orange with henna leaves. Her eyes had a thick black rim of kohl around them. She wore no other make-up, but after she was dressed her mother-in-law placed the red spot of a tika between her eyebrows, pinned red roses in her hair, fastened her wedding jewelry round her neck, in her ears and her wrists and arranged the pendant that hung on her forehead.

When all this was done, an old woman stood up from the corner of the room, and with three paper cones of powder—red, yellow and white—made an elaborate square design on the floor enclosing the place where Pria stood. Several of the women started to chant hymns. The children scampered in and out of the room, neatly jumping over the threshold of every door, where swastikas and other signs of good fortune had been drawn in colored powder. The relatives chattered among themselves, discussing the jewelry and wedding presents. Pria looked at me for the first time and raised her eyebrows in half-humorous resignation.

Downstairs the bridegroom's party had arrived. I was not allowed to join in the ceremonies for Karan, but when I walked past the little prayer room on my way to join the other guests I caught a glimpse of him in a silver brocade achkan, wearing a Mahratta turban and sitting cross-legged on the floor. The old Brahmin sat in front of him muttering prayers, and all around were the male relatives in formal Indian clothes.

The drawing room had been cleared of furniture, and all of us sat on the floor against the walls of the room. In the center a brass urn contained live charcoal and even through the thick perfume of the sticks of agarbati burning in the corners of the room, from time to time I could still smell the pleasant outdoor smoke of the charcoal. The day had already become hot and the servants had drawn the reed blinds against the sun, and this kept the atmosphere of the room dense with the scent of many flowers, the women's attar, the smoke, the incense.

Karan came down first, and with the Brahmin took his place beside the charcoal burner. A few moments later Pria arrived, walking very slowly down the stairs and into the room, her head bent, her eyes looking only at the floor, her mother and Karan's mother one on each side of her. She sat down next to the fire, still without looking at anybody. The priest began the long prayers to open the ceremony.

Hot, uncomfortable and bored, I leaned against the wall, closed my eyes against the triumphant faces of the two mothers, the inquisitiveness of the relatives, the excitement of the children, and thought about Pria and wished with all my heart for her happiness —a wish that she would probably have rejected as unrealistic sentimentality, had she known about it. Did Pria's massive certainty perhaps cover far more fears than I had ever thought about? Perhaps her ordered mind and existence were the achievement of a necessary discipline? It had always seemed to me a natural gift, a birthright, from the days when we had first met at school in England. Even then Pria had retained that sturdy perspective, and unlike me (who tried unhappily to be "good at games") answered the games mistress with confident logic and, in my eyes, with infinite bravery, "But why should I make an effort when I never expect to play hockey again as long as I live?" And all the

blandishments of "being a good sport" or "team spirit," or even
of schoolgirl popularity, were ignored or unnoticed by Pria. She
was never really intractable, and no complaints could be made
about her work. It was her "attitude" that puzzled and distressed
the well-meaning teachers, who on one occasion, in despair at
such commonsensical iconoclasm, had sent her to talk to the
headmistress.

Waiting for her outside, frightened for her and holding my
thumbs as a charm against disaster, I tried to listen to what was
going on inside the headmistress's study. When Pria at last came
out, looking, as always, as though her blue gym tunic and black
stockings were some kind of fancy dress that she was wearing for
the moment but that didn't really belong to her, I whispered,
"What did she say? What did she say?"

"Oh, nothing much."

"Did she give you a terrible ticking off?"

"She was rather more hurt than angry," Pria said with irony.

"But what had you done?"

"That's just it. I haven't done anything—or not enough from
their point of view. She said she didn't like my attitude, that I
didn't show the right spirit. So I told her that these aren't our
customs or our spirit, and in India they wouldn't make much
sense."

"You didn't."

"Of course I did," Pria said surprised. "And I told her that
since I was going back to live in Bombay as soon as I pass matric,
it seemed silly to spend a lot of time on things that only belong
here in England."

Pria never, to my knowledge, told lies, so I believed her account
of the interview, and (to me, who was furtively guilty of currying
favor with girls and teachers) it remained for years in my mind
as a supreme example of courage and integrity. The only thing
the headmistress could do was to write a rather grieved note to
Pria's parents, along with her school report, to say she didn't seem
to show much "enthusiasm." To which, when her father read it
out, Pria replied, "Why should I be enthusiastic about English
things?" though as far as her parents were concerned she didn't

need to defend herself. She was getting an "English education," which is what most well-off Bombay families hoped to give their children, and that would remain a permanent asset in her qualifications for making a good marriage, in a job, if she should want one for a short time, in going to college and in general prestige. All this talk of enthusiasm and sportsmanship could be ignored as an irrelevant, mystifying British eccentricity.

To me her Alice-in-Wonderland approach and her almost priggish knowledge of where she stood in the world were at the same time something to envy and something to deplore. I was unhappy at school, accepting too easily the standards of contemporaries or of the teachers, wanting to make friends, hoping to be good (but not embarrassingly outstanding) at things, but at the same time I felt that for all her placid equanimity Pria was missing something, though I was never sure what.

In the five or six years since we left school, while Pria went to college and I traveled a bit in India but mostly stayed at home, her disturbing, much-discussed "attitude" seemed to be crystallizing if not into a philosophy at least into a way of life. One couldn't help being impressed, and eventually as she married, grew older, had children, grew older still, one would perhaps find out how rewarding—if she were looking for rewards—or anyway how serviceable it would turn out to be. Yesterday's deviation was, after all, I decided, the conventional show of nerves that Pria had claimed at the time.

The prayers and chanting nearing their end, the bride and groom stood up. Karan's mother hurried forward holding two fat garlands made of jasmine, red roses and marigolds intertwined with gold ribbons and fastened with two large gold tassels. She handed one to her son and one to Pria. In the warm, sentimental silence of the room, Karan lifted his garland over Pria's head and gently hung it over her shoulders, round her neck. For the first time Pria lifted her gaze from the floor to Karan's face. Her sari slipped off her head as she placed her garland around his neck, and for a moment there was a kind of arrogance in her look. Then she covered her head again and looked down.

Hand in hand, the bride and groom walked seven times around

the charcoal burner to more chanting from the priest. Finally, standing together before the old man, Pria and Karan bent their heads to where he could reach, and he smeared a little ash from the sacred fire on each forehead.

In a haphazard way the guests and relatives stood up. Pria and Karan stayed with the priest until all of us, chattering in a subdued way, straightening our saris, stretching, had left the room. Later they joined us at the banquet.

On the long veranda that ran the length of the house on one side, the servants had spread bed sheets, and in two lines, facing each other, the places had been arranged, on the floor, for the guests to eat. It was really much too hot in the middle of the day to think about an enormous meal, but appearances had to be kept up and the results of a week's cooking were set before us. Servants bustled about piling onto the banana leaves that were used as plates an endless succession of dishes—rice, chapatis, puris, vegetables of many sorts, lentils, curds, a dozen different sorts of sweets, fruit, more rice: plain, pilaus, sweet rice. We all ate with our fingers, of course, and the relatives living in the house made a special point of tasting every dish to be sure that it met their exacting standards.

Pria and Karan when they came to join us sat together at one end of the veranda. Pria's first mouthful of rice was fed to her by her mother-in-law. Weighted with garlands and jewelry, she sat in a private world, speaking to nobody and eating nothing more. I tried to catch her eye but couldn't. Afterward when we got up to leave I thought I might manage a few words with her, but she had already gone upstairs to rest, and only the relatives were left, chatting and gossiping in little knots all over the house. I went home holding the small package of sweets that each guest had been given.

The wedding reception was held at five o'clock that evening at the Club. Almost a thousand people had to be invited so, naturally, there wasn't room in the Bhutt house. For this occasion Pria was wearing one of her own saris from her trousseau—one that I had helped her choose—a lemon-yellow georgette with a wide gold-and-green pullah hanging over her shoulder, and she seemed more animated. I had arrived early, hoping to be there before she was swamped in greetings and congratulations, but there was no way of escaping from the devoted relatives and in-laws. They formed a solid phalanx around her; she said nothing except that her feet hurt, and turned away to greet new arrivals.

It was a very pretty party with its decorated terrace, the flowers and the saris, the open-air dance floor, the gaiety and the blessings and bursts of laughter, but I left after about an hour. Pria and Karan were moving slowly about among the guests, acknowledging congratulations, saying a word or two to everyone, and I called, "Good-by and good luck" to them over the heads of one of the groups, though I don't know whether they heard. Then I stood on the Club porch waiting for my father's car, feeling lonely and rather sad.

Pria and Karan were to leave the party at half past seven. Their luggage was already in Karan's car. The Bhutt chauffeur would drive them out to the airport. Their immediate families would accompany them in other cars. There would be more flowers, more garlands, more blessings, congratulations and farewells as they climbed aboard the plane. Pria's mother's last words to her daughter would be, "Be thou as Sita, be as Savitri"—dedicate your life to your husband. I thought it would be much better if I didn't go.

I left the next morning for the south, and I didn't see Pria again until that autumn. But by then a lot of things had happened to make me forget the sense of desertion, of something precious lost, that I had the evening of Pria's wedding.

Part Two

✳

THE SOUTH

✳ XVII ✳

THE TRAIN ARRIVED EARLY IN THE MORNING AT CHENUR
station. With a sense of recognition I noticed the damp, smoky
smell of south India, the tepid breeze that came through the compartment windows. As we pulled in beside the single platform,
half a dozen coolies were sleepily winding their turbans, getting
ready for the new day. In the indeterminate light under the platform shelter a row of sleeping travelers, shrouded like corpses,
with shawls covering their faces, scarcely stirred as the train came
to a gasping, shuddering stop. The only activity was in the mail
van, where a voice called something angrily. A man stumbled out
of the ticket room, his hair still disordered from sleep. In a placating voice he replied, Gently, gently. A sack with a locked metal
ring around its mouth was flung at his feet. He smiled, pushing
his hair back. Near him the coffee man was cooling the sweet,
milky mixture, pouring it briskly in a long beige stream from one
brass jar into another and back again.

I gathered my things together, feeling frowzy and muddleheaded,
and opened the compartment door. My mother appeared silently
from the shelter, waving the coolies away. Behind her, Gopal,
bare-chested, his clean white mundu a slender column to the
ground, joined his hands swiftly in a namaskar. I was carrying too

many things to respond, and smiled stiffly, but he had slipped into the train to bring out my suitcases. My mother and I embraced, like distant relatives, pulling apart in a second.

"You shouldn't have come," I said. "I could easily have managed. This is such a terrible time of day."

"I am up in any case. As you get older you need less sleep."

Gopal put both cases on his head and trotted out to find a tonga. My mother and I walked more slowly. She said, "You'll feel better when you've had a bath and some coffee."

"It's a maddening train. Stops at every tiny place."

"It would have to," she sounded amused, "to stop here."

Gopal piled the luggage on the front bench of the tonga, and climbed in to sit on top of it, next to the driver. The carriage tipped forward alarmingly, rocking between its two high wheels. The horse, standing between the shafts with his head down, staggered at the readjustment of the weight. The driver clicked his tongue consolingly, raising his face to stare at us with curiosity as we settled ourselves with our backs to him. They have a special surliness, tonga drivers, oddly at variance with whatever gaiety makes them decorate their horses with bells and caps and red-and-green tassels.

"These packages," I said, shifting about. "I brought you some sweets."

"You shouldn't—"

"The cook insisted on making them. In that basket there are some Bombay mangoes."

My mother smiled. "Alphonsos?"

"They're still the best."

"It's been a good year for mangoes here too."

Jangling and rattling, the tonga moved off. The driver snapped the reins authoritatively. Gopal clutched the wooden framework of the little awning that covered us. I gazed out at the retreating road, fringed with trees, and at the early-morning town where the shopkeepers in the bazaar were just taking down the wooden shutters in front of their stalls, and the women from the country were walking to market, each carrying a shallow basket of vegetables on her head, her back beautifully arched, one arm raised to steady the load.

"Everything is going well in Bombay?" my mother was asking.

"Oh, yes. Life continues as usual. We do the same things, see the same people."

"And how is he?" (In the correct Hindu manner, she never would say her husband's name.)

"Very well. Working hard, of course."

"He always took politics very seriously. Ever since we were married I remember that politics were the center of his life," she said without rancor. "I hope he is taking care of himself. He forgets, sometimes, that his heart is not strong."

"They wanted him to go up to Delhi on some sort of advisory job to do with the Constituent Assembly—"

"Who is it that wants him to?"

"The Bombay Congress committee. But I hope he won't. I'm not sure that he's in things as much now as he used to be," I said, trying to articulate the impression I retained from the meeting with the Congressmen months ago. "I mean, they're very polite but it's the kind of politeness you offer to an old aunt. Situations have changed and the kind of people has changed—"

She interrupted, "They owe him something after all these years."

"I think they realize that, but it's not good enough to be kind."

"Well, politics aren't important," my mother said with an almost ruthless indifference.

"They are to him. He's been left behind."

"I hope—" my mother began but didn't finish the sentence.

"That he'll find compensations?" I suggested. As you found compensations for an empty life, I might have added if I had been able to formulate the idea at the time. She smiled, but still said nothing further.

We left the town in a few minutes, wheeling along in our clattering progress past the small municipal building, the police headquarters set back from the road where a couple of men in wrinkled blue uniforms lounged on a bench in the garden, the King George V Memorial School, the dak bungalow. The paved road ended and in sudden quiet we turned off between the coconut groves, the tonga wheels whispering on the packed earth, the bells on the horse's harness spreading their thin jangle to the countryside.

My mother's house was about two miles out of town. It was small and square with whitewashed walls and a red tile roof. A veranda ran the length of each side, and the whole house was surrounded by a neat, unimaginative garden combining in conventional patterns the dark red earth and the heavy green of hibiscus and jasmine bushes. The boundary was marked by the tall, graceful coconut palms leaning untidily into the far blue sky.

There were four rooms in the house, each of them bare and square, each opening onto the veranda and onto the passage that ran from the front door to the back. The two rooms in front were both living rooms because we used to eat our meals on one of the side verandas. Both the back rooms were bedrooms, one of which my mother shared with my grandmother, who, after the crowded Jalnabad years, could never sleep well at night unless she was somehow dimly aware of movement or of breathing from another bed. The other bedroom was kept for me as there were never other visitors in the house. Each of the bedrooms had a bathroom, partitioned off by a thin plaster wall from the rest of the room, with a separate door to the veranda through which the sweeper, a bent, ashamed old man, crept in several times a day to clean, to replenish the supply of cold water in the big earthenware jar or, in the early mornings, to bring for my bath a brass bucket full of hot water that still held the fragrance of smoke from a wood fire. The kitchen and the servants' quarters were in a separate building at the side of the garden, and beyond them the well and some rather scraggy vegetable patches where the servants grew a kind of spinach, and a big white root somewhere between a turnip and horse-radish, a chili bush, some beans.

The tonga stopped at the gate. My mother and I climbed out and walked through the garden, along the straight path to the front veranda steps, leaving Gopal to unload the luggage and pay the driver. We went first to the living room where my grandmother habitually sat in the mornings. Like the rest of the house its walls were white and undecorated, the floor, polished red tile,

the furniture—a few straight chairs, a small bookcase set on a re-
volving stand, a wooden platform covered with a white sheet—
was ranged neatly along the walls, like a dentist's waiting room.
In the center of the room was a table made of a big, enameled
brass tray supported by six carved mahogany legs. My grandmother
sat in her usual place on the platform, cross-legged, old and fat,
her white hair drawn tightly back into a thin knot, her white cotton sari still (so early in the morning) stiff with starch ballooning
around her. She glared at me but spoke to my mother. "What is
this?" she said sharply. "What is this? Have these girls no
manners?"

My mother gripped my arm. She spoke very calmly to the old
lady. "Amma, this is Baba—"

"Tell her to cover her head when she comes to see me."

Slowly I pulled my sari over my head. My mother crossed the
room and put out a hand tentatively to that immobile white figure.

"These days," my grandmother continued sarcastically, "they
don't even see fit to touch the feet of a mother-in-law." Suddenly,
angrily, she said to me, "Leave your bad breeding with your own
family if that is where it belongs. When you come to this house
you come as a daughter, the wife of my eldest son. Try to behave
with the dignity of such a position—"

"Amma, Amma," my mother interrupted with more agitation,
"This is Baba, Indira, your granddaughter. . . ." She shook the
old cotton shoulder gently.

My grandmother turned to stare out of the open window,
across the garden to the gray, slanting boles of the palms, the departing tonga, Gopal struggling with the luggage and baskets; an
eternity of silence was in the room. "The days come and go," she
whispered, "the days come and go." She looked at me again, still
standing in the doorway, and focused her wide, warm smile on
me. She held out her arms to me. "Come," she said, "my child,
my darling child. I have been waiting for you." I went nervously
across to her. "I have made something special for your breakfast.
After such a long time I still remember what you like!"

"Sweet puris?" I asked, feeling confident again, and recalling from my childhood a favorite treat in her house—a taste that had vanished in me years before.

"What else? Of course sweet puris." She held me away from her with those elegant, slender hands which never seemed to change through the years as her body thickened and aged. "Let me look at you. Good. You look well."

"Tired and dirty."

"But well. I can tell you are healthy. What about your marriage? Have your people in Bombay been thinking about your marriage?"

"Not really," I said, laughing at her in the old way. "Nobody wants to marry me."

"Your mother tells me there is a young man, very eligible, a good family. Have his parents talked to your father about it yet?"

"Oh, I don't know. I don't think I want to marry him anyway."

"Want to?" she repeated reproachfully. "Want to? Who is the master, your wants or yourself?" I said nothing and she told me gently, "It is time you got married."

"I suppose it is."

My mother said, "Come, there is water for your bath waiting for you. It will get cold. I'll tell the cook to make fresh coffee."

My grandmother said, "God protect you. Come back and have your coffee here with me."

In my room my mother sat on the bed, the usual wooden frame webbed with tape and covered with a thin mattress and sheets, while I unpacked some clean clothes. "I should have warned you," she said, "I didn't think it would happen so soon. Did she frighten you?"

"Startled me. What has happened? Is she losing her mind?"

"No, no. She wanders in her mind a little. She is an old woman and she mixes up the past with the present. It is only natural. So much of her life is behind her, it is only natural that she should live in it. Those years have more reality for her."

"It must be hard for you to cope with her."

"Who is to say where reality lies?"

"I know where my reality lies," I said with unnecessary emphasis.

"I hope so," my mother said, smiling. "And she, perhaps, knows hers."

"How long has this been going on?" I asked.

"For some months, now. I expect it will increase. She is an old woman," she said again. "Go on and have your bath. I will finish unpacking for you."

The days in my mother's house were much longer than anywhere else that I knew. The long morning hours would stretch and stretch until I could hardly believe that it would ever again get dark. We ate what we called breakfast but what was really close to lunch at half past eleven in the morning, and it seemed as though a tremendous moment of the day had been reached, a ridge of some kind that one crossed and then breathed more easily walking downhill. In the afternoons I would lie on my bed, half asleep, watching the points and rods of sunlight that came through the reed matting that was stretched across the open doors and the high, small windows. I daydreamed a lot. I had, at the time, no way of judging the previous winter, but I felt anyway this much: that Alix and Nicky had saved themselves. In retrospect it seemed easier to see that the need had been growing for some time and the moment of a kiss, vanished before it had begun, was not, as I had thought, the crucial point of the matter. It had, in fact, meant nothing—both Alix and I had said so at the time, neither of us meaning it. But it served; one needs some excuse. If necessary one invents a necessity. I had never doubted that they were in love, but it took me a stretch of time—and I suppose both of them too—to see that whatever the climate and conditions that it demanded, it was still the thing to salvage. Although I didn't think much about Bombay, the winter had left a residue in my mind, and I thought often of romance. Alix and Nicky, who had dropped so completely from my life, had, at least, left me wondering. Hot, too absorbed in my own imaginings to read, sometimes in those afternoons I would really fall asleep and dream violent, vivid fragments of dreams, and awake sweating and disturbed when my mother called me for tea.

She too rested in the afternoon, but the rest of her day had great order and direction. She got up usually at about five thirty in the morning, before the first rose light filled the sky, and turned the palms black. Sometimes if I woke early and went into the second living room I would find it still full of the smell of incense from her prayers, and would carry in my mind the sound of her soft singing, hymns or the whispered words of a passage from the Bhagvat-Gita. For the next couple of hours she sat on the side veranda, silent, unmoving, calm, her face clear of expression, her back erect, her feet tucked neatly under her, thinking, or meditating, or with an entirely blank mind—hardest of all—I never knew. If one could guess anything from her smooth face and confident bearing it was, perhaps, a definition of those rewards she had mentioned to me so long ago. It was hard to reconstruct in my mind that note of despairing bitterness I had once heard in her voice.

At about eight o'clock we all met for coffee and ate fat little fermented rice cakes with pickles. Often as we sat on the veranda sipping our coffee, not talking much, I would see the cook come wheeling in on his bicycle carrying the day's supply of food from the market in Chenur. He brought me a copy of the newspaper, too, a Madras paper of the day before. Afterward I often sat on at the table for an hour working at the crossword puzzle, or reading items of disparate news that seemed to have no significance in that still house.

My grandmother loved to cook, and every day prepared at least one dish for us. She would bustle clumsily off to the kitchen to heckle the cook or change the arrangements for the day's meals, to inspect the servants' rooms and see that their wives kept them properly swept and clean, that the children were respectful, that there weren't more than the usual three or four relatives staying in the servants' quarters. This was the last area left to her where she could still be bossy and powerful, and refresh her memory of the days when she was the head of a big household, not rich, but with an extensive domain and many people under her government. In the years since my grandfather's death her sons had left to work in various cities of India, her daughters were all married. Living with my mother, now, she had an authority that she could not claim in the house of any one of her sons, and in a small way she enjoyed herself.

My mother's mornings were taken up a good deal with reading, sometimes with household duties. She would smile at me sometimes as she passed the veranda, looking quite young and fresh, no gray in her hair, never beautiful, but pleasant and unforced. And I sat on dreaming in the shade, watching the servants' children playing in the dust or thinking vaguely of a seven-letter word beginning with M.

In the evenings after tea, my mother usually went into Chenur to talk or listen to her guru. She would be gone two or three hours, and my grandmother and I would be left to ourselves until she returned in time for dinner. This was the biggest meal of the day—like all of them, vegetarian (because my mother had given up meat), but with many variations of lentils and rice, curries and pickles, and always a profusion of south Indian fruit. Those evenings with my grandmother were a great pleasure to me, and I think, in a way, to her too. I was her favorite grandchild, the only one that she saw regularly, and we talked day after day about the old life in north India, as the soft southern night came and the huge southern stars hung so low in the sky appeared, and the dry rattle of the palm fronds in the night wind was our only noise.

"Do you remember," she would begin on many of those nights, "the Jalnabad house?"

"Of course I do. Best of all, the mango orchards."

At once she would start chuckling. "You children were my despair! I think we lost more of the crop by your stealing than even from the monkeys."

"But they were so delicious, those tiny raw mangoes."

"That may be, but it used to make the gardener very angry. I've made some sour-mango chutney for you. It should be ready in a few days. But these mangoes in the south are nothing—they taste like boiled potatoes; only langras are worth eating. These are only good for pickles."

Or she would say, "Do you remember the year of the drought?"

"Oh yes, when the refugees came to camp in the garden—"

"—and I was so afraid that you children would catch diseases from them."

"Well, you were more afraid that we would pick up bad language from them." But she wasn't listening to me. She had been reminded of the time, years before I was born, when her two youngest children had died in the great cholera epidemic. Somewhere in her mind the quiet southern evening had dissolved into the sour smell of a sickroom. "Night after night," she mumbled in a painful drone, "night after night." The dry heat of that distant April surrounded her. "Every day I went to the temple and prayed. I promised fifty rupees, I promised my wedding bangles if they recovered." Tears rolled down the creases on each side of her nose. "When they vomited it was black water, black as ink. My children . . ." She looked straight at me. "Where is the doctor?"

"Hush," I said. "Hush. It's all over. It was long ago."

"Why does he not come? Are we too poor for him?" She turned away, answering some remark in her mind. "Yes, yes, all the world is dying. But this is my world, my children. . . . Let him die, he too should die." She covered her face with her sari.

Afraid to disturb her silence I said, "Nani, Nani," softly.

"What is it, my child?" she replied in an ordinary voice.

"What became of old Jagdish?"

"How disrespectfully you speak of him," she said, smiling and amused. "He died some years ago. It was very peaceful. His servant came to wake him one morning and found him dead. And, listen to this, he had quite a lot of money hidden in his house."

"I'm not surprised—just think, an anna a day for all those years." We both laughed because Jagdish, a cousin of my grandfather, had been an established eccentric in our family. He had been miserly in everything, but most conspicuously in the fact that he never bought a newspaper. Every evening he would come to my grandmother's house, walking the mile or so from his own place, stand outside and call to a servant to bring him a chair and the day's newspapers. In the late, slanting sunlight he sat in the garden, carefully read through all the columns, and, still without a word to any member of the family, got up, left the papers on the chair with a stone on top of them to keep them from blowing away and returned to his own house. Naturally, my cousins and I, during the years we spent with my grandmother, watched with unflagging absorption this daily performance. We had many theories about him, but our favorite was that he was saving all his money to give each of the children in the family some magnificent present one day, and we often talked of what we would choose— a bicycle, a doll with real hair that you could unbraid and wash, an English tennis racket. He never did, and I never thought of him except on those chatty, reminiscent evenings with my grandmother in the little southern house, unfamiliar and silent, in a strange landscape.

Eventually Gopal came from the servants' quarters cautiously balancing two oil lamps. He set one on the dining table, and the other in the living room. He wiped the base, turned the flame down so that the chimney would not blacken with smoke, and with his barefooted, noiseless walk returned to the kitchen. In that small, soft island of light my grandmother sat, a big, comfortable figure, her shadow huge behind her on the white wall, her face crumpled with wrinkles and deep pockets of shadow under her eyes and each side of her mouth. Around the outside lamp moths came winging from the garden to bump and whisper and flutter against the glass; small flies with long legs, little, odd insects, like a cloud of dust, floated round it.

"At that time," my grandmother was saying, "we were poor, but I was determined that my daughters would be educated. The other families around us thought me stubborn and unnatural. Why educate the girls?' they said. 'In any case they will get married.' But I said, 'Let them have honor in themselves. They need not learn, as I did, how to read and write from their husbands.'

"There was no school to which I could send them except a Roman Catholic convent nearby. The municipal schools in Jalnabad were full, and in any case I would never allow them to travel so far every day without a chaperone. Most of the girls, it is true, were Anglo-Indians in the convent, but that could not be helped. I had no fears. My daughters had a respectable home so how could association with half-breeds affect them? They were brought up as good Hindu girls, so how could some modern religion from the West corrupt them? But clothes—they were a difficulty." With all that distant arrogance in her voice she continued, "I never expected that they would become ashamed of the clothes they wore. The other girls, they told me, wore frocks. Where should I buy frocks? In some foreign shop? 'Ridiculous,' I said, 'we have always made our own clothes in this family, and if now you must follow some Western fancy and wear frocks to school, very well, I shall make them.'

" 'How?' they asked. 'How will you make them when you have no pattern?' I said nothing, but I thought a lot that night. Some days later I told them to invite a few of their friends to tea. Yes, I was prepared, for the sake of my daughters, to receive Anglo-Indians in the house. As a special treat I ordered kulfi and mangoes for their tea. As you know, both are difficult to eat without spilling." She smiled in reminiscence of her ingenuity and good planning.

"The children came, and before tea was served I told your mother to tell the girls what they would be served. 'Tell them,' I said, 'that I do not wish to send them home in dirty clothes, so they should remove their frocks and have their tea in their petticoats.' It's true," she said, chuckling, "they took off their frocks and none of them found it strange. While the girls were eating I took their frocks to another room and cut patterns in muslin from them. I worked very quickly, and while they were still gossiping and laughing at the table, it was all done. Soon my girls, too, went to school in frocks that we had made for them at home."

Eventually my mother would come back to the house, and almost immediately we sat down to dinner. Afterward my grandmother always wrapped paan for us, picking pinches of different spices out of her old silver paan-daan which held all the paan makings—a big box with an elaborate carved top and designs of flowers and goddesses around the sides. With deft movements she spread the dark red Katha and the lime on the shiny leaves, folded them into squares or triangles, pierced them with a clove and handed one to each of us.

We never stayed up late. Within an hour after dinner the lamps were put out, the activity in the servants' quarters had stopped and we were all asleep. Sometimes I would take the big lamp from the living room into my room with me and read, late into the night, novels about England or France or Russia. The few novels about India that I had read seemed to concern a different kind of life, almost a different country from mine. It was like visiting a place that you have often heard described, of which you have a clear image, but when you see it you find that you were wrong, the house is much smaller than you expected, the garden only casually cultivated, the pleasant woods that you have imagined where one might picnic with the children are treacherous forests, dark and uninviting. And the people—they aren't welcoming friends; they are hostile strangers, speaking a language you don't understand, making jokes behind your back, wondering when you will go. You know them and recognize them, but they are foreigners.

If something woke my mother late at night she would occasionally come into my room, wondering if I had left the light on and fallen asleep.

"No, no, I was reading."

"Can't you sleep?"

"I'm sure I can. I just got interested in this book."

My mother picked it up without curiosity. "Daphne Adeane," she said. "We never had much time for novels when I was young. There were always so many things that had to be done in the house and for the family."

"Well, there were so many of you."

"Yes, nine children." She said thoughtfully, "It didn't seem like too many at the time. Only five of us alive now. Well, sleep well."

"I will. Good night."

And I would return to my foreign novels, finding in them a sympathy for if not an actual glorification of the romance that filled my head. For there are no words in India and no allowance for that young and heady love. Other things, of course, devotion or seduction, and certainly married love—a calm, accepting single-ness of affection—and love of God, or of your children, or love so great that it embraces the world and the universe and demands no form, demands instead a relinquishing of your personality. So I read my turbulent emotions in foreign cadences and dreamed of moments and situations of which I knew nothing.

❋ XVIII ❋

IT WAS SOMETIME IN THE FIRST WEEK OF MY STAY IN MY
mother's house that the schoolteacher came to call. She had mentioned G. R. Krishnan—whom she always called just Krishnan—
from time to time because she saw him twice a week when she
went to the school in Chenur to give Hindi lessons to some of the
students in the morning. The old Hindi teacher had become ill
rather suddenly a couple of months before, and since Chenur was
a Malayalam-speaking area they had had some trouble in finding
someone to replace him. The principal of the school had asked my
mother if she would fill in for a short time, but as the arrangement seemed to work so well they weren't, as far as I could make
out, putting much effort into getting a permanent replacement.

From the way she had talked I had thought of Krishnan as a
middle-aged man, probably fat and respectable with a shy wife
and several small children with large black eyes and heavily oiled
hair. As it turned out he was quite young, rather alert of manner,
a graduate of the University of Madras with, I thought, ambitions.
The principal of the school had come with Krishnan, a nervous
little man who jiggled his foot rapidly as he sat, and laughed uncomfortably after every remark. Both of them were sitting with
my mother at the table on the veranda one afternoon when I
came out of my room for tea. My grandmother, in her usual way,
was planted menacingly in the kitchen to see that the cook produced a creditable tea for the guests.

My mother introduced me and there was a long silence, not
embarrassing but the sort that often falls in Indian conversations.
The principal's knee vibrated up and down, he locked his hands
over his stomach, and both he and Krishnan stared out into the
garden. At last the principal said, "So. You live in Bombay, isn't
it?" He spoke with a heavy southern accent, half singing his words.

"Yes, most of the time."

"Ess. You are estopping here how long?"

"Two or three months."

"Very fine. You should come and see our eschool. Your esteemed mother does very fine work for us at eschool. Gratis." He laughed loudly.

My mother smiled and said she enjoyed it. Krishnan turned to her and continued with something that he had apparently been saying before I came out. "But what we wanted to ask is would you be kind enough to sing for us that day, at the school celebration. The festivities begin at four o'clock and we hope that they will be finished by six."

"I usually spend the evening from five with Guruji."

"Yes, I know. I hoped that for that one day you might come to us."

My mother said, laughing, "I am an old woman, you know. I have no voice any more."

The principal shouted with laughter. "Good lady, good lady, you are too modest—"

Krishnan said, "You must let us judge that."

"Truly," my mother said, "I have not sung for years—I have not even practiced—"

"No practice needed!" the principal interrupted jovially.

"And music? What shall I do about music?"

"Easily arranged," he insisted. "The music teacher will arrange. Do not trouble. He is very fine performer on harmonium. Why not you practice with him a few times beforehand? All will be arranged. Do not trouble."

"Suppose my voice breaks down in the middle?"

"What if? Still we will have the honor of your company. The concert will be short and esweet." He rocked his chair back with pleasure at his witticism.

"Very well," my mother agreed at last, "I will try but I can promise nothing."

"You are itself kindness," he said, bowing to her. "Many thanks."

Krishnan said, "May the eighth is the date of the concert, just before school breaks up for the holidays."

"Ess, ess," the principal shouted, "one crowded hour of glorious life thanks to you, good lady, and then we all depart for well-deserved rest. Mr. Krishnan will kindly bring a tonga to fetch you on that date, and he will also return you here after with no damage to life or limb, isn't it, Mr. Krishnan?" He turned to me. "Can we not persuade this young lady also to honor us? You have inherited your esteemed mother's great talents? You sing no doubt also?"

"No, I'm afraid I don't."

"A little dancing, is it?"

"No dancing either."

"A recitation?" and as I shook my head he added, "No matter, no matter. The pleasure of your company is sufficient. We must not be greedy, isn't it, Mr. Krishnan?"

Krishnan smiled at me and said, "Well, it's all settled. We are really most grateful."

Tea was served with full ceremony. My grandmother helped Gopal to serve the food—the last of the sweets I had brought from Bombay, little salty triangles of pastry studded with black seeds, onions fried in batter, very crisp slices of the big cooking bananas dried and fried and salted and spiced, sections of peeled mango, the soft gelatinous fruit of a special kind of palm that is called nungu—and, of course, tea in silver glasses. She didn't sit down with us and spoke to neither of the guests, and for all the sign they made they might have thought her a servant—except that I knew they knew who she was. She bustled about in her slow way seeing that everybody ate more than they wanted and the tea glasses were constantly full. Even after tea she didn't sit with us, but retired to the bedroom until the guests left, taking my mother into Chenur with them.

The principal extended his farewells down the front steps, through the garden and into the waiting tonga. "Good by," he called, "many thanks, great honor—I shall tell my wife, one day you must have tea in my poor house. You are willing? Very fine. It will be arranged. Good-by," and I could hear his laughter even after the tonga had started.

Krishnan only said to me as they were leaving, "Would you like to see the school sometime?"

"Very much. May I?"

"Most certainly. Some of the work our children do is quite interesting. You shall see it." He walked briskly down the garden without turning.

When the tonga was out of sight my grandmother came out and joined me. Together we sat on the front steps while she questioned me about the guests. Why had they come? What did we talk about? Was the young man married?

"I didn't ask him."

"And he did not mention his wife? Or say something about his children?"

"He seemed to be rather a quiet young man—not that he gets much chance to talk when the principal is there laughing all the time."

My grandmother said in a resigned voice, "But he is a southerner. It is very difficult to tell. They have no manners. Who knows? Perhaps he is married."

I laughed and put my arm around her wide back. "You worry only about one thing."

"It is the only thing worth worrying about. A woman's whole life depends on it. You are no longer very young." She cheered up a bit. "But a southerner. That is not very desirable. How much do you suppose he earns?"

"Not more than a hundred rupees a month—a schoolteacher in a small town like this."

"That used to be wealth in the old days. Your grandfather earned fifty rupees a month when we first moved to Jalnabad. But perhaps his family has money."

"I'll ask him," I said to tease her.

"My dear child—" she opened her eyes wide, and then saw that I was joking. "Are we going to see him again?"

"He asked me to visit the school. I may go."

"Of course your mother will go with you."

"Of course she won't," I said firmly. "She sees the school regularly twice a week as it is."

"You will go *alone* to see this young man?"

"I'm going to see the *school*, not the young man."

My grandmother tilted her head sceptically, but all she said was, "It isn't proper."

"Nani dear, what can possibly happen? In broad daylight, surrounded by inquisitive children, bossy teachers—"

"Still, a girl alone—"

"Really," I said, suddenly irritated, "you make me feel so pleasantly wicked."

"It isn't pleasant to feel wicked."

"Well, probably he'll forget all about it," and I began to tell her about the plans for the school concert, and acted out for her the principal's insistence and jollity complete with an exaggerated southern accent which made her laugh and successfully changed the subject. She wiped her eyes, still chuckling. "I remember so well the time when I first decided to allow the girls to have music lessons. Before that I had felt that it was a vanity, a foolish accomplishment for empty-headed girls. My daughters, I felt at that time, should be more serious and spend their time on their education and their proper work about the house."

In the familiar voice of reminiscence she told me about the woman who had the small house beyond our garden in Jalnabad. "She had moved away long before you were born—deserted by her protector. I wonder sometimes where she went. What becomes of a woman like that? A bad woman, I thought in those days—not a woman of the streets, really, but a member of the dancing-girl community. She was the mistress of a man in Jalnabad, a well-known businessman with a wife and family. A shameful situation—and shameful of her to allow it.

"Sometimes, late at night, I used to wake up to the noise of laughter and singing coming across the garden from the little house. Sometimes I used to get up and stand in the garden listening to them, so angry that tears would come to my eyes. The disgrace of such happenings so close to my house! The children were forbidden ever to speak to her or to her children—they were forbidden even to look over the garden wall. But of course they did, and sometimes I heard them talking about the fine clothes and the jewelry that she wore all day—even to walk about in her gar-

den. It must be admitted he was very generous with her," she said
in a fair, considering tone.

"The children had a little poem,

> Ek roop, roop,
> Saw roop kapra,
> Hazaar roop zevar,
> Lakh roop nakra.

> (One beauty is just a beautiful face;
> It is enhanced a hundredfold with fine clothes,
> A thousandfold with jewelry,
> And ten thousandfold with a coy charm.)

"Occasionally I would hear hem shouting the poem out loud in
the garden to taunt her, loud enough for her to hear. And although
I told them to stop I never really meant it.

"There was a saint who lived in Jalnabad. Often I went to pay
my respects to him or to listen to him when he spoke or read to
us. Those were the only occasions on which I met the woman.
She too was a devotee. Always I was offended and would turn my
face away. At one such gathering, instead of talking to us, the
saint called this woman out of the group. 'You are a singer?' he
asked. She was too ashamed to speak and only nodded her head.
'Then, today you shall sing for all of us,' he said.

"From the minute that she began I realized that she had great
spiritual power. She sang the great devotional hymns of Mirabai
—another woman who was wronged—and we all sat without speaking, almost without breathing for we were so moved. I am sure
that she never sang with such purity or such beauty for her protector.

"As we were leaving I spoke to her and asked her to come and
call at our house. We walked home together and after that we became friends. She gave the girls their first singing lessons, and that,
I am certain, is why your mother always had such a sweet voice.
Even now, in the mornings, when I hear her sing one of the
Mirabai hymns I remember the peace and beauty of that meeting
years ago.

"My only concern," she added irrelevantly, "was how I should address her. In a sense she was a married woman—she had children —but how could I call her by the name of her protector? But she was a tactful woman. Soon she always addressed me as sister, and then, with honor, I too could call her sister. She never told me when her protector deserted her. She never asked for sympathy. One day the children came and told me that the house was empty, the servants had been paid their wages and she was gone."

The evening slid between the palms and the shadows stretched like spiders across the garden. An occasional walker from Chenur passed along the road in front of us. Far away, beyond the rice fields, little smudges of smoke showed where the evening fires were being lit in the houses of the farmers. "Do you remember," my grandmother asked, "the house in Jalnabad. . . ."

I suppose it was only to be expected that I should fall in love with Krishnan. There was a pleasant anticipation about my mood, almost, in fact, a determination to fall in love with someone, and I dare say any young man who had not the dependable familiarity of, well, Hari, would have suited me as well as any other. I had not, at the time, given much thought to sequels, for the exhilaration of the mood was enough. When, after a few days, I received a note from Krishnan asking me to visit the school and suggesting a day, it was as though my impatience and joy in the world had been waiting for this moment to recognize themselves; with certainty and with delight I accepted and went to school the next day with Krishnan's quite ordinary looks and brisk personality already blurred in my mind.

I paid little attention to what he showed me in the school, dutifully admiring the paintings of buffaloes and paddy fields, appearing interested in the topographical map of India built in clay on a large blue tin tray, smiling at the children sitting cross-legged on the floor at the low tables, heads bent over copy books. On the veranda outside the classrooms, Krishnan said, "Will you say a few words to the English class? They're studying *Julius Caesar* for matric."

"That's quite tiresome enough for them—don't inflict me on them as well."

Flippancy didn't make much impression on Krishnan. "You find *Julius Caesar* tiresome?" he asked. "It's considered very suitable for this age."

"Yes," I said, still feeling cheerful, "virtually no embarrassing passages that you have to explain in class. I dare say I'm soured by having had to do it for matric myself."

"Excellent, then you can tell them about the differences in the ways of teaching *Julius Caesar* here and in the school you attended in England."

"How did you know I was at school in England?"

"Oh, I know a lot about you."

Feeling absurdly flattered, I allowed myself to be led into the classroom and chattered incoherently for a few minutes about a play I hardly remembered to rows of serious dark faces which scarcely glanced at me but concentrated on the scribbling of copious notes—one never knew what questions might turn up in the foreign exams.

Afterward Krishnan took me to the principal's office, where he and the five other teachers had coffee every morning. The principal, with his usual blend of pathos and bounciness, laughing and nervous, shouted, "Dear young lady! Come in, I beg you. A chair, Mr. Krishnan, and a cup of coffee, isn't it? You would like some soft drink better perhaps? No trouble. We can get with ice, at once. Pray be seated. In one minute the peon will bring. Until such time, please try the coffee. We, in south, are very fond of coffee, morning, noon and night we drink—isn't it, Mr. Krishnan?"

In the end I drank both the coffee and the raspberry soda pop from the tiny booth across the street from the school.

"How you like our eschool?" the principal continued. "It is most humble in comparison with famous European eschool. In great city of Bombay you have bigger and better eschools, also. In this quiet backwater, I fear, we will not make educational history but must be content with our modest lot. As the poet says, 'The paths of glory lead but to the grave,' isn't it?" he added surprisingly. I nodded my head in general agreement to anything he said. "Ah, perhaps I am mistaken! No doubt the great talent of Mr. Krishnan as guide, philosopher and friend has blinded you to our faults, isn't it?" He jiggled his knee with excitement and pointing to Krishnan laughed delightedly. "What have you to say? Have you thrown dust in the eyes of this young lady? Have you shown her our eschool through rose-colored especs?"

My grandmother, that evening, wasted no time on nonessentials. She asked no questions about the school, the teaching methods or what the children did. She said, "You were pleased with the young man."

"You mean Krishnan?" I said, to give myself a moment.

"Who else? Of course Krishnan. These southern names! What is G. R.? How can one address a man simply as Krishnan?"

"Yes, he's nice," I said moderately. "I invited him to tea tomorrow and he seemed glad to accept."

"That is not surprising. No doubt the food in the hostel is very mediocre. He will be pleased to eat well."

"I dare say that's it," I replied (knowing better). I remembered his real manner with private amusement at the difference. "You must come again and have tea with us," I had said, standing outside the classroom door, waiting for the bell to ring.

"Really?" he had said with alacrity. "That is something to look forward to. When may I come?"

"Oh, any time. Tomorrow? Day after? Is the weekend best for you?"

"Tomorrow. Tomorrow would be excellent."

"Tomorrow then."

He had smiled straight into my eyes as he opened the classroom door, the words, "Until tomorrow," on our lips lost in the shrilling bell.

Years before, the English school, contrary to my grandmother's promise, had not been much of an adventure. I had been too easily intimidated, had been cold and ill at ease. Surrounded by strangers I was lonely for the contained familiarity of the Jalnabad house. It was not the people of my childhood that I wanted, it was an atmosphere both expansive and intimate. But here, I had thought, standing outside the classroom, here at last is my adventure.

My grandmother was saying, "Probably at that hostel they give him nothing but these twists of basan fried in coconut oil—" (to her northern palate anything that wasn't cooked in ghee was a cheap travesty of proper food)—"or even stale jalebies. . . ." This was a phrase I knew from my earliest childhood. For some reason "stale jalebies" seemed to my grandmother the final insult to one's taste. She would never buy sweets from a shop or even a special sweetmeat man (as many people did these days). To her it was only the outrageous laziness of modern housewives that allowed such short cuts, and jalebies, the most delicate of all sweets, had to be served just warm from your own fire. Even the journey from the shop to your house made them "stale jalebies"—the mark of inhospitality. My grandmother was murmuring half to herself and half out loud the various dishes she would prepare for tomorrow's tea. "I'll make some halva from carrots—everybody likes that. And pecoras, onion pecoras of course, they, too, are safe. . . . dahi burras? Too heavy for teatime? Samosas, perhaps—yes, that would be better—very small ones, with the pastry so light you hardly notice it, and inside curried potato with a little tamarind (tamarind is one good thing about southern cooking)—or perhaps peas would be better? Or why not potatoes *and* peas? If we were in Jalnabad, now, I could fill the samosas with minced lamb, or I could even make kebabs. But what can one serve these vegetarians? Even the meat in the south is like string. . . . Never mind. The spinach here is good. I'll coat spinach leaves with a very thin batter, fry them just for a minute and bring them very crisp—crackling, almost—"

"Stop, stop!" I said laughing. "This isn't a feast. It's just one young man coming to tea—"

"That's right," she looked at me with a knowing brightness. "Just one young man. . . ."

"Nani, I do love you. You're the only really scheming woman I know."

She opened her eyes wide at me. "Scheming? I am watching out for the future of my grandchild. That is not scheming, that is the least of my duties now that your mother is learning to lose her family and the world."

"I suppose it's what she wants," I said absently—feeling sorry for her neutral life.

"If not that, at least what she has to do," my grandmother commented, equally absently, unintimidated by her daughter's receding place in life, acknowledging without surprise those other compulsions.

"Please, Nani, don't make an event of Krishnan's coming to tea."

"Why not, since it *is* an event?"

"Well, I don't want it to seem so," I said, unwilling to explain.

She sounded stubborn. "But one owes something to a guest. One cannot forget one's manners. We must receive him with some courtesy. He will expect it—even a southerner."

"But I want it to seem ordinary—"

"What an absurd baby!" She laughed indulgently. "By that you deceive no one, and besides, you please no one, not even your guest—especially not the young man—"

As it turned out, Krishnan, the next day, seemed to prove her right. He was full of admiration for the food and drank three glasses of the special north Indian tea that she had prepared, thick with milk and spiced with cloves and cardamoms and cinnamon. That morning when, as usual, the milkman had stopped with his cow at the front gate and yelled up to the house to announce his arrival, my grandmother had ordered an extra quart of milk for the tea and had, in her accustomed way, watched narrowly while the man milked the cow before her eyes, allowing no opportunity for cheating or watering the milk. She herself held out the silver measuring pot that had belonged to her mother and that she had brought with her to her new home at the time of her marriage. And I, standing on the veranda, watched the scene—the thin, wiry figure of the milkman in his white mundu, my grandmother's broad, implacable back, the caramel-colored cow with her gilded horns and garland of marigolds, her quiet contrasting oddly with the alert suspicion of the two people—and for once I was caught in the anticipation and excitement of preparations for a guest.

To disguise my feelings—they embarrassed my sense of the

casual—I teased my grandmother when she returned to the house. "You would think a Navab was coming to see us—"

"A guest is a guest," she said, paying no attention.

"I thought this was a simple house—"

She turned at this. "Simple or not, we have a standard. There must always seem to be plenty whether there is or not. You should know the story of the Lucknow thakur who was very poor, but who would pick his teeth in public so that people should know he had just eaten a good meal—"

"Or who moistened the corner of his kurtha as an excuse to sit before the village fire—pretending that he had just slipped in a puddle—to hide the fact that he was too poor to afford his own fire—"

"Very well, then. What is the use of a standard if it is not maintained? The price of milk is outrageous—but a guest, after all—"

"All right, all right," I said, full of pleasure. "I only hope he appreciates it."

Fortunately, he did, and was lavish with compliments for the food, the tea, the trouble, and I was warmed by the fact that he had known so immediately how to flatter and comfort my grandmother, even though, afterward, all she said was, "At least his manners are adequate, even if he is a southerner."

All through tea Krishnan's manner was lively, and I wondered how I had ever thought of him as a quiet young man. Evidently he loved to talk and had that delight in theory and complicated thought that Indians accept as characteristic of the southerner's mind. He talked to my mother about music, arguing vigorously about the purity of south Indian music, the "sugary corruption," as he called it, of the Muslims on the music of the north that she knew best—no, Carnatic music was by far superior, the true Indian music. I, knowing nothing about music, having, in fact, always been bored by it in the past, listened to him with fascination and was ready at once to see his point, accept his opinions and prejudices. My mother's good-humored objections gave me a chance to watch, unobtrusively, his attentive face. The wide, frowning forehead with wiry hair springing untidily back over his head, the high, narrow nose, the gentler modeling of mouth and jaw. The whites of his eyes were blue against the dark skin. I watched for his smile and its display of improbably perfect teeth. On each side of his face, just below the cheekbone, the skin was pitted with a scatter of tiny scars. Smallpox when he was a child, I decided, and was immediately impressed by how much about him I didn't know.

"What a thorough Madrassi you are," I said, hoping to learn about him.

"You make it sound like a disease," he replied, smiling with no antagonism, and said nothing more about his home or family or early life that I had expected to hear described. Gradually, over the next few weeks, I learned that he was not concerned with personalities. He felt, I suppose, that one's background offered up no secrets, or, if it did, they did not matter to him. It was the moment, the idea, the accomplishment that interested him. If, for instance, I made as I sometimes did a remark like, "Isn't the principal marvelous?" (meaning, of course, "Isn't he absurd?"), Krishnan would reply, "Yes, he is. A very competent administrator. It's hard to know these days which course to steer—with everything in India changing so much—and he manages to keep the framework of an English educational system without allowing the students to lose touch with India—a touch that grows every day more important," and, naturally, I would be shamed into silence and save my giggling and my gossip for my grandmother.

Once I said to Krishnan, "You must have been such a solemn little boy. I wish I'd known you then."

"Really?" he said, surprised. "Why?"

Uncomfortable at having to explain a moment of sentimentality, I said, "Well, I don't know. Because children are more accessible, I suppose."

"In my experience I haven't found it so. They're much more secretive than adults because they don't yet know what can and cannot be kept private."

"Well, in a classroom—" I said, nettled.

"An artificial situation, I admit. But still you learn a good deal about their character seeing them day after day, and can still never tell how they will turn out."

"Is that important? To be able to predict?"

"Well, one can always explain in retrospect—it means nothing, only perhaps imagination, and not always that—certainly not understanding."

I said, "I dare say only a child can understand another child."

"A child only understands the condition of childhood," Krishnan said meticulously, "which is quite another matter. Otherwise they would remain friends when they grow up and that hardly ever happens, and they usually explain it by saying that their lives have separated them or their interests have changed—"

"That they have grown apart."

"Yes, that is the more accurate phrase. They have grown out of childhood—the thing that kept them together."

Krishnan was always willing to talk endlessly in generalizations like this, but when I insisted, "But what were you like? Clever? Naughty? A joy to your parents?" he only replied, "Most children are a joy to their parents, surely?"

That first time he came to tea, however (I didn't count the time that he and the school principal had called at the house to discuss the concert), there was scarcely an occasion for personalities. We talked about music and Sanskrit and philosophy—or rather Krishnan and my mother talked, and I was content to watch him and listen and catch the occasional rapid smile he offered directly to me, as if we had a different and exclusive method of communication, or as if we had a private appointment later and could afford to be distant now. We hadn't, of course, but I imagined him thinking, as I was, that our circumstances determined our conversation. What, except impersonal topics, should we allow in front of these others, my mother sitting erect at one end of the table, never fidgeting unnecessarily, my grandmother hovering in the shadows of the living room, just inside the open door, watching plates and glasses with a professional anxiety? I suppose I was dimly aware of my mother's pleasure, too. If my father had included her in his life, had discussed and argued with her, talked, laughed, made jokes, considered her opinions and her presence, respected the value of the education my grandmother had struggled to give her, would things have been different? Would she have been happier? Watching her smiling across the tea table I thought she looked content. Perhaps it had all worked out for the best. Perhaps the joy could only come after the wish for it was gone. But perhaps I felt that only because I did not want to be bothered with anything but my thoughts of Krishnan, and compassion takes up time.

In a way I was glad of the distance forced between Krishnan and me, of the electric air of being silent conspirators, the importance it gave to a quick exchange of looks, an accidental meeting of hands on a plate of sweets. I leaned back in my chair, half dreaming, half alert, conscious of looking well in my red cotton sari, offering the contrast of youth and eagerness to the white-clothed figures of other generations.

When he got up to leave Krishnan shook hands with me instead of making a namaskar, and to me the reason was obvious— I hoped the others hadn't found it so. In faulty, stumbling Hindi (getting the forms of address all wrong) he thanked my grandmother and complimented her extravagantly on the food. No excuses were needed for his coming to tea the following day—the matter fell into place with an inevitability unhoped for in the most flawless stratagem. He would bring the school music teacher, who did not know our house, out here after school so that my mother could talk to him and practice for the concert.

"Of course you must both have tea with us," she said.

"But please go to no trouble," Krishnan replied, smiling at me, and I knotted my fingers behind my back and smiled in response, thinking, until tomorrow, just until tomorrow.

All the morning I was full of energy. I washed my hair, rubbed sandalwood oil into it, and walked up and down the veranda with my hair streaming down my back, feeling the dampness soak through the towel across my shoulders, through my choli, to make a sweaty patch between my shoulder blades. I saw my grandmother bustling through the house, busy domineering in the kitchen—two guests today, and a challenge besides for nothing of yesterday's tea must be duplicated.

I picked flowers from the garden even though it was the wrong time of day. ("Early in the morning," my grandmother had often told me, "before they are tired from the day.") Hibiscus never seem at home indoors, so I chose cannas, deep yellow, veined with red, and tried to make of them a more graceful arrangement than the gardener's usual stiff, symmetrical bouquet. But cannas are intractable, the effect was amateurish, I decided that the vase was the wrong shape.

At the table on the veranda I sat down with pen and ink and paper before me to write letters. A newsy one to my father, with many details of everyone's good health, the exact condition of the weather, the Hindi lessons my mother gave, the plans for the school concert, and ended with several insincere inquiries about Shalini and my brother.

The letter to Pria was more muddled. "You really must come to Chenur one day," I wrote. "It's very quiet, of course, though like most of Malabar it isn't proper country or proper town for that matter but at least it isn't the suburbs either. Hari, I'm sure, would be very scornful—country should be country and grow things, in a serious way. I don't know what I do with my time but I'm not bored and the days vanish away into the past too quickly to register. Perhaps it's because southerners are surprisingly nice, anyway the ones we see most, from the school where my mother teaches, are quite amusing." Suddenly revolted by the disingenuousness of this, I wrote, "Pria, how I wish you were within talking distance—one does need one's own generation. One's elders know about all the wrong things and the reticences are insurmountable. There is a schoolmaster (inevitably this sounds dull) in Chenur, G. R. Krishnan. I think . . ."

The postman arrived. He propped his bicycle against the veranda railing, took off his shoes and came up to me smiling. I shuffled through the thin stack of mail. Two postcards in Hindi for my grandmother; she had an active, mysterious correspondence with countless second-cousins, great-nieces, relatives by marriage, always on buff-colored plain post cards. A magazine for my mother, the *Kerala Journal of Philosophy*, a letter from my brother addressed in a clear script that had scarcely changed from his schooldays, and a wedding announcement from someone I had never heard of. Nothing for me.

When I returned to my letter I stared at the paper and at the words "I think . . ." in my handwriting. I couldn't imagine how to finish that sentence. What had I thought that I could tell Pria? I folded up the letter and put it away in the suitcase in my room to be unpacked weeks later in Bombay. Half past ten. A whole hour before breakfast. I walked about the house fretfully, and later put my hair up, spending such a long time on twisting it and pinning it that my mother and grandmother had already sat down at the table before I joined them for the midday meal.

❋ XIX ❋

"RADHAKRISHNA BO-OL MUKE-SÉ—

"Radhakrishna . . ." My mother's voice from the inner room repeated the phrase over and over to the vulgar whine of the harmonium, each time varying it slightly, adding a different flourish.

Krishnan and I still sat at the table on the veranda, dawdling over the last of the tea. My grandmother sat outside with us that afternoon, perched cross-legged on her white platform, her hands active with knitting needles and a quantity of wool of a rather ugly tan.

"Her voice suits that kind of song very well," Krishnan said in a pause. "Lyrical, direct. It was popularized by Saigal, you know. One must be at home with the mentality of the north to do it justice."

"Why the north?" I asked, not much concerned with the answer, listening to his voice against the resuming music behind me.

"One doesn't really grasp the appeal of Krishna in the south."

Remembering something Pria had once said disdainfully, I repeated her words with laughter. "Too much boyish charm?" I suggested. "A way with the ladies? Too lucky altogether—the best of both worlds?"

"Well, not quite in those terms," Krishnan remonstrated, laughing with me. "We are more absorbed by austerity and a more impersonal force, not someone like ourselves."

"But that's exactly the thing I like about Krishna—"

"Perhaps, but liking is something else. I was talking about worship."

"Oh, worship. I don't think I've ever tried to formulate what I think about religion, though it has bothered me sometimes. In Bombay I took an American girl to—"

Krishnan pounced on my words enthusiastically. "That's our trouble! We *must* formulate what we think about religion." He wasn't interested in my anecdote about Alix, but I didn't care because I was quite irrationally revived by his inclusion of me in his problems—"our trouble." "It's very hard to know what to do in schools, for instance" (and I noticed how his words ran together when he was on his own topic). "Should we have religious instruction or not?"

"I don't know. It's one's own concern, I suppose."

"Not at all!" He slapped his hand on the table. "What is all our greatest literature? Our best music? Our finest art? Even to some extent our politics? Religion, of course religion! How should we teach our children about their country without teaching them religion?"

"Well, why shouldn't our children" (I repeated his phrase for the sound of it) "be taught religion then?"

"Ah, but we must be very careful. We must distinguish between religion and superstition—the curse of India—"

"So they always tell us—"

"Not without justification. And we must distinguish between philosophy and mythology. We have the oldest and the greatest philosophy in the world; we mustn't abuse it. You can see the problem with which it confronts educators in India?"

"Oh yes," I said, and added out of curiosity, "Do you see yourself as an 'educator'?—you know, like gardeners being horticul-

turalists or American undertakers being morticians—though
'undertaker' is pretty peculiar itself."

He frowned at the irrelevance. "It's all the same. So you see,
one must teach them religion without involving oneself in the
forms of worship. And then one is confronted with a yet more
subtle problem, for often it is the *forms* of worship themselves
which constitute our best art. . . ." His voice ranged on explor-
ing intricacies that I didn't follow while I watched his hands,
restless and emphatic, and thought about the life of a schoolmaster. At best a cramped house, not much money . . . some
years, at least in the beginning, in small towns . . . eventually,
perhaps Madras, the university. . . . I smiled at Krishnan.

"You agree with me?" he asked.

I nodded with no idea of what he'd said, but sure that I agreed
anyway.

Krishnan left early that afternoon because my mother was going
to Chenur to talk to her guru and the tonga that had brought
Krishnan and the music teacher out to our house was to take
them all back together. I walked to the gate with them, and then
wandered back to the veranda to sit idly at the table and listen
to the receding jangle of the tonga bells.

"What are you knitting?" I asked my grandmother. (The tonga
must have turned off our little track onto the wider road to
Chenur.)

"A shawl."

(They must be talking loudly above the sounds of the clattering horse, the rustle of wheels, talking about the rehearsal.)

I said, "Surely you don't need a shawl here, it never gets even
chilly." ("I'm very much out of practice," my mother would be
saying. The polite music teacher would reassure her, "No, no. Not
more than two or three rehearsals will be needed.")

My grandmother counted stitches with quick jerks of her forefinger. "It's for your Aunt Susheila."

(By now they would be arranging the day for the next rehearsal.
If Krishnan said, "I enjoyed listening to you, and the songs are
beautiful," perhaps my mother would suggest, "Then you must
come to the next rehearsal, too. . . .")

"My Aunt Susheila?" I repeated dimly. "She can't be going to have a baby. She must be sixty."

My grandmother stared at me. "What's the matter with you, Baba? Susheila is in Mussourie. It's very cold there."

(She would be saying, "I'll expect you both, then." Tomorrow? More likely the day after. Or even later . . .)

"Of course, yes. I'd forgotten," I said.

"You should keep more in touch with the members of your family. One day you will find them a comfort."

(Or then, again, she might be saying, "I'll see you at school on Tuesday; if you have a free period after my Hindi class we could practice then. . . .") "Eventually, I suppose, one needs comfort," I said. "But only when one is old—"

"Are you immune to old age?" my grandmother asked with amusement. "You, too, will need some reassurance through the years."

(Will the school music room be free? Surely they will have to rehearse here. . . . surely that will automatically include Krishnan? It is a group of a sort, cohesive. . . . Surely it will seem rude if he is not invited too?)

"Mm. I expect I will, of one sort or another," I said.

"It is hard to see these things as only natural when one is young."

Our conversation meandered on along well-worn lines, trivial, allusive, endlessly predictable, while the short, golden evening filled the garden, gave way to the dark blue night, and at last Gopal came with the lamps.

The hot, hot afternoon stayed breathless around me (lying on my bed) with a substance quite distinct from ordinary air, as I wondered about Krishnan. I had deliberately asked my mother nothing the evening before, tormented but pleasurably certain about our next meeting. Life in a town like Chenur allows for no accidental meetings, and for all my novel reading I could think of no way to arrange it, but knew, all the same, that it would some-how arrange itself. In England people go for walks. In other places one could count on parties, perhaps, or dances or some plotted social occasion. Here, the school principal might invite us to tea, my mother, of course, and me and possibly Krishnan. "My dear ladies, come in, come in, we are most sensible of the honor. Be it never so humble there's no place like home, isn't it?" Four chairs would be set in a row on the veranda. "Sit, sit please. I shall place myself here, the thorn between two roses, isn't it, Mrs. Goray? Mr. Krishnan, I rely on you for stimulating conversation. . . ." He wouldn't introduce his wife—in fact she might be too shy to appear at all, and one would see only the darkened eyes of the children staring with wild speculation from between the folk-weave curtain across the doorway to the living room. There would be a good deal of formal, polite, boring talk among us. It was not the kind of meeting I had in mind.

If my Hindi were better, I thought, I could take over my mother's classes at the school. There twice a week at least, even on such neutral territory, we could find our own occasions. But the end of the school term was so close, and in any case my Hindi would never do. However, I would, I decided, make some effort to study Hindi seriously.

I imagined a Bombay dinner party—Jay's New Year's party, specifically—and saw myself standing on the terrace in Alix's pose, half turned toward Krishnan standing beside me. "Can you hear the surf? The sea is much closer than it sounds." We would walk together down the terrace steps, through the dark gardens to the sea wall. Through the noisy rushing of the water I would scarcely hear the whispered words, "A happy, happy New Year to us." But the picture held no reality and I soon abandoned it in favor of more highly colored dreams of quite impossible occasions, rescues, elopements, rendezvous in foreign countries, incredible accidents, fate.

At teatime, feeling rather silly, I shook back the afternoon and wondered briefly if Pria ever caught herself in such absurdities. I was glad I had never finished the letter to her. Staring at myself in the bathroom mirror, I pulled at my hair peevishly with a comb, damped it and dragged it into a tight, unbecoming knot on the back of my head. I put on a sensible white cotton sari which was still rigid with starch and made me look fat. I walked out to the veranda in time to see Krishnan wheeling his bicycle up the path from the garden gate.

He stood at the veranda railing, holding his bicycle in much the way that the postman had waited the morning before. There is something very intimate about sharing a railing. You can look into someone's face without embarrassment, connected by the wooden beam, without commitment.

He smiled a little uncertainly. "I just dropped in—"

"That was always acceptable in Jalnabad."

"Jalnabad?" He tilted the bicycle carefully to rest and put his hand on the railing.

"Where my mother's family lived. People were always dropping in."

"I see. I came to ask if you would help me correct some essays that my matric class have done on the character of Cassius."

"Oh, Cassius," I couldn't help laughing. "I always liked Cassius. The rest seemed so self-righteous."

"You find them self-righteous?"

"Well, and I've never liked fat men anyway."

Krishnan laughed too. "Cassius is only an excuse. I just wanted to come to tea."

"I'm glad."

"The hostel gets on your nerves after a while, and you only see the people that you see every day anyway."

And that's another excuse, I thought, but said, "My grandmother will be in a panic that she hasn't cooked something special for you."

"Anything from her kitchen is certain to be excellent."

From the doorway behind me my grandmother said, "Why is he standing in the sun? Ask him to come in and sit down."

After tea we actually did correct the essays, arguing mildly about small details of the play, while my grandmother sat with her knitting and her obtrusive respectability, but the thing we really accomplished was a kind of ease between us, a fading of the sense of guest and host, that made it possible, in the days that followed, for Krishnan to come to tea almost every day, for my grandmother to produce only one special dish (instead of a feast) beyond our usual tea, for Krishnan to feel that an absence, not a presence, needed the explanation. In the succession of late afternoons that became the focus of my days, Krishnan nearly always brought his work and sometimes I helped him and sometimes I just watched, pretending to read, or wandered with a pleasant restlessness about the veranda or the living room, seeming to occupy myself with fabricated household tasks—flowers, inevitably, or winding my grandmother's tan wool. She sat placidly with the ugly shawl growing from her needles—she could never bear to sit long with idle hands—her slender fingers moving, elegantly expert, the active bones concise in their small movements.

Once, watching her hands, I said, "Do you remember the bangle man that used to come to our house in Jalnabad?"

Krishnan paused in his work to listen, and she smiled without looking up. "He was hard to bargain with, but his selection was the best. He used to get some of his patterns from Lucknow."

"I can't wear glass bangles now. My hands are too big."

"Size is not the difficulty," she said, "your joints must be soft."

I had a sudden, clear picture of the bangle vendor squatting in the courtyard of our Jalnabad house, surrounded by all the girls in the family. We would choose the colors we liked and he would pick them out of his basket four or six at a time, impossibly small in size, and knead our fingers and our hands so that the knuckles of the forefinger touched the knuckle of the little finger and the thin glass circles slid along to rest tight against the wrist. His hands were not gentle, and he would fold the children's palms with a force that was almost painful, but in a moment there was the band of green or red or purple sleek across the bony arm, and all the time his shallow basket lay open with the sun glinting on the fat coiled snake of bangles inside it. My grandmother took the tiniest size of all—smaller than the children—and her hand was so supple that it collapsed like the bones of a bird when you held it.

"Well then," I said, "I am too old and stiff to be able to force glass bangles on my hands now."

"You should never have gone to that English school. It's the diet they give you."

"Diet?" Krishnan asked, interested.

"Porridge," I said.

"And too much meat," my grandmother added. "It makes the bones hard. You cannot be graceful if your bones are hard."

"Do you not eat meat?" Krishnan asked politely.

"Of course; I am from the north. But meat should be a suggestion in a meal, a delicacy to add interest to the rice and vegetables. You should not eat just a piece of meat and consider it a meal. You should not make meat the main item. Use it in passing, as you would show a talent for playing the veena at a social occasion, not to make much of, but to heighten another pleasure."

"I see," Krishnan said, and he sounded as though he had been given a valuable piece of instruction.

"I never thought of meat as an accomplishment," I said.

"Besides," my grandmother said, paying no attention to us, "too much meat in the diet makes childbearing difficult. That is well known."

Krishnan said, "I see," again, and I looked out at the garden with some constraint.

"I had no trouble with my children," she finished in a matter-of-fact way. "It was considered an indulgence in my time."

Apart from short passages of talk like this, my grandmother might have been entirely unaware of us, of Krishnan working and of me sitting about, but afterward, when he had left, she wanted to know in detail what the English talk had been about. "Work?" she would ask. "Is that all he talks of? His work? Has he no family? Surely we have friends in common—he seems to come from a good family. Does he mention no names? No relatives of whom we might know?"

"Perhaps none of his people are in the north."

"But we *know* some southerners."

It was easy to repeat our conversations to her because they always seemed to me to be conducted on two levels. Krishnan, for instance, once said, "I wish there were some way to repay you all these evenings at your house, but there is only the hostel."

"Where the teachers in the common room—I suppose you have a common room?—would be shocked by the appearance of a stray girl."

"But I'd invite your mother, of course."

"Of course. That's the snag," I said, feeling that we understood what we meant.

He smiled. "Exactly. Because the hostel is very run-down and the food is bad. That would be a poor return for her hospitality."

"Exactly," I repeated, smiling too, and knowing that we both added in our minds, What's the point, since in any case we wouldn't be alone?

When I told my grandmother this, it seemed to her perfectly proper. "It is right of him to wish to make some return, and right of you to refuse on your own behalf and for your mother. I see that at last you are acquiring some sense of propriety. It is very difficult for a man alone to entertain. He should get married."

"Yes, he should," I said, cheerfully meeting her approving look.

Perhaps this little exchange stayed in her mind for some reason. At least, the next day, just as Krishnan was leaving, she looked up from her knitting and said in a suddenly bitter voice, "You are leaving again?"

Krishnan replied pleasantly, "I'm afraid I have already stayed too long. I must get back."

"Must?" she said acidly. "How many necessities we invent for our convenience! Will Bombay and its politics suffer so much if you stay away a little longer?"

Krishnan looked surprised, but not alarmed. I said, "Nani, you are dreaming again—"

She interrupted me with an impatient movement of her hand. "Don't make excuses for him, child. Nobody doubts your loyalty to your husband."

Krishnan said, "Please—I had better go—"

"Go, go, by all means, since in any case you will go—"

"Nani, look at me. This is me—"

"I must say what I feel." Her eyes were still on Krishnan. "You should not leave your wife in this condition. Her first child, after all."

Krishnan started to say something, but she continued, frowning and ill-tempered. "I have never held with this habit of returning to your mother's house to bear your children. A woman needs only one person with her then—her husband. At least take her with you."

Krishnan backed away to the veranda railing, and I watched his retreating figure across the garden, wheeling the bicycle, while I murmured ineffectually to my grandmother. "Responsibilities!" she said sarcastically. "Don't talk to me of responsibilities. We cannot agree on that. But remember everyone needs solace—even you—in their life . . . at some time . . ."

I sat beside her and took her hand and said very loudly the first things that came into my head. "I am Baba, your granddaughter. It is nearly seven o'clock. We are in Chenur. It has been hot today. Probably it will get hotter, we can expect no rain for at least six weeks. Krishnan has just left on his bicycle—"

"Has he left?"

"Yes. Krishnan has gone back to the hostel."

"He was late today." She shook her hand free of mine and picked up her knitting needles again. "You should learn to knit and sew," she told me in her usual tone. "They are useful accomplishments and they are pleasant to look at. This Western education is all very well, but not much use—"

"I thought you believed in education for girls?"

"Naturally. But that doesn't mean that you should neglect the other skills. My daughters were given both (and that makes it easier to get along with a mother-in-law) so why shouldn't you learn too?"

"Did you arrange my mother's marriage?" I asked, for the first time really wanting to know.

"No," she said, seeing that this question logically followed our train of thought. "Hers was the only one I didn't arrange. It arranged itself. Your father was in Jalnabad to plead a case—he was just beginning in those days—and he stayed with friends of ours. They came to call one evening and brought him."

"And he saw her and decided at once that this was the girl he wanted to marry?" I said hopefully.

"He made the proper inquiries first."

"Were you pleased?" I asked. "Was she?"

"I was pleased to have her settled even though his was a Bombay family. Our friends who acted as go-betweens assured me that he had a fine future in his law work, that he was honorable—that he wouldn't, for instance, marry again—but in the end there is only one's judgment—"

"And she too was relieved to have her life settled for her?"

"Well, in those days, remember, an educated girl was not so much in demand. Many people considered it a drawback. And we were not rich; the dowries we could offer for our girls were scarcely more than the minimum."

"I see," I said coldly. "One is expected to consider oneself lucky."

"Nowadays, it seems, education is an asset."

"For more than marriage surely. Anyway, that isn't what I was thinking of."

"I know," she replied in her placid voice, "you were always a dreamy child. Even years ago when you used to stay in Jalnabad I remember you were always staring. It's a bad habit to get into; it keeps you from seeing things as they are."

"It seems to me that there was so much more to stare at in those days. The days were so full of things."

"Childhood is bound to be a busy time. There is something very sad about small meals," she said, returning comfortably to her world of reminiscence. "In those days I used to put on the table a stack of puris too high for the small children to see over and great bowls of curry and chutney, and the fruit had to be picked twice a day. In a minute, it seemed, the food had vanished—"

"You used to smile, I remember, and tell us not to be greedy."

"I smiled? I expect I did. There are few things more satisfactory to a woman than to see the meal she has prepared eagerly eaten. Once, when my cousin Ramji and his family came to dinner . . ."

The night, again, and the moths that punctuated our evenings, the penetrating heat of high summer, the soft, sporadic crackling from the garden, the cloudy lamplight, a raised voice calling something from the servants' quarters, our Chenur night again.

I had half thought that Krishnan might not come the next day,

but my grandmother didn't remember his disordered departure—
or didn't think it worth remembering—and prepared as usual for a
slightly elaborate tea. As it happened she was right, and we both
saw Krishnan's neat figure in its white drill trousers and open shirt
arriving at half past four, unstrapping a little stack of books and
papers from the carrier rack of his bicycle, frowning and smiling
his way into the house.

That evening he didn't do much work, and we talked at length
about schoolmastering—that is, he talked, and I listened spell-
bound to those carefully maneuvered phrases designed to tell me
all kinds of things privately in public. "It's a wonderfully satisfying life in spite of its irritations," he said, and seeing, I suppose,
my bemused expression, explained in the tone of someone being
painfully fair, "I mean there's a lot of routine—"

"As in any job."

"Oh yes. And the pay is very little, and that means that we
live always on the edge of poverty."

"But that doesn't matter, surely, if you're interested and feel
that the work is worth while." Some reassurance was expected, I
could see, from me.

"It doesn't matter," he said buoyantly. "You see, I really enjoy
teaching."

"That makes it much harder to feel put upon," I remarked idly.

He looked severe but took no notice of my comment. "Education is the only hopeful program for our country that will not
plunge us into political extremities, and for a teacher that is a
most rewarding thing even if he hasn't enough money to educate
his own children properly. Don't you agree?"

"Well, one can't really plan for one's children."

"But one *should* plan, that is our trouble—"

"What I mean is, in any case there's no telling how one's plans
will work out. I suppose we can only be sure that they won't work
out the way we expect."

"Possibly. But there must be planning; otherwise in a country
like India nothing will get done. And for the planning you need
experience, and for that you need people who will continue to

teach under the present conditions for the value of that experience later on. That is one of the compensations."

He was telling me, of course, that our life needn't be lived forever in a small town like Chenur. Here he was gaining his "experience." If he was underpaid, living uncomfortably, working obscurely, this was only for a time. Eventually there would be a wider life, conditions that might appeal to me, company that might please me. He had, in short, that thing that my grandmother hoped for in sons-in-law or grandsons-in-law, a Future. I nodded, accepting his terms, the present difficulties and the eventual satisfactions. "I can understand that," I said, "it might even be fun Trying to Make Ends Meet, as it's usually described."

"*Fun?*" Krishnan said, shocked at this flippancy.

"Well, not exactly *fun*, but you know, a challenge, like working out a problem in algebra—not, of course, that I understand algebra, having been to an English school."

"Didn't they teach you algebra in England?" Krishnan asked, momentarily distracted.

"Well, yes, they did, but it's conventional not to understand it. Like getting history mixed up and wondering what a surfeit of lampreys are—or is." I must try not to be silly, I told myself, but without too much conviction because I was feeling rather elated.

Krishnan looked very puzzled and said, "I see." He added severely, "Poverty isn't *fun*, you know."

"I was hoping you wouldn't say that."

"It's true."

"I know it is. But we wouldn't be poor, I mean really poor. We'd be hard up, which is quite different, and we'd Manage Somehow, which always sounds so brave."

"Perhaps it sounds simple if you have always lived in luxury, a house in Bombay, a family that—"

"You're right, you're right," I interrupted quickly, determined to put myself in a better light, "but Indians who have even the necessities *have* to get insulated against poverty; I mean, they're already rich. I think," I said, hurrying on, away from the moment when we had talked as though we really were going to get married, "the only thing that would bother me—if I were a schoolmaster, that is—would be losing touch with my pupils after they left school. It seems sad that one should be such a big part of their lives—gossiped about among themselves, one's temper watched, or one's approval sought, an object of hero worship, possibly, one's private life a subject for speculation—and after all that, you never see them again."

"The best of them often make a mark of some sort, and you are fairly certain to hear of them again."

"But not hear *from* them."

"Well, for that you'd have to build up a friendship with the students outside the classroom while they are still in school. It's a practice among Western educators, I'm told, and I admit it's a good idea. But you must have a place to which you can invite them, a home of your own—"

I was touched by his clumsy approach, but unable to help him. "Yes, a home," I muttered, "of course—"

"Next year, things will be different," he said shyly, and stared with fixed attention at the garden. "Next year I think I may have a home of my own—"

Terribly embarrassed myself, I could only say, "Well, perhaps."

Krishnan started to say something else but changed his mind, and I was relieved that our conversation went no further. The silent busy presence of my grandmother, the tea table with remnants of food on plates and tea growing cold in the glasses, Krishnan and I sitting opposite each other, rigid and bashful, the bright garden and the shaded veranda—all this made to my mind quite the wrong setting for a proposal.

After an uncomfortable pause he said, "I'd better get some work done."

Afterward my grandmother and I sat as usual on the veranda and talked about Krishnan. "He seems to be an ambitious young man," she said, "and that is a good thing. If he is serious perhaps he will rise in his profession. (But southerners—how can one tell?—they talk so much, and without direction. They are full of ideas—as if ideas had a life of their own.) It is not a bad profession. His prospects are good—after all, an M.A. from Madras University, that is not to be taken lightly. He might rise in the Government Education Service, and that means a pension and provident fund. We must consider those things too. Or a professor in his old university—again a good post and a respected position. . . ."

I spaced out my replies between her comments, "Yes," and "Yes, he is," and "I expect he would," but dreaming all the time of another image, remembering the fluid movements of his hands, listening to the sound of his voice inside my head, the intimate public things he said, talking to me—but for anybody to hear. At last I couldn't bear my grandmother's musing voice, her calculating remarks, even the gentle making-allowances character of her thoughts. "I'm in love with him," I said loudly.

"What?" she said confused. "What? Love?"

"I'm in love with Krishnan."

She stared at me with angry, alert eyes. "Love? What do you know of love? You are not married."

"I know I'm in love."

In disgust she said, "You talk like a Westerner. I always told your mother not to send you to school in England. It was a great mistake."

"She didn't much care about English schooling."

"No doubt it was your father's wish and of course she was loyal. He talked to her of 'advantages' and listened to no advice. I suppose you mean you want to marry him."

"I do want to marry him, but that is not what I meant."

"What else could you mean?" Then in a voice that was suddenly shrewd she asked, "Baba, have you been seeing him? Have you been meeting him somewhere outside?"

"No, no . . ."

"Well, for that, at least, one can be grateful. After your shameless way of talking, you can see why I should wonder."

"I'm sorry I told you," I said, close to tears. "Why should you make everything so dirty? Why should you want me to feel ashamed?"

"Any woman feels ashamed. How else should she be modest? When you are married it is all different. Then, if you speak of love you will know what you are talking about—though I hope you never speak of it."

I leaned back against the veranda pillar, conscious of the hard square wood between my shoulders, eyes almost closed, unwilling to look at her.

"Come, come, my child," she said gently. "It is nothing to cry about. Every woman wants to get married. It is quite natural that you should too. I will speak to your mother. There is certain to be a mutual friend who will mention the matter to his parents. We will arrange that they ask for your horoscope—"

"Oh no!" I said, outraged.

"Don't worry," she smiled. "Leave it to me. Most probably his parents will be pleased at the opportunity—"

"No!" I interrupted desperately.

"Yes, I assure you. They couldn't, after all, be so wealthy or we would have heard of them. You will have a good dowry, and that is always a consideration—we will see that someone hints of this to his people—"

"Please, Nani. Please don't do anything—"

"Of course there is the difference of community," she continued, ignoring me, settling things in her own mind, "but the caste is right. I think we will have no trouble persuading them. It will be respectably arranged—"

"Nani, listen to me." I realized I was almost shouting. "*Please* don't do anything, I beg of you. I couldn't stand it. Don't you understand? I want *him* to ask me."

"Naturally. That is only proper. The request must come from *his* people. We will merely prompt them a little. Otherwise—who knows? The idea might never suggest itself to them."

"I mean him *personally*. Krishnan himself must ask me."

My grandmother said in honest bewilderment, "When will he ever have the occasion?"

With panicky cunning I thought quickly. "He could write me a letter. Yes, I have a feeling he will write me a letter. And please," I pleaded, "I would so much prefer that. It would be more—well—*private*. Can't you see?"

"What extraordinary ideas you have," she said indulgently. "But what if he doesn't?"

"I think he will. I *know* he will. So, at least until then—"

She smiled at me in her warm, experienced way. "Come and sit near me. You are a child still. Such a silly child." She put her arm around me and pulled my head to her shoulder. "Sometimes you remind me of my great age. I have seen eighty years of India —about eighty, that is, it might be more, one doesn't know exactly—and I should be beyond astonishment. In my last life I must have died young to be, now, so forgetful of experience. The world changes, and I remain, like some stunted creature still ready to be surprised at it. Long ago, in Jalnabad, there used to be such a woman, poor, half-naked, she used to wander about the roads and sometimes came to our kitchen to beg for food. Her hair was matted and hung about her face, and the children used to chase her and tease her and call, 'Crazy woman, crazy woman! Where is your comb?' But she wasn't crazy, she was simply a child. In her mind she must have been seven or eight. No wonder she didn't comb her hair." She patted my shoulders. "And now look at me. That woman could be my sister, for the resemblance between us grows. I live in Jalnabad though for years others have owned our house, and in my mind I too return to my youth and forget the present world.

"You know, my mother remembered the Indian Mutiny and the lawless days when all the women stayed inside the house for fear of wandering English soldiers and the horrors they might commit. It was a terrible time, and she and the other young girls in her house never forgot it. Even when I was a child whenever our elders wished to frighten us into good behavior they would whisper to us, 'The white man is coming! The white man is coming!' and we imagined the white man capable of such barbarous things that we ran to obey whatever the immediate command might be—to wash our hands before the meal or tidy our rooms— and it took us many years to learn that this was simply an adult's trick. And now, just look at your old Nani, she hears foreign ideas from her own granddaughter. The people that she most dreaded speak to her through her child's child. But the sad part is that I, at my age, should be surprised. The West has come to us now in a new way, a much more insidious way. Will this, too, be a conquest?"

Calmed now, as I suppose she intended, by her long, rambling talk, I said, "You sound like Hari. He's always telling me I'm half Western."

"Hari," she said, seizing on the essential point. "The boy in Bombay?"

"Well, Poona, really."

"A much more suitable match for you from all I hear."

"But I'm not in love with him."

"Love is not necessary for a good marriage; devotion, yes, and children, and respect, and honor for a woman, but not love."

"But yours," I said, feeling I had a point, "yours was a happy marriage? You loved your husband?"

"Yes, I was happy to be married," she replied, changing my meaning, "and in the end I loved my husband."

" 'In the end'?"

"At first I was simply obedient. It was years before I experienced also the glory of loving. It came to me gradually through many days and nights when at last I knew him as I know myself, when there were no more discoveries, when there was no longer need for forgiveness or understanding or expression, then I loved him as I have loved nothing else on this earth—more, even, than my children. When he died I, too, wished to die for I could not find in myself even a love for God except with him." She paused, thinking of the old days, and added after a moment, "You can see that when we talk of love, you and I, we talk of different things."

"Yes, I see that. But the thing I talk of, that love, is it less valuable, less glorious?"

With utter conviction she said, "Of course. Just think—what is it, this 'love' of yours? A little excitement, a little impatience, much imagination—is that enough to found your life on? Can you base the structure of your feelings, your fulfillment, your children, your whole being on so little?" I hadn't known until that moment that my grandmother knew me so well or had understood, long before, the things I spoke of. She said with a sigh of something like boredom, "Yes, it's high time you got married. But for pity's sake don't live on dreams. There's no nourishment in them."

I had been moved by her conversation, but didn't yet realize that my feelings about love could be undermined by some quality, some toughness in the fiber of her thoughts. It's all very well for her, I thought; she is an old woman, her life is over, she'll die soon. I hadn't yet allowed the idea that it might also be best for me, that something incontrovertible in my blood or earliest upbringing responded to her attitudes and convictions. It took Krishnan himself to complete the circle, to show me that the story that began with the Nichols and their effect on me would never reach an ending that they could approve of, that the exoticism they represented, their strange approach to life, their unfamiliar concept of personal relationships, would eventually be overruled by the timbre of love in an old woman's voice and the off-hand common sense of an ordinary young man. In other words my preoccupation with romance began, in my mind, to seem cheap. Or perhaps it was simply that I came to the end of a delayed and fanciful adolescence.

❊ XX ❊

THERE ARE SOME CLOTHES IN WHICH YOU ALWAYS ENJOY yourself. I had brought one such sari with me to Chenur—an old one, but still my favorite. It was a shot silk, green and blue, like a butterfly wing, that heavy Madras silk that gets softer and more lustrous the more you wash it. I decided to wear it on the day of the school concert because I was determined, that day, to be very happy. Even the early morning was wickedly hot, the kind of white intensity that powders over roads and gardens like dust and drains all color out of the sky. After lunch everyone stayed very still in the darkened rooms, veranda shades and window blinds drawn against the blinding afternoon.

It would have been cooler and more appropriate to wear cotton, but I wanted to look pretty and festive so I shook out my silk sari and put it on. It draped itself right the first time. With it I wore a choli of a kind that was popular in Bombay, although the older women thought the design unseemly. It fitted very tight over the breasts, had narrow sleeves but no back at all, and fastened only with two strings tied across the shoulder blades and just above the waist. My grandmother had collected a handkerchief full of jasmine from the garden with the sweet and heady smell of the south. She had woven them into a wide, curving band for me to wear in my hair, tucked round the knot on the nape of my neck. I smiled at myself in the mirror, ready to be excited and amused.

We started off that afternoon in the mad and inexplicable muddle that always seems to accompany such occasions. First the school principal sent a tonga out to our house which arrived far too early and stood about on the road by the gate for nearly an hour. Just as we were ready to leave, Krishnan arrived in another tonga. He ran up to the veranda, where we met him. "What is this?" we cried. "What is this? We thought you weren't coming!"

"Why not? I took it as arranged," he said in some agitation. "Look, I have brought a tonga to pick you up."

"But we assumed, since the principal sent the other tonga—"

"Does he not trust me, then, to see you safely to the concert?"

"No, no, couldn't be. Surely not—"

We decided to go with Krishnan and dismiss the other tonga. We hurried down to the gate, but by then the first tonga driver had vanished and nobody seemed to be able to find him. His horse nibbled fastidiously at our jasmine bushes, shifting his position a few inches occasionally.

"Where can he be? This is really too bad."

"I will leave a message with the servants," I said.

"Yes, yes," Krishnan and my mother agreed, and I ran back, calling across the garden, "Gopal! Gopal!" But as I was talking to Gopal, the tonga driver reappeared, looked around, apparently took in the situation, hopped into his tonga and drove off. "What has happened?" I shouted to my mother.

"Who knows?" she replied. "Probably he has returned to the principal."

"But who will pay him for all this time?"

Krishnan looked worried. "Come on, come on!" he called. "We must not be late."

"But what about the *principal?*" I yelled, losing my head.

"We will settle when we see him," he answered impatiently.

At that moment my grandmother emerged from the house wearing her sandals—something she did only when she was going out. "And where is the tonga?" she asked briskly.

"Gone, gone—" I replied.

"Why is it gone?" she asked irritably. "I wanted to go to the market."

"*Market?*" I said incredulously. "At *this* hour?"

("Hurry, hurry," Krishnan called. "What is the matter?")

"What is wrong with this hour? Since you have another tonga in any case, I thought I would use the first. I, too, must have an outing occasionally."

"But there's nothing in the market by afternoon. You should have gone this morning."

"There was no tonga then," she said reasonably.

"I know, but—"

"Really, Baba, don't argue with me."

"But listen—" I said desperately.

("We must go!" Krishnan shouted. "What is the delay?" my mother asked.)

"My dear Baba, you children have no consideration of your elders. How can I go to the market in the mornings?"

"I know, I know—"

"I have all my household duties to take care of. I cook. I watch to see that the servants are doing their work. If I didn't do these things, who would? Surely, I too am allowed a little relaxation of an afternoon—"

"I must go—"

"And what about the tonga?" She turned away before I could reply. "Very well," she said, with magnificent restraint. "I shall remain here while you all enjoy yourselves. Go along. Don't think of me."

("We are late—come on!")

"Good-by. Nani—look, I'm sorry—we'll be back soon—"

I rushed back to the waiting tonga. My mother was already sitting inside. Krishnan jumped up in front next to the driver. I climbed heatedly on the back seat. We arrived at the school long before anyone else. Even the principal was not there.

A huge canopy had been erected over the cricket pitch behind the school. There was a wooden stage at one end of it with a number of straight chairs ranged around the edges. On the ground, in front of the stage over the sparse, withered grass, big fiber carpets of faded but different designs had been spread. This was where the audience of parents, guests and children would sit.

We stood about in exasperated silence for a while, and at last the principal arrived with a small gang of boys in Boy Scout uniforms who were helpful in the most determinedly useless way. At one moment they wheeled off like a flock of birds and began to take the chairs down from the platform. Krishnan hurried toward them. "What are you doing? What on earth are you doing?"

"Taking the chairs down, sir," one of them said busily.

"Put them back," Krishnan commanded.

"Well, sir, the principal said—"

"*Put them back!*"

"Yes sir," the boy said, making a Boy Scout salute. He briskly started to put chairs back while the others continued to take them down.

"*All* of you," Krishnan shouted. "Where will the speakers sit?"

"On the chairs sir."

"How can they if the chairs aren't on the platform?"

"Yes sir."

"Now, as fast as you can, all the chairs back on the platform."

"The principal said, sir, that the speakers wouldn't be able to climb on the platform, sir."

"Yes sir," they all agreed.

"Then go and find some steps. Don't strip the platform."

"Yes sir. Where are the steps, sir?"

"Go and ask the school caretaker. Use your heads for once."

"Yessir," they said obediently. The leader blew his whistle enthusiastically and they all went scurrying off in a dark blue formation toward the school building.

For the first time that afternoon Krishnan smiled at me. "Well, everything seems to be done," he said, looking around at the transformed cricket pitch. "I expect it will go much better than one thinks when it actually begins."

But in a few minutes the Scout leader was back at our side. "Please sir, have you got a bedspread, sir?"

"What?" Krishnan shouted. "Speak up, now, don't mumble."

"A bedspread, sir!" the boy yelled.

Krishnan said ominously, "Are you trying to be funny, young man?"

"No sir, the principal said—"

"Why do you want a bedspread?"

"For the musicians sir."

Krishnan took a deep breath and said with heavy sarcasm, "Are the musicians ready to go to sleep so soon?"

"Nossir."

"Well then?"

"They can't sit on chairs when they play sir, and the principal said that if they sit on the bare platform sir they'll get splinters in their—"

"Yes, yes," Krishnan interrupted hastily, "I see."

"Yessir," said the boy reproachfully.

I wondered hysterically whether the principal could possibly have said such a thing, while Krishnan and the boy went off to find a suitable piece of cloth to spread on the platform.

At last the parents and children began to arrive, fathers stiff and rather ill at ease, striding purposefully ahead of their families as if they wished to accept no connection, mothers sauntering more benignly in their wake, sometimes holding the hand of a small, painfully neat child, or watching indulgently while the school children clotted together in whispering, giggling groups. They appeared to be straggling in, but surprisingly quickly, and with some imperceptible organization of their own they arranged themselves on the mats under the marquee. Some of the more excitable boys were racing around the crowd, others sat subdued near their parents. The Boy Scouts were self-importantly directing people here and there. One batch of parents got steered into the school building to the refreshment room by mistake, and then were quickly extricated from there and appeared, still sheepishly clutching sweets and sandwiches, to be settled with the rest of the audience under the canopy.

Krishnan and I sat at the far end of the first row where he could keep a nervous eye on the parents and on the doings backstage. One of the masters bustled up to him. "What about tea?" he said. "Are there to be no refreshments? Have arrangements broken down?"

"Later, later. We must get them through the speeches and the concert first—"

"But some people have already taken food. Others wish to go also. It looks bad."

"It can't be helped. Get them all out here. If we don't start soon it will be dark before we finish."

"What to do?" the man said despairingly. "No arrangements for lights, is it?"

"Of course not—much too expensive."

With much worried clucking the master hurried off to do what he could.

There was a yell and confusion at the back of the marquee where one of the poles threatened to collapse. All the audience turned around to stare and shout. The people nearest the platform stood up to get a better look. Just then the principal appeared on the stage and yelled, "Friends!" Nobody paid any attention. "Friends! Friends! I have the honor—"

Someone beside me said, "We shall all be smothered. It's coming down—"

"I have the honor to welcome you to our annual concert—" he continued, desperately jaunty, gazing stricken at the backs of the parents.

"Can't they do something? Better perhaps to remove altogether the pandole—" my neighbor said.

"After a term of hard work, and high accomplishment, we come with our heads 'bloody but unbowed' "—he laughed miserably—"to the end of the school year. . . ."

The Scout leader appeared beside us; obviously remembering Krishnan's order to "speak up," he said emphatically, "Please sir."

"Ssh!"

"But *sir*, the pandole is falling."

"Find the caretaker. Quickly."

"Yessir. I found him sir."

"Well then?"

"He is having tea sir."

"For God's sake tell him to *stop* having tea and mend the pole."

"It's not the *pole* sir."

"I don't care *what* it is."

"Nossir."

"Now hurry and get the caretaker."

The boy blew a piercing blast on his whistle. The audience turned to stare at our corner. The Scouts rushed for the school building. My neighbor asked with alarm, "Is it a fire?"

The principal was shouting, ". . . so this is an occasion both of greeting and farewell. As the poet says, 'Parting is such sweet sorrow,' though I dare say some of the members of the fourth standard find only the sweets, not the sorrow." Since virtually nobody heard this little sally the principal chuckled again, by himself. "Before we go on to . . ."

Somewhere a child began crying and a minor distraction was provided by the mother standing up in the middle of the crowd to take the screaming baby away. The caretaker came running from the school, wiping his mouth, and behind him, like a dark blue tail of a comet, streamed the Scouts, each carrying a more-or-less lethal weapon. Intense interest focused on the corner of the marquee with its leaning pole.

". . . much pleasure in introducing to you, my old friend Dr. Venkatakrishnanaiyer, well known in this community as a scholar, as a . . ."

With sharp cries of direction and encouragement, the caretaker organized the Scouts to hammering pegs and holding the pole upright. The audience muttered warnings. My neighbor said, "Look out! They are bracing it on the wrong side."

"Ssh!" Krishnan hissed.

"After all, I should know," my neighbor said huffily. "I am an engineer."

". . . has kindly consented to favor us with his presence, and put at our disposal his great knowledge of Sanskrit language. . . ."

The pole gradually veered upright. More hammering. A deep sigh of relief from the audience, a little scattered applause and a few cheers for the Scouts. The marquee was once again secure, and the parents smiled at each other, the children looked hopefully around for more excitement.

". . . will open our school concert with a Sanskrit blessing. Come forward Dr. Venkatakrishnanaiyer, hence with denial vain and coy excuse. . . ."

The front rows had sat down, the people at the back made themselves comfortable. Everyone turned his attention to the stage but seemed not at all surprised to see, instead of the plump, bouncing figure of the principal, a thin old man with long hair, an elaborate caste mark on his forehead and an exalted expression. In a high, penetrating voice he began to intone the words of the blessing, and once he had started there seemed to be no way of stopping him. On and on he chanted, while the children fidgeted and whispered, while Krishnan looked anxiously at the slanting rays of sunlight, while I wondered whether a teacher's wife would feel she had to attend such functions. I suppose it was only about twenty minutes, though it seemed closer to an hour, before the blessing was over and the speaker returned to his chair. But just as the principal rose to introduce the next dignitary, the Sanskrit scholar returned to the front of the stage with a fat manuscript in his hand.

"For the sake of those who have not studied Sanskrit," he said, "I will now give an English rendering of the blessing."

Beside me Krishnan muttered, "We'll have to cut the concert short."

My other neighbor asked, "There is perhaps an interval for

tea?" When no one replied he got up and left. Several other people saw this, smiled understandingly and followed him out.

There were two more speeches, one from an official in the Chenur Public Works Department and one from the Assistant Collector of the district, but at last the concert itself began with an interminable veena solo by the music master. This was followed by group songs from some of the students, a drum solo, some music and a dramatic recitation of "The boy stood on the burning deck, Whence all but him had fled," which was somewhat enlivened for me by a child in the row behind who added, in a telling whisper, "And when his feet were burned away, He stood upon his head." The concert ended with my mother's two short songs. The principal returned to the stage to give the closing address, but most of the parents were determined by then to get to the refreshment room, and he bellowed out his cheery words to a rapidly diminishing audience, and again gestured despairingly to a few rows of unresponsive backs. Through the rising chatter of parents, guests and children, I heard his last sadly jubilant words, ". . . for those who will not be returning next year and may have forgotten in this last term of their carefree boyhood that life is real, life is earnest, a message of heartfelt encouragement. Like the other great men of your country, may you also leave behind footprints in the sands of time. Tea and cold drinks will now be served in sixth estandard form room."

Standing on the steps, still laughing inwardly at the speeches and absurdities of the afternoon, I watched Krishnan saying good-by to the parents and guests on the path in front of the school. The principal was rocking with jollity and fussing about near by. My mother was talking to a group of women in the school passageway behind me. The late southern evening colored the school walls with gold light. There was a deeper resonance in people's voices. The women's saris showed new warmth of red and yellow and orange. I leaned against the railing of the steps, easy, in no hurry, conscious of a jolt of pleasure when Krishnan turned and smiled quickly at me.

In a short pause between good-bys and end-of-term courtesies to parents, Krishnan ran up the steps to stand beside me for a minute.

"These things take so long. I'm sorry to keep you waiting. They all want to know how their children are doing."

"Only natural. I don't mind waiting. Actually," I said idly, expecting only a conventional response, "we can easily get ourselves home as soon as we find a tonga. You mustn't feel you have to see us there 'without damage to life or limb' just because the principal committed you to it. If you have things to keep you here, I mean. End of term leaves you with lots of odds and ends to finish up, I expect."

Krishnan looked relieved but a little dubious. "Well, if you think—" he began.

"Oh yes," I said quickly, apprehensive all at once, my comfortable mood gone, thinking vaguely, I believe I expected this. "It will be perfectly all right. Really."

"Well, it will take us a little while to close the school up." Krishnan's voice was considering, practical. "And then I have my packing still to do, though that won't take very long."

"Packing?" I held tight to the railing, refusing to accept his tone, unable to accept this as an ordinary moment, feeling an imminent disaster of some sort.

"Yes, didn't I tell you? I'm leaving for Madras tomorrow."

"Leaving?"

"My people are there, as you know, and well, this year . . . especially . . . I have to get back there early. . . ."

"Especially?" I felt very foolish simply repeating odd words out of his remarks but I couldn't wake myself up enough to do more than that, to comment or ask for explanations.

Krishnan looked at his feet, stretched out a hand to rest it beside mine on the railing. He was embarrassed. A step above him, I looked down at his bent head, and was touched by the confusion in his manner, the line of his jaw, the pull of the long tendon from behind his ear to his collarbone.

"Especially this year because, well, I'm to be married. There are many preparations and my mother wants me there."

I could think of nothing to say except, "You never told me."

"Because I haven't thought much about it. It's all been arranged for such a long time." His voice held no breath of guilt, only shyness.

"Do you *want* to marry her?" (I had to ask it.) "This—this girl, I don't even know her name."

"Saraswati. Yes, I suppose I do. It's my mother's dearest wish —we've known the family for years—and besides, a wife will be a help to me. Hostel living gets uncomfortable after a while. I need a home." His words, his manner allowed no emotion from me. One couldn't contemplate a scene—one couldn't even talk of feelings.

I was pleased that my voice held only ordinary curiosity when I asked, "This Saraswati—what is she like?"

"Oh, a very good girl. Educated. She's a college graduate. And quite fair." He was watching another group of visitors preparing to leave, assembling on the path, looking around for tongas. He was only half concerned with what he was saying, had a smile ready for the parents, was poised to run down the steps and continue his cheerful farewells.

"I see. Well, I should wish you—"

"Excuse me," he interrupted. "I must just see these people off." He hurried down to stand, the competent, agreeable schoolmaster, with the departing guests, remembering people's names and children, embedding his good-bys in encouraging remarks of a good term's record or a little more work next year.

When my mother came out of the school and stood beside me on the steps, and I said, "No point in waiting around here. Krishnan has things to finish up anyway. We might as well get a tonga and go home now," she took it quite as a matter of course. We found a place in the group around the principal, and he shouted when he saw my mother, "Good lady! you were the life and soul of our party! Music hath charms but we need an artistic lady like you to prove it to us. You put our poor estudents to shame with your performance—"

"You mustn't flatter me," my mother said, laughing.

"No flattery! Why gild the lily? Isn't it?" he asked, looking around for confirmation. "We will never forget your kindness and your first-rate voice—"

"Well, that's very—"

" 'A thing of beauty is a joy forever'!" The principal bounced joyfully.

"We must say good-by now, and wish you good holidays—"

Krishnan had found a tonga for us, and we climbed in eagerly. He stood beside it a moment, speaking to my mother. "I have so much to thank you for—your hospitality, and so many evenings I've spent—"

"Not at all. It was a pleasure, and you've kept Baba from being lonely—"

"Well," he smiled at me in a friendly way, "I've appreciated your kindness. We'll all meet again next year, perhaps. Until then, good-by—"

"Good-by, good-by," we said, "take care of yourself . . . good holidays . . . good-by . . . good-by. . . ."

We drove home in silence. My mother never expected conversation, and that evening I was grateful for her withdrawn serenity. I stared out from the back of the tonga at the coconut palms, the banana trees, the red earth slipping away behind us, keeping my eyes wide open as I used to when I was a child, so that the wind would dry my tears before they fell, afraid to blink, unable to speak, unwilling, yet, to think or remember.

All through dinner that night my mother talked much more than she usually did. I was too thankful for her unaccustomed volubility to question it at all, and I noticed that my grandmother directed all her inquiries about the school concert to my mother— naturally, perhaps, because I had only been a spectator—but I didn't interrupt to embroider my mother's thin and modest account of the afternoon, as I would normally have done. I don't know if my grandmother noticed that. Certainly she didn't turn to me as she would on other occasions with requests for a more detailed description of somebody's clothes or what jewelry the wife of the principal wore, or what Krishnan had said. I lived through the afternoon again, at second hand, gradually bringing myself to reconstructing in my own mind Krishnan's last few, brief sentences, gradually taking in his mood, his manner, the commonplace announcement of his marriage—an event arranged by his mother, to a suitable girl, a practical discharging of affairs, a normal handling of an ordinary matter, accepted by Krishnan, even welcomed in a way. My own feelings began to seem overblown.

I found that I was hungry and ate a lot, and immediately after dinner felt sleepy. I rose from the table saying that I was going straight to bed, and, in our habit, that seemed in no way extraordinary. My grandmother made a slight gesture in my direction, immediately suppressed, and I caught a quick exchange of looks between her and my mother, the meeting of a glance, no more. I don't know what they guessed or thought—if they thought anything—about my uncharacteristic silence and a manner that must, I suppose, have seemed strained, and since I never talked about Krishnan to anyone again, I never knew whether their easy lack of curiosity was a merciful tact or just a dismissing, as a subject of conversation, of somebody who had no further place in our lives.

In my room I moved with deliberation. I set the oil lamp down in its usual place on the table. I took off my nice butterfly-wing sari, noticing that at night it was more blue than green. I folded it carefully and hung it over the towel rack so that the wrinkles would smooth out of it by morning. I untied my choli with the daring open back, pulled the tight sleeves gently over my elbows and dropped it into the big basket of clothes to be sent to the dhobi. Then I kicked off my sandals and lay down on my bed in my petticoat. I could smell the sweet, withering jasmine as my head pressed the flowers into my pillow, and an occasional flutter against my neck reminded me that the buds, limp and brown now, were loosening from their string. On the ceiling was a yellow circle of light with two inexplicable arcs of shadow crossing in it. The corners of the room were misty with deeper shadow. After a moment I found that I was not, as I had expected, going to weep.

At least I shall never see him again, I told myself. Already it is in the past, and if I don't remember then it will be even more quickly obliterated because at least I shall never see him again. But at the same time I was searching back over the weeks just past for reassurances of some kind—What did I do? What did I say? I scoured old conversations for those evidences that had, at the time, seemed so apparent. A gesture, a phrase, a look of secret understanding—they were now too flimsy to grasp, lost before I could formulate them. My mind moved in more conventional patterns and I found myself framing, instead, such questions as, Did I throw myself at him—or could it have seemed so? and, What could he have thought? A fast Bombay girl? A cheap little piece? Even alone in my room, lying unwatched on the bed, I felt my shoulders tense with shame. No, more likely he wanted an audience—certainly he found an appreciative one—he was pleased with the change of scene, the good teas, the quiet evenings. "Hostel living gets uncomfortable. . . ." But tomorrow by this time he will be gone. There can be no occasion at which we meet. At least I shall not see him again. I was, so I realized, more consumed with humiliation than regret.

I searched my mind for sadness and discovered that it was not for the loss of Krishnan but for some other loss which I tried only cautiously to define. I'll miss him, I thought, I'll miss the excitement of seeing him come up to the house from the gate, wheeling his bicycle, I'll miss the impatience of waiting for teatime and those public-private conversations, that magic conspiracy of ordinary words and interior meanings. Then, more clearly than any remembered conversations, I thought (without summoning it) of my grandmother's voice saying, "A little excitement, a little impatience, much imagination—is that enough? . . ." At last I felt the burn of tears in my eyes and knew what I was crying for.

The moonlight of the south is like no other moonlight that I know. It is warm, for one thing, and it is very bright. It is more like living in the daytime of another planet with different qualities of light than in the familiar night of your own. The moon rises red and menacing, softens slowly to gold and hangs close over your head, somewhere between the trees and the sky. On a night of the full moon I walked in the garden listening to the distant drumming from some village dance and thinking about Krishnan.

The house was patterned with segments of dazzling white where the moonlight reached the walls and wedges of black under the veranda roof and in the cavernous open doors. I heard my mother's voice calling, "Baba, Baba . . ." softly from the veranda steps.

"Yes, I'm here." I walked toward the house and saw her standing on the steps, half in shadow, with her hand on the wooden railing.

"It's late," she said in a puzzled voice.

"I know. It's this moon."

"Ah, the moon . . ."

I stood there in the full moonlight like someone on a stage, my faceless shadow sharp on the white wall. "I don't know what it is about the full moon. . . ."

"Yes, these last moons before the rains."

"But only here, only in Malabar. Northern moons are different, somehow. And in Bombay—"

"Bombay?" she said as though she had never heard of the place.

"In Bombay you hardly know whether there is a moon or not."

"I remember it over the sea sometimes. It was very beautiful even there in Bombay."

"Why did you leave?" I asked without meaning to.

"I had to leave," she said, no surprise in her voice. "I had my own enemies."

"Enemies? In Bombay?"

"In myself." I could hear her smile although I could hardly see her face in the shadow. "Love, anger, desire, affection, pride— what other enemies are there?"

"And it had to be here? Couldn't you have stayed in Bombay?"

As though she were explaining a simple problem to a child, she replied, "I was unskilled. I had to work with a teacher. It could have been anywhere, but my help was here."

"Now you are happy?"

"Is happiness what you want?" she asked me with infinite compassion in her tone.

"Yes," I replied, remembering dimly a toast that Alix and I had once drunk to happiness. "Of course that's what I want."

"Oh, my poor child."

"Aren't you happy? Isn't that what all this has meant?"

"I haven't learned fully yet," she said noncommittally.

I insisted, "But when you *have?*"

"I shall be at peace."

Not love, not happiness, I repeated to myself, not excitement, not even doing good, not caring, not life. "Well," I said, uncertain and now suddenly rather embarrassed, "I suppose we should be going to bed. Would you like a glass of water? This heat . . . When will the rains break?"

"Any day now, perhaps next week."

We went into the house together. In the corner of the passage inside the back door the big earthenware jar full of water always stood. Beside it was a silver tumbler. I tipped the jar to fill the tumbler, remembering before I tasted it the wet-earth taste of the water. My mother leaned her head back and neatly poured the water into her mouth without touching the tumbler to her lips. I did the same, and before I had finished my mother had, without saying anything more, gone into her room and closed the door.

Part Three

✤

THE MONSOON

✤ XXI ✤

I NSIDE OUR BOMBAY HOUSE THERE WAS THE UNMISTAKABLE atmosphere of illness—not a smell, exactly, but an air at once oppressive and chilling. The ayah had been waiting at the front door for our arrival. Hushed and pleased and full of doom she followed us upstairs reciting the theatrical story of my father's heart attack. The weeks of overwork, not eating proper meals, just a tray in his study and most of the food untouched as often as not when the bearer took it away, the collapse at the head of the stairs, the miraculous fluke that made him fall against the wall rather than against the banister (because surely he would have pitched right over the rail, a tall man like him, and fallen down the stair well to crash onto the marble floor of the hall), the hurrying, panicky servants, the telegram to Chenur summoning my mother and me, the visits of the doctor, the medicine, the special diet. . . .

My mother appeared to be listening attentively, but she probably wasn't because she interrupted absently to ask for tea to be sent up, and walked immediately to my father's room. I stood in the doorway uncertainly while she crossed to the bed. Her back looked as calm and easy as ever, her hands unfidgety. She sat in silence on a chair by the bed waiting to be spoken to.

Across the darkened room my father's voice sounded unexpectedly vigorous. He spoke first to me. "Come in, Baba, and close the door; those wretched servants whisper and chatter in the passage all day." He turned his head very slightly toward my mother. "There is no cause for alarm," he said.

"You have always had a weak heart."

"No, no. I have never had trouble with my heart. It is merely the hot weather. It has been unusually hot this year. And perhaps," his voice suddenly faded, "I have been working rather too hard. . . ."

"You are no longer young," my mother said.

"I suppose that is it," his words trembled to a whisper.

"You need plenty of rest and a calm mind."

My father did not answer. I smiled at him, still standing just inside the door, but got no response. There seemed nothing to be said.

My own room had that unnatural neatness and unfriendly aspect that I had often noticed when I returned there from visits south. One of the servants had put my suitcases away in the dressing room, and I sat on the edge of my bed, unwilling to begin unpacking or even to bathe and change. Even when the ayah brought in tea, I left it cooling on the table, too lacking in energy to pour it into a cup, put in milk and sugar, stir it, drink it. Instead I listened to the ayah telling me that when Shalini had been told of my father's attack (and I knew with what reluctance the ayah must have telephoned her), she had wanted to come at once to stay in the house and attend to everything herself. But the ayah had cleverly outmaneuvered her. First she had told Shalini that the bearer slept on the floor outside my father's door in case he should need anything during the night, and then that he would have to be lifted even to sit up for his meals—not to mention other necessities—and obviously this was work for a man. As a final argument she had asked Shalini, what about the children? Clearly they couldn't come to stay in the house as well because absolute silence was essential. On the other hand, wouldn't they feel neglected if they were left motherless?

I couldn't help giggling at Shalini's predicament. Imagine missing such an opportunity for devotion. She had never really been able to hold her own against the ayah. Though perhaps she had consoled herself with pleasantly important conferences with the doctors, with ponderous, detailed reports to my brother, with fussing in the kitchen over nourishing food, with daily visits and telephone calls to her friends. . . .

Suddenly the idea of Shalini moving into the house and gradually taking over its management made me realize for the first time that my father might, in actual fact, die. It became in that moment a matter that, known for years, took on its first reality. I felt that some acknowledgment was due from me. I felt that somehow the part of my life that was concerned with him must be set in order. Somewhere there was a question to be asked that could only be answered by him. If I loved him, and I now knew that I did, no longer expecting him to be the person he couldn't be, there must be some communication that I could give or receive. Suppose there was never another chance, what would I regret? But even in that moment I realized that such an exchange belongs to life, that death doesn't finish or explain or even alter very much. Yet in that short stretch of time, sitting on my bed in a room growing slowly familiar, watching the ayah, the neglected tea tray, the stripes of light and shade on the floor, I missed and longed for my father more than at any time in my life.

The monsoon broke a few days after we reached Bombay. All afternoon the sky had been a weird, ominous yellow and eventually the sun had dipped into the sea in a wild plunge of improbable purples. After that the wind that had fitfully rattled the trees and the reed blinds all day, and had sent the dust pirouetting and fogging across the garden, steadied itself into a constant drive. The great canvas awnings that had been stretched some days before over windows and verandas to keep the rain from beating into the house cracked angrily in the gale. In the sudden suspense of a lull you could hear the distant threshing of the sea or the flurry of fans inside the house. Indoors the gloom was charged with meaning, the smallest words echoed with enormous implications; a question about the dinner hour was a judgment, a refusal of a second helping a death sentence. The awnings to which we

were still unused so early in the monsoon enclosed the house in
an impenetrable isolation.

For days the servants had been gasping about the coming of
the monsoon, and in that steamy climate of anxiety it was easy to
imagine it accompanied by disaster. Too late, and the planting
would be useless, a barren and expensive guess. They thought
continually of their villages, the family plot of land, the beginning
of a new season of growth, or—with the experienced association of
Indians—of failure, of famine and despair.

For five days, at the Mahalaxmi temple, there had been prayers
and offerings for the opportune arrival of the monsoon. The ayah
had donated a rupee to the temple funds for the sake of her half-
forgotten, distant and indifferent and close family in her village.
"It is always the same," she told me, "you pray for it to begin,
and then you pray for it to end." Too long, too much rain and
the harvest is ruined, the scanty wealth rots in the fields.

That evening I stood on my veranda and watched the curdling
sky. From the southwest came the first shredded fleeing clouds,
then the great inky banners and then the serious clotted mass
that brought the rain. Behind the clouds was the mutter of
thunder, almost inaudible in the sound of the wind, and occasional
flares of lightning that lit the bending trees, the squat houses, the
rushing street, for a brilliant, dark green second.

The rain poured down the gutters, hammered on the earth of
the garden, rattled on roads and blinds and roofs; somewhere in
the house a door slammed; and I slept all night with the sound
of the rain in my head and woke in the morning, pleased and
optimistic, to a new liquid city, the grass already springing green
on our lawn, the streets glassed with wide puddles, and men, like
large, angular water birds on thin legs, walking to work, their
dhotis tucked high, barefoot with their sandals in their hands,
children drenched and playing in the water, people in flooded
cars or stranded buses laughing with each other, the servants with
a three-month reprieve, all of Bombay with a carefree energy.
Even my father said to me that morning, "Now that the heat is
over I can do some work." He smiled at me. "Tell the bearer to
come up; I'll explain which files I need." But the doctor wouldn't

allow him to work. Six weeks of rest was the order, complete rest, and then he would see.

In those six weeks I had many occasions to talk to my father because he had been forbidden any visitors except the family, and even we were only permitted to sit with him for half an hour or so. My mother, of course, spent as much time as she wanted with him, but for the most part she simply sat in silence in his room or occasionally read her books.

My own friends were all away from Bombay—Pria and Karan still in Ceylon, Jay in Kalipur, Hari in Poona, I supposed, the Nichols? Probably Alix was still in Kashmir; I didn't know. I thought once of phoning Nicky's office—surely he had to be back at work—but I hadn't thought of them for a long time and it seemed too much trouble to begin again. So I spent most of my time at home or at the Club and went to the movies occasionally with my brother and sister-in-law.

In the mornings I used to sit for a while with my father and read him the newspapers. At first I had had some dim idea of censoring the news for him because he was supposed to be spared as much anxiety as possible, but he was much too shrewd to be taken in by such amateurish tactics and told me that his heart might be failing him but his head definitely was not. He smiled at me tolerantly. "Senility is a disease of the mind," he said. "I hope my heart may collapse first."

He didn't like to hold the paper himself because nowadays his hands shook in a terrible, uncontrollable dance. Even when he read a book which could be steadied on a rack across his chest he preferred to do it when there was nobody in the room to see the fluttering of the turned page. He told me this quite casually, and added, "Vanity dies harder than the human animal. A singularly tough quality. I often think it is underestimated by our—ah—philosophers." (I wondered if he meant my mother—an uneasy chasm of bitterness if he did.) "It enables people to achieve what is otherwise well beyond them—perhaps more than they deserve." (Not bitterness, then; simply a recognition of things as they had happened.)

The news itself was, at that time, calculated to disturb almost any Indian, sick or well. Day after day I read to him stories of the country's agonized division, of murders, riots, atrocities. I read him editorials about the columns of destitute refugees jamming the roads to Delhi, carrying their children, their pathetic bundles, a salvaged cooking pot, a bag of wheat, a remaining fragment of wedding jewelry. I told him in detail about the great disaster at one of the great northern rivers where thousands of hysterical Punjabis trying to reach safety had met the refugees flooding in the other direction. It had been an enormous, futile tragedy. Bullock carts driven by screaming, panicking drivers, overloaded with household possessions, the useless accumulations of years of secure living, had been forced into the river to drown. The water flowed red as the sunset from the killing on the banks. A floating child, a sodden veil, a toy, a cow, a body, a wheel, a turban—anything—would be washed up miles down the river for weeks. The crowds, no longer aware of meanings or of purpose, trampled and smothered each other to death.

"Can't they *do* something?" I used to ask, conscious that this was a childish question.

My mother only answered, "No child is born without blood," which made me angry.

My father said, "What can be done now? It should all have been done before. But there is no place for patience just before success. We will pay for this every day for years to come. There was no planning. There should have been planning. . . ." But he didn't seem to be listening to his own words, and in a minute or two, after I had read him the news, would always return to the question of how soon he could get back to work. The case he was working on—a small case, of no political importance, in fact, of no particular importance at all—obsessed him. He talked of it and thought of it constantly. Once when the doctor told him it was not urgent and could wait until he was well enough, he lost his temper. "A small man is in small trouble so it can be ignored? I'm afraid I do not function in that way. I feel my responsibility to my client very deeply! These champions of the peasant in the field—they look for issues to shake a nation! I may not know the peasant, but I am reasonably sure that his problems are small ones—a question of five rupees or a handful of rice. Who will deal with small troubles? Who will fight for the five rupees? No. It's an unimportant case, you all tell me. Don't think about it. It can wait for your convenience. I tell you—"

The doctor interrupted nervously to calm him and make lots of soothing comments about, "When the cardiogram is steadier . . . a couple of weeks of complete quiet . . . your illness has been more serious than you assume . . . not yet quite out of the critical stage . . . don't want to bring on a relapse. . . ."

My father tired quickly, and would say in an exhausted voice, "I shall soon be stronger. . . ." In the dark room, with the small, unpleasant appurtenances of sickness near him, the bottles of pills on the bedside table, the thermometer in a glass of cloudy liquid, the jar of Horlick's, the extra pillows, he retired behind his eyes to a private country with a sick man's authority, and we all left him alone. If he ever felt strongly about the things I read him from the newspapers, or had angers or sadnesses about the emerging government, the new nation, he never expressed them to me. He reserved his occasional explosions to trivialities, his comments and speculations to his case, and fragments of conversation to the progress of his health. It seemed as though his personality had taken shelter in some cave that one couldn't penetrate, and had left only a thin old man, lying quietly under the sheets, a bony face with faint lines of pathos showing around the mouth, waiting for something.

One evening early in July Hari came to the house to call, and it was with quite unexpected pleasure that I greeted him. The familiar, irregular face and the air of prosaic assurance seemed an enormous offer of comfort in the sick and silent house. We sat in the big drawing room—seldom used except for parties—while the monsoon rain hissed and thundered outside the windows. He had heard of my father's heart attack, and had come to inquire about his recovery. He had arrived in Bombay that morning to see about clearing some pump machinery through customs for the Poona place. He would be in town for a few days.

After I had given him my father's news and had told him that no visitors were allowed as yet, there was a pause, rather an awkward one, with both of us remembering that evening that seemed a great deal more than only three and a half months ago. He was the first to smile. "You look as though you need a change," he said. "I'll take you out to dinner. We'll go to a Chinese place, and to a film afterward, if you'd like to."

"Just by ourselves?" I had never been out alone with Hari before.

"If your parents have no objection."

"Oh, they won't object. They'll be pleased, if anything. They terribly approve of you, you know."

"Well, I'm glad somebody does," Hari said easily, and, as it turned out, the whole evening was as easy as that. We ordered far more food than we could eat, ordering things that sounded bizarre in their English spelling on the menu and laughing about the tremendous air of conspiracy that a Chinese restaurant offers, about being hurried into a little partitioned-off room, with the curtains drawn and the sound of whispering and somehow immoral laughter from the other cubicles.

We stood in the restaurant doorway afterward, watching the rain bounce through the arches of the arcade that covered the sidewalk. Hari put his raincoat over my head and shoulders—it smelled of a mixture of cigarette smoke and rubber, and gave me a momentary feeling of dependence that the wearing of someone else's clothes is apt to do. He gripped my arm, and together we ran across the streaming street to his car, bustled into the front seat, slammed doors, smoothed back disordered hair. Moist, laughing, we turned to each other as if we had shared a small adventure, like people with a secret, excited, ready to talk trivialities.

"Lord, what a night!" I said. "We never really prepare for monsoon rain. What is Poona like?"

"Cool and gray. Almost no rain. Very good riding weather, though."

"Riding. Do you know, I haven't ridden since that summer ages ago when you taught me. I think that was the happiest holiday I've ever spent."

"Really?" Hari looked at me almost with disbelief. "I never thought you much liked the Poona place."

"How little people know about each other. It reminds me of Jalnabad, as I told Pria the weekend we were there, but with an added freedom. All she could say, though, was that the house needed children."

With a return to his usual practical tone Hari said, "Yes, it's a very healthy climate."

"In several ways," I said, but Hari didn't ask me what I meant.

The movie, when we reached it, was fairly empty, the pelting rain and the wild, windy night must have kept most people away, and because of this we looked around with some curiosity to see who else was there. After the short films and trailers, when the lights went up for the intermission and a succession of advertisements was flashed on the screen, we walked out into the lobby to see who that we knew was still in Bombay. There were the usual slender young men in the gallery—office workers, clerks, students perhaps, in white drill trousers and open shirts—and the Anglo-Indian girls in very high heels and flowered dresses, dark hair in elaborate arrangements, dark eyes searching, some women in saris, not speaking to their husbands, some foreigners. No one we knew, but a typical crowd.

It was when we were leaving the theater after the main feature that I saw someone ahead of us who seemed to me familiar. The short, square back, the lazy walk, something about the white jacket—"Jay!" I called, "Ja-ay!" But he didn't look round and since other people in the audience moving slowly out into the rain turned to stare at me, I didn't shout again. Later I thought I must be mistaken. Jay couldn't be in Bombay. Anyway, if it had been Jay he would certainly have heard me. Since he hadn't turned, obviously I had made a mistake. I hadn't noticed whom he was with—if he was with anybody—if it really had been Jay.

When I got back to the house and Hari, smiling and promising to call the next day, had left, I walked through the downstairs hall half aware that there was some change in the house, something rather disturbing. I noticed, then, that too many lights were on. Usually only the hall light was left burning for me, but that night

I could see the brillance from the dining room and kitchen marking great yellow oblongs on the veranda, and more light and the sound of movements from the bedrooms upstairs.

My mother met me on the landing with her finger across her mouth for silence. In my room she sat on a chair and pulled her feet up under her. "He had another attack a short while after you left."

"The doctor—?"

"The doctor came, of course, and gave him an injection. He is sleeping now."

"Will he be all right? What did the doctor say?"

"A slight attack. No need to worry yet. But we must exert even greater care."

"What else must we do?"

"He must not see newspapers. Even letters must be read by us first, and anything connected with his work or politics or anything that might cause him to worry must be kept from him. Naturally, no visitors."

"But he can't be completely cut off. It will drive him mad."

My mother said indifferently, "It must be done."

"Well, he will know you're doing it and that will worry him much more."

"He may not know. We have not seen yet what effect this will have on his mind."

More than the news of the attack, this remark shocked me. "His mind? Surely his mind can't fail him?"

"I don't know."

"Is it a possibility?" I insisted. "Did the doctor say so?"

"We can't tell yet. But, yes, it is a possibility."

Apparently my mother didn't sleep at all that night for she came into my room early next morning, her eyes deeply shadowed with fatigue, and said, "He has just woken up and is asking for you. I am going now to rest, but call me if anything troubles you."

I dressed quickly and went in to see him. He was propped up on several pillows, looking for once far from immaculate. The gray grime of unshaven beard showed on his jaw and marked shadows under his cheekbones. His breathing was heavy, his mouth bitter. "Sit down, Baba," he said, and there was a new rasp to his voice. "Sit down, and don't talk."

I sat in an armchair by the bed watching him and waiting for an indication of some kind that he was relapsing into childishness or that he was no longer aware of present realities or for some decay of that admired intellect. But he seemed to have nothing more to say to me and lay staring at the ceiling fan. His only movement was the occasional flicking of his pupils as they followed the turning blades. In that hypnotic silence I must have fallen asleep and suddenly it was noon and the bearer was standing in the doorway with a tray.

I started up, beginning an apology, to help arrange the bed table, but my father lifted a trembling hand. "Why not sleep? What is there to be said?"

"Can you manage by yourself? Do you need help?"

"No. The cup will make an irritating noise rattling on the saucer, but I do not need help. Not yet . . ."

He ate scarcely anything, a couple of mouthfuls of soup, and then he seemed too tired to lift the cup again. "Baba," he said, "what are you going to do?"

"I have nothing particular to do today. Do you want me to take your tray away?"

". . . after I'm dead?"

Carefully I replied, "You're not dying."

He turned his head away from me impatiently. "You and the Patel case . . . two pieces of unfinished work."

"A person isn't anybody's work. Don't worry about me."

"We have never understood each other. Your nature is full of things . . . that are not inherited from either your mother or from me. . . ." There was a pause in which he breathed heavily. "It concerns me . . . that I do not know . . . what your consolations will be. . . ."

Not the intellect or success of my father, nor the driving, satisfying years of work that were more valuable than the price of loneliness, nor my mother's painfully grasped peace and strength of not-loving, not-wanting, not really anything definable. But I was gradually formulating in my mind something learned in

Chenur that seemed to me to be a solid enough compensation. It would have comforted my father if I had been able to express it.

"I think I know the terms in which my life must be lived," I said, sounding foolish, "and that is something."

He lay silent, eyes closed, chin trembling. The habits of reticence were too strong, I discovered, to be broken after so long. I couldn't tell him what he wanted to know, that somehow, I now felt in charge of my life (though not entirely in command). One makes one's own adventures, and I no longer expected outside things, or those feelings that I had wanted to think were stronger than anything, to form my decisions in love, in marriage, in all the rest.

I said, "I wanted to tell you—the day we came up from the south, I was thinking about you and I wanted to tell you that—" at the last second I couldn't say, "that I love you, and hadn't known it before," it sounded entirely too dramatic.

"What did you want to tell me?"

"That I shall be all right," I said lamely. "You really mustn't fret about me. The doctor says—"

"Damn the doctor! I shall go to my end at my own pace." He sank back exhausted by his outburst.

"I'd better go and let you get some rest. You're supposed to sleep in the afternoons."

"I have a long time in which to sleep. I have the rest of my life in which to sleep." He seemed amused by his remark. "Stay with me, Baba, until I sleep."

I sat down again and he closed his eyes. Distantly his voice whispered, "You'll have some money . . . a third, and the rest . . . between your mother and my son." I listened attentively to the hoarse, cloudy words. ". . . never be without plans. You must be thinking . . . this house, of course . . ." then, surprisingly clearly, ". . . impossible to live with Shalini. She would try the fortitude of a saint. . . ."

When I was sure he was asleep I left the room. From then on my days changed entirely, with my father's room their center and the outside world growing daily more remote. He could not bear to be alone; in a way it was the most pitiful thing about his illness. The man who all his life had preferred his own company to any other, whose self-sufficiency had amounted to arrogance, was now consumed, as his sickness never consumed him, with loneliness, with a dread of solitude. He even fought against sleep.

My mother and I took turns sitting with him all day, and, after his evening sedative, staying with him until he slept. Would it have been better if he had needed her like this years ago? I thought. At night the bearer brought his blanket and bedding roll and slept now on the floor at the foot of my father's bed instead of in the hall. I don't know what reassurance we gave him. He seldom spoke to us, but occasionally out of his interior world he would ask a sudden, brisk question. "Have there been any calls about the Patel case?"

"No. Mr. Patel knows the situation—"

"If he calls, tell him he is in safe hands. I will win his case for him." Every day his voice dimmed more quickly. "It is just that at the moment I am working very hard . . . it takes a great deal of work simply to go on breathing . . . to make my heart beat . . . to push the blood through my veins. . . ."

Once, when I had thought he was drowsing, he said, "Baba, do you want to travel? You could if you wished."

"Not particularly. I'm not very good with strangers."

"Like your mother. After that first visit to London she never even wanted to return with me for your winter holidays. She always said she preferred to wait and see you at home in the summer."

"I remember. She didn't like the cold."

"And she felt she hadn't time to think, that she became too busy with unimportant details. She had a special tone of voice for politics and for my work." He lost interest. "Perhaps she was right. It is harder work to think than to work . . . but too late now . . . not enough energy now . . . only to lie here."

Sometimes out of some continuing train of thought would come some comment one couldn't answer. ". . . wish for the perspective of some future historian to tell you what you already know. If you are human you are responsible, responsible in your moment and your context. Who is to say what matters? History plays tricks on us all. . . ." Or, as on one occasion, he would suddenly bark a sentence like, "The only treachery is to delude oneself!"

"What?" I would say, startled.

"Baba? Where are you?"

"I'm here."

"Don't go away."

"No, I won't." And his mouth would relax, his eyes close again.

"I dream a great deal. I wish I could sleep without dreaming. Pieces of this and that . . . the old days . . ."

From time to time there would be days that were punctuated with the petulance of a child. "Why is the room so dark? Where are those miserable servants? Tell the bearer to pull the curtains. I can't lie here in this cellar. I'm not in jail." Once, when the servant who shaved him in the mornings brought water that was too cool for my father's satisfaction, he sat up in bed angrily and with a burst of temper swept the bowl of water onto the floor. He sank back weakly, saying, "It's little enough to ask," with helpless tears in his eyes. Another time, when he asked me to read the newspaper to him and I told him that he was supposed to rest, he said, "That won't disturb my rest."

"Well, there's nothing much in the paper anyway."

He glared at me and said bitterly, "You are determined to make an invalid of me. I will not have it. Bring me the paper, I shall read it myself."

But he lost interest in things quickly. By the time I had brought him the newspaper he had closed his eyes and did not speak. The paper lay on the bed beside his hand, neglected.

During the few days that Hari was in Bombay he telephoned every morning. I began to look forward to his calls as my one remaining contact in the hushed routine of our house with the vigorous, ordinary doings of the world outside. It was almost as if I, too, were recovering from sickness. His voice carried its own suggestion of the clear air and health of a different life. He always asked after my father in his quick, unsentimental way which (in contrast to Shalini's tearful phone calls) seemed a reassurance in itself. I was in no mood for inflated emotions.

Hari told me small items of news about our friends—Karan had written to him from Ceylon, asking him to look for an apartment that might be suitable for Pria and Karan to move into when they returned in October. "I think I've found one that might do. Quite nice. Rather old-fashioned. When your father is better, will you look at it and see if Pria would like it?" Or, "Did you know that Jay is selling his horses and closing down his stable? He has very kindly offered me first choice."

"Are you going to buy any?"

"I thought I might take a couple of the Indian-breds. The Arabs had better go to someone who will race them. After the rains you must come up and try them. You may find you still like riding." There was always the tacit assurance that soon this illness would be over, and moments of another sort of living to keep in my mind as an antidote for the sickroom tensions.

Sometimes Hari related the most recent anecdotes that people were telling each other in Bombay. Had I heard that the Viceroy had issued calendars to all the government officials concerned which read, "Sixty more days to Independence," and progressively as each leaf was torn off, "Fifty-nine days to Independence," "Fifty-eight days . . ."? Did I know that a rather amusing crisis had developed over what to do with the pictures of the English king that had for years decorated government offices? They would have to be taken down after Independence, but to burn them or tear them up might seem to be lese majesty and wouldn't be at all in keeping with the cordial spirit that everyone hoped to maintain with the departing British. Could one just store them, piles and piles of them, in some godown until they moldered away?

"Wonderful," I said laughing. "How fortunate we are not to have insoluble problems like that."

"Well, not entirely insoluble. I suppose they could be shipped off to other colonies."

"Or be used on the covers of those chocolate boxes we used to get in England."

Hari sounded cheerful as he said, "Anyway, it's exercise for one's ingenuity." Later I remembered that he never compelled me to feel grateful for sympathy, and then I found that I was grateful for that.

The day he was leaving for Poona he stopped at our house on his way, to say good-by and to convey his mother's formal respects to my mother. He stayed only a few minutes and, as he was leaving, asked, "Is there anything I can do? Anything I can send you?"

"Something to read," I replied. "I seem to have a lot of time."

"Novels?"

"No," I said with unnecessary emphasis. "Something entirely factual, about real things."

Hari smiled. "Factual? Like Euclid?"

"No, no." I looked away, embarrassed by my touchiness. "History perhaps. Yes, send me a nice, solid history of the Mahrattas full of dates and footnotes."

"I would have thought that you'd prefer the Rajputs. Their history has so much more literature, and they have all the good stories. They manage to produce a hero for the slightest occasion —or what they call a hero, a great, romantic dashing failure—"

"But that's exactly what I don't want!" I snapped.

Hari was silent for a moment, and then with a change of tone said seriously, "I agree. The Rajputs loved a hopeless fight, a brilliant display of courage and then death. They were so impressed by their young men dressed up like bridegrooms for a war, the touching farewells to weeping wives, the last cups of wine and the last words before they fell, that they always seemed to forget that actually most of their battles were lost." I listened carefully for disguised meanings but could tell nothing from his voice or manner. He said, "Well, I'll see what I can find for you," and ran down the front steps to his car.

The warm, humid weeks of July and August passed in the slow routine of the sickroom. In the middle of August—I had almost forgotten it myself—there were bursts of firecrackers from the street, singing and shouting from neighboring compounds that carried through to my father's room. There was no rain that afternoon, and under the hot clouds processions of people paraded down the road carrying banners, wearing their festival clothes, celebrating, yelling slogans, laughing and congratulating each other. From time to time we heard, distantly, the brassy music from a military band.

"What is all this noise?" my father asked. "What is the date today?"

"The fifteenth. It's Independence Day. People are celebrating the holiday."

"Independence," he whispered, "independence . . ."

That evening I listened to the radio downstairs, turned down very low. There were many speeches—the Viceroy, the new President, the Prime Minister—there were many accounts of the celebrations in Delhi, of the parades, the crowds, the festivities, the banquets, the rejoicing. The whole elaborate business of a transfer of government had been effected. It seemed very simple that evening—a matter settled from one day to the next. And, as such things do on the radio, the gaiety and triumph sounded rather forced. All night there were shouting and the far-off explosions of crackers. From my bedroom window I could see the occasional flares and sparks and stars of fireworks.

Through the next few weeks my father's condition wavered a little in each direction, but the general trend was toward an increasing weakness. He was unco-operative and seemed uninterested in the process that the doctor called "keeping up his strength." He slept fitfully, with longer intervals of troubled wakefulness, and the doctor said he couldn't increase the sedatives. Now his chin trembled almost as much as his hands. His breathing became outrageously labored. He seldom spoke or moved, simply lay in bed, a gaunt, gray man snoring and blowing with ghastly difficulty.

We had brought in all the equipment that would be necessary when he would need an oxygen tent, but in the end we never used it. Early in September he had a third and fatal attack. The trained nurse who had lived in the house for a week before his death had called the doctor in the night. Together they had worked to save him, but it had all taken so very little time and had been decisive from the beginning. Afterward people said, "At least he died in his sleep. That is something to be grateful for." I didn't think about the idiocy of this remark until much later, because no one had told me how busy you are kept after a person's death.

All that day my brother and Shalini were with us. She wept a great deal, and every time I thought she had stopped, some new thing—my father's watch on the table, or a reminder in a remark one of us made—would bring on a new freshet of tears. The doctors, the servants, the priest, the phone ringing, certificates and strange men coming into the house, unexpected meals, the ayah in hysterics. The day grew into some grotesque marathon of endurance. My mother spent most of the day in her own room, praying, and that night she wanted to spend alone with my father's body in his room.

The next day there were hundreds of arrangements to be made for the cremation and for the accompanying ceremonies and prayers. In the evening, just before sunset we went down to the strip of rocky sea shore where the funeral pyre was built and covered with a thick layer of flowers. My father's bier was carried in procession through the city streets, accompanied by the clanging, regular beats of a cymbal. My brother and several members of the family walked beside it, barefoot, their heads uncovered, near the men who carried the litter. Behind them streamed the mourners, like all of us, dressed in plain white, and a large group of stragglers who had attached themselves to the party, idle members of the perpetual crowds on the Bombay streets, probably wondering whose funeral this was.

My mother and I had seen the procession start off from the house, and then had driven to the precincts of the temple by the sea where the pyre had been erected. There we waited in the late-afternoon drizzle while the last rites were performed and the pyre lighted. It burned surprisingly quickly—an hour, perhaps, and it was over. The evening bells from the temple were clattering out to the sea. On the horizon once or twice we saw behind the clouds the flaming pennants of the sunset.

Damp and speechless, we drove home where more relatives were already gathered waiting for us. The next day we received the casket of ashes—really a very small box, bewilderingly light to carry. My mother would travel with them to Benares to scatter the ashes in the Ganges.

For the next few days, and less frequently over the next weeks, I sat in the big drawing room all day, properly dressed in white, and received the condolence calls from hundreds of friends, acquaintances, business associates, politicians, ex-clients and colleagues of my father's. Somewhere among them was Mr. Patel, whose name had been in my father's mouth more than any member of the family in his last days, whose case was never won by the famous lawyer. I found his card on the table one evening, but no impression remained in my mind of his looks or figure or manner. The days slipped by in a mist of weariness and formalities, or a longing to be alone, and of instant, sudden sleep. It was nearly the end of September before I really had a chance to think about my father, and by then a kind of reality had vanished, a three-week insulation had cut me off from him.

✳ XXII ✳

"BABA? MY DEAR CHILD, HOW ARE YOU?"

"Oh, you know," I said, feeling better at once for hearing Jay's husky, mumbling words on the telephone.

"They tell me," he said, slightly mocking, "that it is all illusion —life and death, all maya. They are probably wrong, but it's a comforting thought to concentrate on at times like this. Complicated, of course, like those plays within plays that I've never understood, or dreams within dreams—however, even that probably helps. Keeps your mind busy sorting out the intricacies."

"Jay, I am so terribly glad to hear your voice. What are you doing back in Bombay?" In the last days of September, a couple of weeks after the trickling, indecisive, shabby end of the monsoon, the city was particularly uncomfortable. The air was clammy and insinuatingly hot, with no wind from the sea to make the evenings fresh. Paint peeled off the houses, and great patches of greenish mold grew under the eaves and near the gutters. All Bombay had a dank and seedy look.

"It is, indeed, excessively steamy," Jay said. "It makes one wonder about the Turks, doesn't it? I mean, what kind of national masochism made them invent the Turkish bath? If, of course, they did invent it and it isn't just another example of that irritating British trick of foisting unpleasant things off onto other nations, like Dutch uncles or French leave or Russian roulette or even, I suppose, Welsh rarebit—"

"Or German measles and Siamese twins," I suggested, laughing for the first time in weeks. "There's even a repellent vegetable we used to get an awful lot in school called Swedes."

"Well, there you are," he said. "Perhaps we are being hard on the Turks. But what I really phoned about was to tell you how extremely sorry I was to hear about the death of your father." (I blessed him silently for not saying The Sad News or The Passing.) "He was a great man," Jay continued, "and I don't suppose we gave him enough credit during his lifetime. Probably in a few years . . . by which time it will do him no good. I suppose the vultures have been gathering in great numbers. Shall I come and call? Or are you very tired of condolence visits and seeing people?"

"Jay, I would much prefer it if I could come and see you."

There was a faint reserve in his voice as he said, "My dear child, I'm staying out in Juhu."

"The farther away the better. I'm feeling smothered by this house."

"Who will be there to deal with the callers?"

"Shalini will love it."

Jay's voice said, smiling, "I dare say. You're certain you wouldn't rather I came to you?"

Rather surprised by his insistence, I said, "Quite certain. When may I come? This evening?"

A pause. Jay said, and it struck me as curious at the time, "Why not? You might as well come this evening."

If I had thought about it I could have guessed that there was going to be something peculiar about that evening because Daulat Singh greeted me with quite unaccustomed cordiality. Jay was sitting out on the veranda, alone, looking out to the blackening sea of evening. The beach, swept clear, sand packed hard by the monsoon, was deserted. There was still no wind, and overhead we could hear the spasmodic creaking from the coconut palms.

Jay got up unsteadily when I came out to the veranda. His jacket was half open and there were patches of sweat under his arms. His face was shining and he held a glass of whisky in his hand. He was very drunk.

"My dear Baba," his voice was still under control, "how extraordinarily good to see you. Come in, come in. Sit down, or as my brother would say, take a pew."

"I can't tell you how wonderful it is to be here. It feels like a reprieve of some sort. How is your brother, since you mention him?" I said formally, disturbed by Jay's manner. He was always careful when he spoke of Kali.

"In excellent health, I have no doubt. He elevates the simple matter of being healthy to a high and serious art, or perhaps I should say to a religion complete with ritual, scriptures, saints, acolytes. . . . Acolytes? Do I mean anodynes? . . . Well, anyway—"

"Are they still in Kashmir?"

"*He* is still in Kashmir," Jay said with odd emphasis.

"And she? Did Kashmir turn out to be too much of a bore?"

"Ah," said Jay, with a conspiratorial wink, "that's asking. Who is to say where she may be?"

"Not Kalipur, certainly. Much too hot at this time of year."

"Perhaps a warmer climate suits her after all. Much, much warmer. . . ." Jay laughed at some joke I didn't understand. "Yes, I think she will find it much too hot in the end."

Uncomfortably I wondered what Jay could be talking about. A love affair? A scandal? Had she decided to go to Europe alone? I sat facing Jay with my back to the sea and asked no more questions. Jay clicked his fingers in the familiar way and Daulat Singh reappeared to fill his glass again with whisky. Jay, looking at it thoughtfully, said, "I find this more effective than champagne. You won't join me? No, I thought not. Wise girl. Though why I say that, I don't know; by the time you have wisdom you will probably need this as well." He held up his glass and took a big gulp.

Determined somehow to shake off the uneasy atmosphere, I said, "I'm so surprised—pleasantly, of course—to see you back in Bombay. I had thought that you were still in Kalipur and probably wouldn't be back for ages. Once, some weeks ago, I thought I saw you at the movies, but it must have been someone else. I called, and they didn't turn round—and they must have heard—but it was a most startling resemblance—"

"I've been in and out of Bombay a couple of times," Jay said vaguely.

"All summer I've been envying you," I continued, "knowing how much you love Kalipur and thinking how happy you must be up there instead of sweltering in dreary old Bombay. I know it must be hot in Kalipur, but I'm sure it makes a great difference if you love a place, and then you probably don't mind the heat at all. I know my mother doesn't mind it in Chenur. Do you have to be very outdoorsy? Or is it all state work and papers and conferences? Or is that all Kali's department? We know so little about your Kalipur life. You never—"

"I have no more Kalipur life," Jay interrupted softly.

"But, Jay—"

"So where should I live now? A man must keep his honor, you know. Or so they say. They say an awful lot of foolish things, but the trouble is that by the time you know how foolish they are, you are trapped by them, committed to them. If you cheat at cards you are a scoundrel. If you deceive your wife you are something of a fine fellow—envied, anyway—it's all in the telling. It's all in what you are committed to. I can't go back to Kalipur, which, as you say so simply, I love. How can you make friends after a betrayal?"

"But Jay, you never betrayed anyone in your life. Did you?"

"No, I don't think so."

"Well then—"

Almost inaudibly Jay said, "A sin of omission." He stared into his empty glass, and clicked his fingers.

"Why are you in Bombay? What has happened?" I didn't know whether to be cross or worried.

"I am in Bombay because it is my—what do you call it?—my home. That's right. My home." He waved his arm to indicate the three rooms, the veranda, the light bamboo furniture, the cheap matting, the casual furnishings of a beach house. "Here it is, all of it." He looked at me seriously. "Do you read the papers, Baba?"

I nodded.

"Well, go on reading them. The headlines will probably be enough."

Daulat Singh, returning to the veranda with Jay's new drink, paused suddenly in the dining room. From where I sat I could see into the room, and watched him hesitate and then wait politely for someone coming out of one of the bedrooms that we used for changing our clothes when we spent the day with Jay in Juhu. The woman who walked out to the veranda ahead of Daulat Singh was a stranger to me. From her looks and diffident manner I thought, at first, that she might be some sort of palace retainer from Kalipur, or even some widowed aunt or cousin with simple tastes. She came in barefooted, in a white muslin sari and a loose white blouse. She wore a long necklace of alternate gold and black beads, two gold bracelets and tiny single diamonds in her ears. Plump but still graceful, she had what Shalini would call "a comfortable figure." Her face was wide and placid, a smooth, experienced face, full of acceptance and kindness, expecting nothing. Her hair, showing gray, was held in an enormous bun on the back of her head with an elaborate arrangement of hairpins. She joined her hands in a namaskar to me.

Jay, watching me, had not turned round and did not get up from his chair. "Of course," he said, "you haven't met Sundribai." As she sat down at some distance from us, at the end of the veranda, he said, "I wasn't sure that she was feeling like coming out this evening. Perhaps I should have warned you. I don't know what I should have done without her these last couple of months. And recently, since the end of the monsoon, she has been really most accommodating. She has come to live out here, which is not particularly comfortable for her. Before, she always refused, except for an occasional weekend, naturally. Don't worry, she speaks virtually no English." I had looked nervously in her direction, entirely uncertain of how to behave. I had never before met somebody's mistress.

"Oh Jay—" I whispered helplessly.

"She has a very beautiful voice. When I can't sleep she sings to me. Perhaps I shall ask her to sing after dinner. And when I've had too much of this," he held up his whisky glass, "she is very soothing. She scratches my head. Daulat Singh, on the other hand, is very bossy. He fusses and suggests remedies—"

"Jay, do stop it," I said at last.

He raised his eyebrows at me coldly. "Do I shock you? I thought everybody knew."

"Rumors. There have always been rumors about you, Jay, ever since I can remember."

"Ah yes. Rumors. Like the salt in the Bombay air, an inescapable if corroding ingredient. You can dine out on this for weeks." Suddenly Jay slid forward in his chair, resting his elbows on his knees, staring at the floor. "My dear, please forgive me. I know I am behaving with quite appalling vulgarity, and there is enough of Kali's damnfool Englishman in me to make me regret it. If you prefer, we can talk about the heat and what our friends are up to."

"I don't really prefer. Actually, I'm rather inquisitive. How long have you known—er—her?" I didn't want to say Sundribai's name out loud.

Jay smiled in his unexpected, young way. "Oh, years. Even before my wife left me. She had many good reasons to leave, but Sundribai wasn't one of them. Always most scrupulous and unobtrusive. Though Kali, of course, saw her as the only reason. He felt very sorry for my wife. I did, too. What was she to make of a poor and puzzling creature like me with one foot in each world?"

"She was orthodox?"

"Of course, yes. So she found Bombay disturbing and, well, wicked. And in Kalipur when Daulat Singh and I would go off messing about with the crowds at festivals, or in the villages, sitting at the fire in the evenings telling stories, or becoming excited about the local fairs and markets, it didn't seem dignified to her. Her family had been warned by friends at the time of our marriage that I was 'wild,' and she soon saw that they were right. She lives —quite happily now, I think—with her family and our two daughters. Meanwhile, there is Sundribai who thinks I am demented, but doesn't seem to mind."

"Good God, Jay, what a lot about you I don't know. Did you meet in Bombay?" I wondered what fantastic party or gathering of people could possibly have brought them together. She looked too respectably dowdy, almost embarrassingly so, to have her origins in Kamatipura, the red-light district.

"She was a remarkably promising singer, you know. She came to Kalipur to perform at a music festival. That was where I first heard her. She came up to the palace later to sing for us." He smiled at her with great affection. She didn't respond, just sat there gazing with owlish contentment at the two of us. "We understand each other," Jay said.

Dinner, to me, was a chokingly awkward meal. I kept feeling that Sundribai should in some way be brought into the conversation, though just how I couldn't think. I spoke only Mahratti, and Hindi with a bad accent, while she spoke only Gujerati. Her food was brought to her on a thal—rice and vegetables—and she sat at the end of the table with her feet tucked under her; she seemed quite at ease but ate nothing. Jay told me that he had often tried to persuade her to eat while he was at the table, even to the point of ordering Daulat Singh to serve her then in spite of her wishes, but she would never touch the food until he had finished. Jay himself pushed his food away impatiently and sipped his whisky, watching me. Self-conscious and clumsy I gobbled some of the huge dinner, clattering forks on plates with an alarming noise, and feeling that everyone could plainly hear me chewing each mouthful.

When Jay and I left the table to have coffee on the veranda, I noticed that he was now quite obviously staggering. His speech was thickened and his whole face and body loosened to flabbiness. He retained, however, a curious dignity and insisted on apologizing to me in complicated constructions for allowing me to come out to Juhu that evening. It was no good saying, "But I wanted to —asked to, in fact," because he kept saying that it was really for his own selfish protection.

"Must find a new life, my dear child, must get some new people. Be sorry to lose you . . . very fond of you. . . ."

"You won't lose me. Unless you're going away somewhere—are you?"

"I shall be busy. Very much—ah—occupied." He chuckled in his old way.

"But you'll be in Bombay. You'll be seeing all of us as soon as everyone gets back."

"They are all going away," he told me solemnly, "on long, long journeys. Far, far away . . ."

"Jay, what are you talking about? Where is everyone going away to?"

"Away from," he corrected sadly. "Away from me. You will go too, Baba . . . far away. But I shall be busy. In any case, I shall be too occupied."

I decided to humor him. I had never seen him as drunk as this. "What are you going to be so busy with? It all sounds very grand and important."

"Oh yes. It's very important. More important every day. I'll be busy with this." He held up his glass again. He toasted me silently with the whisky. "This consumes a lot of time. And I consume a lot of this. Fair's fair. There isn't room in one's life for friends and whisky. It's very insulting, but of the two whisky is more important . . . and more reliable. . . ."

When Sundribai came out he asked her to sing. I sat still, drinking coffee, thinking, How can she possibly sing immediately after dinner? and, What an extraordinary evening this is. Thinking, Poor Jay, he is all in pieces. Thinking, How will I ever describe Sundribai to Pria? "You'll never believe it, she embarrasses you not because she's furtive and rather glamorously improper, but because she's so modest and sure, an old and trusted friend of the family or a poor relation who knows her place but, you know, has her standards." I could hear Pria saying, "What can Jay be thinking of? It must be some kind of hysteria." Thinking, Jay has such an air of disaster, can it all be because he's so drunk? Hallucinations, perhaps? All this muddled talk about betrayals and going away on journeys? Poor Jay. This is a farewell party about something, but I'm not sure what.

Sundribai's voice rose sweet and true, the voice of a young girl, in the darkness of the veranda. She sang a favorite and famous song about the child Krishna, a delicious baby bouncing his ball, a mischievous little boy stealing a pat of butter and running away, but smiling so bewitchingly, apologizing so endearingly, that you must forgive him. He is entirely charming, the child, the god, and I hold out my arms to him to embrace the little boy, I put my lips to his face to kiss the child, but I receive—oh—I receive the kiss of a lover.

"Beautiful . . . beautiful," Jay muttered, "like rain at night . . . a flute in the hills . . . like wings, like birds flying. . . ." His voice became indistinct. The Juhu shack might have been built on the edge of a cliff; beyond the railing of the veranda there was nothing but night. The lamplight from inside that filtered out caught on Sundribai's bangles, on Jay's white trouser leg, on my coffee cup. Sundribai began another song, rather happy, with trills and laughter. Her voice was disembodied, like a bird's, unreal, very high and cool. She sang several songs, while I listened to the soaring, dropping notes, and tried to imagine the sturdy, housekeepery figure that sang them.

When, at last, I got up to go, I thanked her and made a namaskar to her which I don't suppose she saw, and turned to say good night to Jay. He didn't get up, and when I leaned close to him I saw that he was asleep. The half finished glass of whisky was on the table beside him. His fat little hands hung from the arms of the chair. His damp, wrinkled white suit was pulled around him in cuts and ridges. And that wise and chuckling face was all disintegrated in sleep, the eyes lost in brown folds, the nose that you never noticed bracketed with deep lines and that drooping, comical mouth slack, unconscious. He sighed deeply and shifted in the chair.

I hadn't heard Sundribai move, but suddenly I felt her touch on my arm. She pulled me away, begging silently for silence. We crept away together like conspirators, smiling, understanding, worried, unable to say a word. Daulat Singh saw me to the car; he was brisk and polite. "Return soon," he said with considerate authority, and left me, feeling astonished, to the long drive home.

Slowly people were trickling back into Bombay. Those who could avoid even this diminishing stickiness of early October were still in the hills, but husbands were back at work, filling in somehow for a couple of weeks until wives and children came back to the city. Houses were repainted, gardens and trees no longer sodden. Dinginess was lifting off Bombay with the sea wind, with the new, cooler weather, with the fishing boats out again, Chowpatty and Marine Drive again thick with strollers in the evenings.

A letter from Pria said that she and Karan would be back in Bombay in a week, that Karan felt terribly guilty about having stayed away so long and would give up his vacation next year, that he had only been able to manage this much because he was "inspecting" and "conferring" with the Ceylon branch of the business and had managed to get a month's extension for that. "Actually, of course, he can hardly stand being away from work, and that's why he's all involved with the Colombo branch. I knew when I insisted on a six-month trip that he would probably get restless, but facing people as 'newlyweds' is such an embarrassing bore with everyone looking at you with that shaming speculation and watching your waistline. I hope we can return as an Old Story. I must say, I feel very settled." Settled, apparently, to her satisfaction, too. Married life, she wrote, was very relaxing. It gave one a pleasing authority and a surprising amount of time to oneself. I could hardly wait to talk to her; all at once I wanted her very much to be back in Bombay. I had a lot to tell her and ask her.

When she did come back, however, we talked mostly about her. She looked extremely well; I had forgotten how beauiful she was. Almost at once she told me, "I think I'm going to have a baby— swear not to tell because I'm determined not to show it until I'm at least six months gone." Pria. Pria with a baby. I don't know why I was so amazed—she had always said she wanted a baby as soon as it was decently clear that that wasn't why she'd married Karan—and she didn't seem at all changed, except that there was a new excitement in her, and I suppose I was jealous of something so exclusive.

"I don't know what to say. I'm terribly pleased, Pria, if you are."

"Oh, me. Karan's the one who is really exalted. A man and a father are two different things, you know."

We sat among the packing cases in their new apartment, converted from the top floor of an old house on Malabar Hill. The furniture was scattered around us still looking temporary and uncozy in its new place. Pictures and books were still in boxes, rugs rolled up and tied with string lay along the walls, a powdering of sawdust, bits of newspaper, splinters of wood on the floor and in corners. Cupboards were opened, clothes half unpacked. The big, uncurtained windows were open to the highest branches of the trees in the garden. The afternoon sun spilled all over us.

Pria said, "Tell me about your father. Letters are quite useless." So I did, all about his illness and the things that weren't said, the slow decline and the silence. Pria said nothing at all, and after a long time asked, "Well, now what?" which was something I had carefully not thought about. "Soon the papers will be sorted and the legal things settled. Your mother will go back to Chenur, and Shalini, if I know anything about her, will be panting to move in. What will you do?"

"That's just what he asked."

"Well, you'd better decide. You could stay with us, of course, but that would look funny and people would say, 'What's the matter with the Gorays? They always were a peculiar family and now they aren't even speaking.' And Shalini would have such a good time being a martyr. And anyway, staying here would only be for," we both counted rapidly, "six months."

"I'll have to think of something. I could get a job."

"That doesn't settle where you live. Besides, getting a job is a last resort. It's much better and far more realistic to get married."

"I dare say. But one can't just start methodically to search for a husband."

Pria shrugged her shoulders. "I don't know why not. Everybody does. Some people are sensible enough to admit it—to themselves, of course."

"Oh well," I said, unwilling to hear one of Pria's lectures so soon. I got up to walk about the rooms and look undecidedly into packing cases. "So much has happened," I said. "I feel I've changed."

"I think you have," Pria said thoughtfully, "though I'm not sure how."

"I'm not sure either. But I can tell you one thing—"

"Oh Lord," Pria interrupted, "people always start a criticism in that way."

"Well, I used to think you were missing something—even at school, and then later too."

"Of course. One can hardly help that. Surely to expect everything would be greedy." Pria turned to me with a new diffidence. "Forgive me for being so dogmatic. I don't know why I feel the need to badger you."

Because I couldn't talk about Krishnan, I started to tell her about Jay, and the strange evening in Juhu with him and Sundribai. She was properly attentive and full of curiosity. "Fancy!" she said. "A kept woman and so uninspiring. It doesn't seem right, somehow. They are inextricably connected in my mind with pink silk lamp shades and chocolates before breakfast. One could even imagine squalor but not a well-meaning aunt. What do you suppose Jay is up to? Didn't he explain *anything*?"

Even without Jay's explanations, in a few days we—and all of Bombay—understood a great deal of what had happened in Kalipur. The story was spread across the morning papers, and the editorials were headed, "Kalipur Scandal."

The story itself was simple, rather well planned and outrageous. All over Bombay that morning in the houses of our friends, telephones were jangling and people were discussing and guessing and supplying contributory incidents until we had pieced together a fairly good picture of the whole affair. Early in their Kashmir holiday the Maharani and Kali had been sitting, one evening, in the bar of Nedou's Hotel surrounded (we could all picture the scene) by their usual flock of sporty hangers-on. At some point the Maharani had looked around the dark brown room and said vaguely, to no one in particular, "Really, it's too much. If they are determined to take away our rights and privileges in our states, surely there is something we can do to get away from this government—this government of the common man. They couldn't have chosen a better name for themselves—*common* is exactly the word I would use to describe them." People around her murmured in a general sort of agreement, probably depressed by this familiar refrain of hers. "You are all so spineless!" she had suddenly flared. "I, for one, am going to do something about it. I refuse to sit about here to be bored and uncomfortable and bullied by politicians. At least I can have one last fling—Europe, America— next year they probably won't allow it. At least I can amuse myself while it's possible. . . ."

People had thought that this was just cocktail-party talk and had not paid too much attention. Later they remembered and wondered if she had already plotted something more than a holiday. She left Kashmir soon after to stay for a few days in Kalipur, where she collected the equipment she considered necessary for a trip to Europe. Her trunks of pastel saris with their sequins, their gold tracery, their delicate embroidery. All her personal jewelry—presents from Kali and things she had bought herself. And several million rupees' worth of state jewelry—that is, heirlooms that were kept in the state treasury, part of the wealth of Kalipur, worn by each Maharani during her reign and passed on through generations.

She had traveled modestly, with only her personal maid, as a gesture to the austerity of the times, to vanish into her usual places of pilgrimage—Paris, Cannes, Monte Carlo, London, Aix-les-Bains. So far the only odd thing about her trip was the fact that for the first time she had traveled to Europe without Kali.

In August, she had gone to spend a few weeks with her friends the Parsons in America. There the excitement started. Incredibly, she had sold the state jewelry in New York. She had managed to get (so the Bombay rumors said) something over a million dollars for it. One could imagine her saying with considerable satisfaction, "There now. It may not seem much to Americans, but I can manage to live very nicely on it. After all, I can't be forever cooped up in Kalipur. . . ." To an Indian reporter in New York who had managed to reach her and question her, she had said indignantly, "What do you mean by state jewelry? We are Kalipur State—the Maharaja and myself. It is our jewelry. We can do whatever we wish with it. And who will stop us?"

Pria and I discussed it all at enormous length in horrified excitement on the telephone. "But she must have gone off her head," I kept saying. "She must have known it would get into the papers. It was certain to make a scandal. She can't be sane."

Pria's voice came thoughtfully over the wire. "I don't suppose she cares. She found a way to go on living her stupid sort of life, so she took it."

"But she always went on and on about being rulers. It was a kind of hysteria."

"Well, exactly," Pria said. "Being a ruler." Both Pria and I knew that it would be a very different matter when the States were merged into India and the princes would become constitutional monarchs with virtually no power. "Now," Pria was saying, "the only claim Kalipur had on her life is gone. She never really liked the place."

I said, "What I'd like to know is, what about Kali? Surely he'd consider it stealing." And thinking of the party months ago when all of us were uneasy listening to foolish, baffled Kali who couldn't understand what was happening in his State, added, "Anyone could have told him—"

"He might even have listened," Pria interrupted. "But I expect she would have managed to get her own way somehow. They are really very strong, those determinedly self-indulgent women—"

"Poor Jay," I said. "No wonder." I thought about him sitting and drinking in his Juhu shack, reading the morning paper on his veranda, waiting for the phone to start ringing. "Pria," I said, "let's go and see him. Now, at once. Not phone or anything."

We got there about noon and Jay was sitting much as I had

imagined him. He put his glass of whisky down as we came in and, almost without greeting us, said, "Have you heard?"

"Yes," we said meekly.

"Isn't it outrageous? Isn't it absolutely the limit? How can they be serious about Prohibition?"

"Prohibition?" Pria said as if she thought Jay were raving.

"You mean you haven't heard? They're really serious about it. It's to start with two dry days a week—that means that clubs and hotels and bars can't serve anything alcoholic on those days. Then the number of days will gradually be increased until liquor can't ever be served. Are they running a girls' boarding school or a government?"

"Is it just public places?" I asked, fascinated by Jay's absorption in what he was saying. "Can you drink at home?"

"For a while. But you'll need a permit, and they set a quota of how many bottles a month you can buy. It's absurd—and cheeky—this policing of morals. And think of what a blight it will be on the parties of the future. How will people stand each other without liquor?"

"Jay," Pria said gently, "we came to see you because of this morning's news."

"As well you might," Jay said indignantly. "If they really carry through with this nonsense, I shall have to leave Bombay. Go live in Antibes with all the other soaks. It will be very inconvenient, but I don't know what else we can do."

"About the Kalipur business," Pria insisted, and Jay stared at her unforgivingly, almost with dislike. His face was both puffy and deeply creased, his clown's mouth rigid. "We came to say we know you're not involved, that we're your friends and we want you to remember that and tell us if we can help."

"If Her Highness has anything to communicate to you, I'll let you know," Jay said with ludicrous pompousness.

"Oh, don't be such an ass," Pria said impatiently. "She can go hang herself for all I care."

"I beg your pardon. You are speaking of my brother's wife." After a moment he added consideringly, "That doesn't sound as good as 'the woman I love.' "

Pria and I relaxed, and she said, "Don't take it too much to heart. Anyone that knows you knows that you had nothing to do with all this."

"But who knows me?" Jay said vaguely. "The Kalipur people are the only ones that matter, and there I am one of this—this family."

"It'll blow over soon."

"Not in Kalipur."

I asked, "What will happen to her?"

He finished his whisky, and snapped his fingers for Daulat Singh to bring another. "Prison perhaps if she returns to India. Exile certainly—exile from Kalipur, that is. They don't want trouble with the States just now, so I expect it will be exile. And she is a woman; probably that will be in her favor."

"And Kali?" Poor stupid, well-meaning, bumbling Kali.

"Yes," Jay said almost inaudibly, "there's a tragic figure. They can't prove that he is implicated, but nobody will believe that he isn't. He will be a gentleman, I have no doubt. He'll behave very correctly, according to his incomprehensible code—stand by her, and all that. Take the blame. Get confused in the cross-questioning. Make a nonsense of it. Out of his element. He'll say things like, 'What right have you—' and, 'I fully endorse my wife's stand—'" He sighed deeply. "Oh God, what a mess. Exile, I suppose, for both of them."

"And for you?"

"Exile, too—not by order of the court, but how can I go back?" Jay, who loved Kalipur, whose secret strength was in Kalipur, whose tolerant good humor with life stemmed from some warm intimacy he felt with Kalipur, fat, sad, half-drunken Jay needed nothing from us, not even affection.

"Jay," I said, touching his arm to make him look at me, "it can't change their feelings about you."

Jay smiled at me patiently, a little amused. "Baba dear, it's my feelings that are changed."

Pria said, in clear, practical tones, "There's no point in being so tragic about it all. If Kali really does have to go, then his elder boy becomes the Maharaja. And since he's too young to rule, they'll have to appoint a Regent. And obviously, Jay, you're the logical choice. Altogether a much better arrangement, *I'd* say."

Jay said formally, and without much interest, "If they offered me the Regency I'd have to refuse."

"Oh *why*, Jay?" I asked. "Why cut yourself off?"

"It's too responsible a job, and I have no sense of responsibility." With a sudden change of manner Jay said, "Listen, I'll try to explain something. Once I told Sundribai a story about a man I knew. He was married but had been keeping, very discreetly, a mistress as well. At some point—I forget, now, what precipitated it—he decided he wanted to divorce his wife and marry his mistress. He was a cautious man. He set about the matter with an almost military sense of strategy. He was not going to be blackmailed by his wife into parting with a large alimony. He prided himself on having preserved a magnificent obscurity around his life with his mistress. He felt he deserved congratulations when his wife, swayed by whatever persuasions he used, accepted a generous settlement instead of alimony and gave him a divorce. Before he could announce his marriage to his mistress, his wife had already made her own announcement. She was going to marry a man he had never heard of. When she wrote to him she added with unnecessary malice that she had known for years about his mistress and had only wondered why it had taken him so long to make up his mind and to release her so profitably. Now, what do you think Sundribai said to that story?"

"She thought it funny?" Pria suggested.

"She was shocked?" I said.

Jay shook his head. "She said, 'How sad that there should be so little trust in a marriage.' And all at once I could see nothing in the story but the sadness of those piddling little treacheries. This summer in Kalipur, after I knew what my sister-in-law was up to, something of the same sort happened to me again."

"You decided to marry Sundribai?" I asked incredulously.

"No, no!" Jay laughed explosively. "No, that would never do. I meant the same sudden change in a viewpoint. I looked back on my life as drowning men are supposed to do, and saw it all in terms of my irresponsibility. Everything—the life I've led, my marriage, even my love for Kalipur—I couldn't accept the meaning of any of it. Suddenly I knew that I could only do what I've done, be what I've been because I was a younger son, because there was always Kali doing the other things." He smiled lazily at Pria and me, and clicked his fingers for Daulat Singh. "You two," he said. "You've often felt sorry for me having a brother like Kali. You shouldn't. Kali has been my only excuse, my only security, in a way, to be the creature I am, my only reason for not learning all this long ago. If Kali goes, I must go too."

Jay took a sip of his fresh drink and leaned back in the chair. For once Pria didn't know what to say, and I, constrained by this atmosphere of guilt, couldn't bear to look at either of them. Jay went on talking dreamily. "Have you ever walked into a room that you know well, have lived in, and seen it, for the first time, lit only by moonlight? You know how the shapes and colors change? How there are great caves and wells where before there were carpets or tables? You know how, in that moment, it's a stranger's room with no welcome for you? Or how—"

"Stop it, Jay," Pria said quickly. "You must pull yourself together."

Jay chuckled again, but no longer with the indulgent charm that we expected from him. "Oh, I enjoyed being the eccentric black sheep. Make no mistake. It's a cheap way of winning sympathy. But now . . . You see, don't you, why I can't go back to Kalipur?"

When we left we were full of promises to come back soon, to see Jay again in the next day or two, to have Jay over for dinner, drinks, something. But in the end we never did see him again. First it was because Pria was getting her apartment settled and my own plans were so unformed. Then it was because Juhu was a long way to go for the off-chance of finding Jay at home and gasoline was still rationed. Jay himself never called us and never invited us out. And later, when one or the other of us did telephone him, he didn't want to leave Juhu, didn't want to come to dinner or go out at all. Then it was because he either refused to come to the phone, or if he did was so obviously drunk that one thought twice about inviting him to a party only to have him reeling about and muttering and going to sleep in a corner. And finally, because we heard that Jay had left Bombay and the shack in Juhu had been sold. But that wasn't until nearly the end of the year, when the Bombay Season was in full swing, everybody was terribly rushed, what with the cool weather, racing, parties, new faces in the city, the new excitement of the first season under Independence; a modest season, comparatively, but still it didn't leave one much time to compare it in quality or extensiveness with the previous year. Somewhere, I supposed occasionally, Jay was sitting and desperately drinking, alone in spite of Sundribai and Daulat Singh.

About the only other decisive thing that happened to me that year, the year that decided so much of my life, was a long conversation with Hari one Sunday in December. In the weeks immediately after my father's death he had been in Bombay and, of course, had come to call and offer his condolences. There had been several other people there and we were surrounded by formalities and an oppressive feeling of being strangers. After that he had phoned occasionally to ask if he could help with anything, and once we had met at dinner with Pria and Karan. I wasn't going to parties, and so the dinner was a quiet one, just the four of us, an intimate housewarming. We were Pria's first guests in her new apartment.

Pria had made her own atmosphere there. If I had been looking for contrasts to the impractical charm of Alix's drawing room that had so impressed me, I could scarcely have found a sharper one. Pria's furniture was what we called "good," by which we meant expensive and lasting but not beautiful. Her sofa was covered with printed Indian cotton, and the same material hung as curtains on each side of the window. She had been extravagant with one of her chairs; it was upholstered in a silk brocade from Hyderabad. The only picture, placed above the sofa, was a Jamini Roy of milkmaids watched by Krishna hidden in a tree. I remembered it from Pria's bedroom in her family's house. Everything was very clean, the furniture highly polished, the curtains stiffly starched. Pria said to Hari, "We were delighted with your choice of an apartment. How do you think the room looks?"

"Very nice," Hari said, meaning nothing by the comment. I thought, one could entirely redecorate his Poona house, throw away the calendars, buy some decent pictures, paint the furniture and insist on Kashmir carpets in every room, and he would say, "Very nice." Probably, in that case, he would mean, "If you're pleased . . ."

"Baba?" Pria was saying. "Do you like it?"

"I think it exactly suits you." To myself I described it as a "no-nonsense" room.

"Mm." Pria said smiling, "I must think about that remark."

Throughout the evening Karan was subtly exhilarated and gave elaborate deference to Pria, so that even if I had not known she was going to have a baby I would have guessed it. Hari talked easily, familiarly, about Poona, about horses, about events of the past summer. Pria sat, composed and beautiful, radiating a settled contentment, a quietly triumphant achievement of something. It was an entirely uneventful evening, but it stayed in my mind as one remembers a cool winter day in the steamy rains of high summer.

I drove home with Hari, sitting far apart from him in the front seat of his car. My father's car, driven by the chauffeur, followed behind us. We stopped, as usual, for a few moments at the corner of the Hanging Gardens, looking through a break in the trees at the Maharani's Necklace curving away below us in bright points of light.

Hari said, "One day, I suppose, they'll finish the reclamation project and then Marine Drive will stretch all the way to Colaba."

"It'll look pretty, I think, but we'll probably have to think of a new name for it. I dare say the 'Maharani's Necklace' won't be fashionable by then."

"It already has unfortunate connotations. There'll be a lot of changes, I expect."

"Does the idea worry you?"

Hari sounded mildly surprised. "No. Why should it?"

"I can't imagine."

Hari said almost apologetically, "I think in a rather different context. These big shifts—governments, ideologies—well, country life goes on in much the same way, you know, improving a little I hope. In the country all our changes are slow."

"A year ago I would have welcomed changes—any changes."

"Not now?"

"Now I'm choosy about my changes. There's a lot in our past that I hope we won't lose."

When we reached the house Hari asked me rather abruptly if he might come to tea the following Sunday, and I said Yes, with pleasure. The intervening days were filled with a good deal of anxiety, but by Sunday I had more or less decided what I would say to Hari.

After tea we walked about in the garden, pausing by the beds of tuberoses and the jasmine bushes, hearing the shrill laughter of the servants' children beyond the wall, watching the golden sunlight of evening on the city roofs, and beyond them the sea. We scarcely looked at each other.

Like everybody else, Hari asked me what I was going to do, and I told him that I was going south with my mother in January. All the events of last May in Chenur already seemed part of a remote and inexplicable past. She, I knew, wanted to get back to Chenur—it had already been over six months since she left—and she had waited only for me to make up my mind. "Besides," I added, "I can't keep Shalini out of the house any longer."

Hari said nothing at all, and we walked again around the little path that encircled the pond.

I started a sentence, "The other evening at Pria's," and let it trail off thinking that there really was no way of leading up gracefully to the speech I had prepared. It took all the courage I had and I think, perhaps, it was the only brave thing I'd ever done. So I held my breath and said very quickly, "Hari, do you still want to marry me, because if you do I want to too."

Hari still said nothing, and, unable to look at him, I asked more calmly, "Do you want to know why?"

In an ordinary sort of voice he said, "I think I know why."

"Well, you're partly right. But it's only the thing that made me decide *now*, not the thing that made me decide. I mean, it's really not that I see marriage as a . . . I mean as a *solution*."

"Hardly a solution." Hari sounded amused. "More like a new set of problems."

"Well yes, but ones that I now want to cope with."

"The state of matrimony? Not me in particular?"

"You make it sound so insulting. I'm not in love with you, if that's what you mean—though I'm not sure what *that* means."

With surprise he said, "I didn't think you were."

"But it doesn't matter, does it?"

"No, it doesn't matter."

"Because it's only a reason after all, isn't it? One reason among others—beauty, or money, or wanting to go to bed with someone, or because your parents arrange it, or because you think you'll never have another chance, or you don't know what else to do."

"What else would you do?"

"Well, I'm not sure. Get a job, perhaps, or study something. Fill in time—to keep a measure of dignity, really—until somebody else asks me to marry him."

"And you would accept?"

"I expect so, if it were within reason."

"I see," Hari said in a voice so distant that I was suddenly certain that he was going to say no. I should, I thought in Shalini's revolting phrase, have "played my cards better"; I suppose it would have seemed to her the lesser insult.

The best I could do was to say, "We agree about a lot, don't we? I mean, marriage to you wouldn't be, as they always promise you, a gamble."

"No," he said, and out of the corner of my eye I watched him shake his head, "no, it wouldn't be a gamble, I was always sure of that."

"And, really, there is plenty of room in a marriage. Space to be or become the person that you are going to become, space for silence or for love or for loneliness or bitterness or comprehension or disaster or—"

"Enough, enough!" Hari was laughing. "A gamble, after all?"

"Well, no. Except to the extent that your life is, or you are."

Up and down the garden we walked. There was already that rise of intensity that evening brings. Pink and orange African daisies, the buds on the coral bushes, the red velvet of the curling roses asserted themselves with new authority. The sleepy afternoon, the time for the white flowers, was gone.

"Oh look—a peacock!" The large, ungainly bird perched on the wall, its small, stupid head pecking in all directions with a hysterical nervousness. We stood still and watched it stretch the incredible blue of its neck, rearrange its wings and feathers fussily, its crest dipping and trembling.

"I wanted to ask you a question," Hari said. "Why did you say 'no' before?"

It had seemed the only answer at the time. "I wanted the decision made for me—by you, or someone, or something."

"To be swept off your feet?" Hari asked with unexpected irony.

"Well, I didn't want to have to answer. I didn't want a choice."

"But everything is choices."

"I know. Within birth and death. Pria thought I was influenced by the Nichols."

"Those Americans?"

"They were in love." Hari and I sat on the low wall, next to the steps leading into the sunken garden. I asked, "Do you remember that day we all spent in Juhu, the day of the beach party?" I stared at him rather deliberately, making him, in the end, look at me. A serious, considering face and beautiful eyes. I said, "I enjoyed myself that day, didn't you?"

We faced each other warily and in silence, with the intimate involvement of enemies or lovers. "Yes," Hari said at last. "I always thought I should marry you, Baba. I'm glad you want to. I'm glad it's settled."

Set in Linotype Electra
Format by Katharine Sitterly
Manufactured by The Haddon Craftsmen, Inc.
Published by HARPER & BROTHERS, *New York*